ANY GIVEN DOOMSDAY

"Handeland launches the intriguing Phoenix Chronicles urban fantasy series with a strong story . . . the demons' evil plans and vividly described handiwork create immense suspense for the final battle."

—*Publishers Weekly*

"Fascinating. A fast-paced thriller that will have readers looking for book two." —Kelley Armstrong

"A fresh, fascinating, gripping tale that hits urban fantasy dead-on. Don't miss this one." —L.L. Foster

"Sexy, dangerous, and a hot-as-hell page-turner! Lori Handeland world-builds with authority."

—L. A. Banks

"Handeland is back with a striking new series, narrated by a heroine thrown headfirst into a fairly apocalyptic scenario . . . With sex and power intertwined, Handeland looks to have another winner of a series on her hands!"

—*RT Book Reviews*

Titles by
LORI HANDELAND

Sisters of the Craft

In the Air Tonight
Heat of the Moment
(coming July 2015)
Smoke on the Water
(coming August 2015)

The Phoenix Chronicles

Any Given Doomsday
Doomsday Can Wait
Apocalypse Happens
Chaos Bites

The Nightcreature Novels

Blue Moon
Hunter's Moon
Dark Moon
Crescent Moon
Midnight Moon
Rising Moon
Hidden Moon
Thunder Moon
Marked by the Moon
Moon Cursed
Crave the Moon

The Shakespeare Undead Series

Shakespeare Undead
Zombie Island

Anthologies

Stroke of Midnight
My Big, Fat Supernatural Wedding
No Rest for the Witches
Hex Appeal

Praise for the Phoenix Chronicles by
LORI HANDELAND

DOOMSDAY CAN WAIT

"A striking series . . . with a decidedly sexy edge. Readers again view the world through the eyes of ex-cop-turned-humanity's-savior Liz Phoenix [in] this complex mythology."

—*RT Book Reviews* (4 stars)

"We really enjoyed it . . . and are looking forward to [more] in this series." —*Robots & Vamps*

"Cool . . . exciting." —*Lurv à la Mode*

"Fascinating, vivid, and gritty."

—*Fallen Angel Reviews*

"Handeland does an amazing job of packing so much punch into the pages of this story without ever leaving the reader behind. *Doomsday Can Wait* ups the paranormal and emotional content of the series, adding strength to the heroine and a more human touch to one of her closest allies. This is an action-packed series that urban fantasy readers should thoroughly enjoy, and I'm looking forward to seeing where the author takes us next." —*Darque Reviews*

"Handeland pens another tale that captured my heart... with captivating characters [and] an absorbing plot that will keep readers on the edge of their seats."

—*Romance Junkies*

In the Air Tonight

Lori Handeland

St. Martin's Paperbacks

IN THE AIR TONIGHT

For information address St. Martin's Press, 175 Fifth Avenue, New York, NY 10010.

ISBN: 978-1-250-02012-3

Printed in the United States of America

St. Martin's Paperbacks edition / June 2015

St. Martin's Paperbacks are published by St. Martin's Press, 175 Fifth Avenue, New York, NY 10010.

10 9 8 7 6 5 4 3 2 1

Prologue

Scotland, four hundred years ago

Three men with large, hard, dirty hands lifted three infant girls from their cradles.

"No!" Prudence Taggart cried, and a crockery bowl fell off the table, shattering against the floor.

Roland McHugh, the king's chief witch hunter, flicked a finger in her direction, and two other dark-clad men dragged her out the door of the cottage. Several more yanked her husband, Henry, along behind. Those not occupied hauling the five Taggarts from their home built a pyre. From the speed at which they completed their task, they'd done so before.

"More than one soul in a womb is Satan's work." McHugh's lip curled as he contemplated the sleeping children. "How many lives did you sacrifice so your devil's spawn might be born?"

Both Henry and Prudence remained silent. There was nothing they could say that would save them, and they knew it.

Since King James had nearly been killed, along with his Danish queen, in a great storm he believed had been brought about by witchcraft, His Majesty had become slightly obsessed on the subject of witches.

However, as he didn't want to seem backward and

superstitious to his English subjects, who had very little regard for the Scots in the first place, he had been forced to commission a secret society, the *Venatores Mali,* or Hunters of Evil, to do his bidding. In McHugh the king had found a leader who hated witches as much as he did.

Their captors lashed Henry and Prudence back-to-back against the stake then formed a circle around them. McHugh snapped his fingers, and two lackeys appeared with torches.

The witch hunter removed a ring from his finger and a pincher from his wool doublet then held the circlet within the flame until it glowed. He pressed the red hot metal to Henry's neck. The scent of burning flesh rose, along with a nasty hiss, and the livid image of a snarling wolf emerged from Henry's flesh.

"Are you mad?" Henry managed.

"Sometimes the brand brings forth a confession."

"Shocking how pain and torture make people say anything."

"It did not make you." McHugh shoved his ring back into the flames, and his gaze slid to Prudence.

"I did it," Henry blurted. "I sold to Satan the lives of your wife and child to bring forth our own."

"Of course you did," McHugh agreed.

He was convinced magic, sorcery, witchcraft had been involved in the deaths of his loved ones. Nothing would change his mind. Not even the truth.

Some people could not be healed. McHugh's wife had been one of them. By the time he had fetched Prudence, the woman had lost far too much blood, and the child was already dead.

McHugh pressed his ring to Pru's neck. She stiffened until the stake creaked. Lightning flashed, and somewhere deep in the woods a tree toppled over. Wolves began to howl in the distance—a lot of them—and the circle of hunters shifted uneasily.

"I confessed, you swine."

"You thought that would save her?" McHugh tut-tutted, then he snatched the blazing torches and tossed them onto the pyre. The dry, ancient wood flared.

Henry reached for his wife's hands. They were just close enough to touch palm to palm. "Imagine a safe place where no one believes in witches anymore."

The forest shimmered. Clouds skittered over the moon. Flames shot so high they seemed to touch the sky. When they died with a whoosh, nothing remained but ashes and smoke.

And the men who had held the three infant girls held nothing but empty blankets.

Chapter 1

The Present

I understand that my dream of being normal is merely that.

For one thing, I'm adopted and everyone knows it. In a town like New Bergin, Wisconsin, adoptions are rare. Strapping Scandinavian farm folk produce blond-haired, blue-eyed children quick as bunnies. Which means my blue-black hair and so-brown-they'll-never-be-blue eyes make me stand out like the single ugly duckling in a lake full of swans. Even before factoring in that I'm an only child.

The *only* only child in New Bergin. Which doesn't necessarily make me abnormal, but it doesn't mean I fit in either.

No, what makes me abnormal are the ghosts. As the freaky little kid in the movie said: *They're everywhere.*

At first my parents thought my speaking to empty corners and laughing for no reason was cute. As time went on, and people started talking . . . not so cute anymore.

"Should we take her to a psychiatrist?" my mother asked softly.

Ella Larsen always spoke softly. That night she whispered, yet still I heard. Or maybe one of the ghosts told me. I'd been four at the time. My recollection is muzzy.

"Take her to a psychiatrist?" my father repeated. "I was thinking of taking her back."

Perhaps that was the beginning of my feelings of inadequacy in New Bergin, or at the least, the birth of my incessant need to please. If I wasn't "right" I could be returned like a broken chair or a moldy loaf of bread.

I stopped mentioning the ghosts the next day. I never did see that psychiatrist, although sometimes I think that I should. I'm still living in New Bergin. My name's still Raye Larsen.

Once I stopped chattering to nothing my father and I came to an unspoken understanding. He coached my softball team and took me fishing. I pretended to be Daddy's girl. I had to. I didn't want to go "back."

According to my records, I'd been abandoned on Interstate 94, halfway between Madison and Eau Claire. Whoever had left me behind had not liked me very much. They'd dumped me in a ditch on the side of the road—naked without even a blanket.

Assholes.

Luckily for me it was a balmy July day, and I was found before I had succumbed to even a tinge of sunburn. I'm just glad it wasn't November.

My mother died when I was twenty. Cancer. Haven't seen her since. The one ghost I wouldn't have minded turning up a few times and not a word. I don't understand it.

As I hurried down the sidewalk to work my best friend, Jenn Anderson, appeared at my side. "You wanna slow down?"

"Not really," I said, though I did just a little.

We weren't late for a change, probably because I hadn't waited for Jenn. We worked for the New Bergin

School District, Jenn as the attendance secretary, me as a kindergarten teacher, and walked to school together each morning.

In choosing my occupation, I'd tried to get as far away from the dead as possible, figuring I'd be safe from ghosts in a kindergarten classroom.

Boy, had I been wrong. As previously mentioned: Ghosts are everywhere.

While I might have come to teaching for a reason that wasn't, I'd discovered quickly why I should stay. Good teachers could be made, but the best ones were born, and I was one of them.

Who knew I'd be great with kids? Not me. That they were honest and happy and full of energy, and being around them made me feel better than anything else was an unexpected bonus.

I'd even started to consider that I might want a few of my own. Perhaps if I created a family from scratch, rather than joining one already in progress, I'd feel like I belonged somewhere, to someone, and that constant emptiness inside might go away.

Of course finding a man in New Bergin wasn't easy. They were the same ones that had been here all along, and I wasn't impressed.

They hadn't been either. Though I tried to be like everyone else, the fact remained that I wasn't. In truth, the only people who had ever accepted me as I was, and loved me for me no matter what, were my mother and Jenn. Which was no doubt why I loved them the same way.

Jenn and I had met on the first day of preschool and become BFFs. No idea why. We were so different it was scary and yet . . . we worked.

Even without the long, perfect mane of golden hair and equally gorgeous face, complete with a pert little nose—although *this* Jenn's nose was actually her nose, plastic surgery being a no-no in New Bergin—the name Jennifer Anderson was too close to Jennifer Aniston for high school kids to resist. When she'd begun dating the only Brad in town, she'd just been asking for it. As a result, one did not mention *Friends,* or Brad for that matter, ever. Do not get her started on Ross.

Jenn, who was several inches shorter than me, had to take three steps to my one. The flurry of her tiny feet, combined with the spiky ponytail atop her head, made her resemble a coked-up Pomeranian.

"Where's the fire?" she asked.

A breeze kicked up, making her silly hairstyle waggle. For an instant, I could have sworn I smelled smoke; I even heard the crackle of flames.

But if there were a fire, the local volunteer fire department would have been wailing down First Street by now. Which meant . . .

I turned my head, and I saw him. Nothing new. I'd been seeing this one for as long as I could remember.

Clad in black, he reminded me of the pictures in the Thanksgiving stories I read to my kids. Puritan. Pilgrim. One or the other. Although why the Ghost of Thanksgiving Past had turned up in Wisconsin I had no idea. According to the stories all those persecuted Puritans had lived, and died, on the East Coast.

Maybe he was Amish.

Neither case explained the sleek black wolf that was often at his side. The creature's bright green eyes were as unnatural as the creature itself.

Every time I approached, they melted into the woods,

an alley, the ether. Unlike all of the other specters that just had to talk to me, neither my Puritan, nor his wolf, ever did.

Jenn snatched my elbow. Considering our daily walk, you'd think she'd be in better shape.

I slowed, and as soon as I did the man in black—no wolf today—went poof. Now you see him—or at least I did—now you don't.

He'd be back. Most of the ghosts went on, eventually—wherever it was that they went—but not that guy. Someday I'd have to find out why.

"Sheesh," Jenn muttered. I'd started speed-walking again. She stopped, leaning over and setting her palms on her knees as she tried to catch her breath.

I kept going; the sense of urgency that had plagued me as soon as my Keds touched First Street that morning had returned.

"You—" Deep breath. "Suck!" Jenn shouted.

I quashed the temptation to comment on her shoes, which were too high for walking and too open toed for a northern Wisconsin October. But then, as Jenn always pointed out, she didn't have to chase children. Ever.

The days of a school nurse had gone the way of the dodo. If children became sick, they were sent to the office—Jenn's office—then sent home.

Certainly they puked, or sneezed, but usually not on her. Her fashionable clothes discouraged it—today's body-hugging red sweater dress appeared fresh from the dry cleaners—and her attitude ensured it. The instant a student walked into her office, she jabbed a pointy, painted nail at the bank of chairs against the far wall. If they puked or sneezed, they did it over there.

Jenn always told me my comfortable jeans, complemented by soft tees and sweatshirts, often of the Packer, Brewer, Badger variety, invited disaster. Maybe so. But at least I matched everyone else in New Bergin.

Except Jenn. Funny how *she* was the one who fit in.

I reached the cross avenue B—those New Bergin founding fathers had been hell on wheels in the street-naming department—and stopped so fast I nearly put my toes through the front of my shoes.

Gawkers milled about, blocking the sidewalk and spilling into the road, but since the police had roped off the avenue they weren't in danger of becoming chopped suey.

Brad Hunstadt—yeah, that Brad, Jenn's Brad, make that ex-Brad—stood on the inside of the rope, arms crossed, face stoic. He'd only recently joined the force following the relocation of another officer to Kentucky to be nearer to his grandchildren.

Before that, Brad had been kind of a loser. He might be pretty—like the famous Brad—but he'd never been a candidate for rocket science school. He'd graduated from high school, gone to tech school. I'm not sure for what because he'd never worked for anyone but his father, the local butcher, until now. Jenn and I figured his daddy had paid someone off to get Brad out of his business and into another.

As I approached, my gaze was drawn to the woman standing at the edge of the crowd, staring at the dead body propped against the wall of Breck's Candy Emporium—home of twenty-five different types of caramel apples. The staring itself was not remarkable. Who wasn't? What was remarkable was that this woman could be the twin of the one she stared at.

She was a stranger—believe me I knew everyone—in a place where strangers stuck out, even when they weren't covered in blood and lying dead on the ground.

I'd seen hundreds of ghosts, but each one still made my heart race. They were *dead*. I could see them. It was hard to get used to, and really, I probably shouldn't.

"Huh." Jenn had caught up. "I can't remember the last time we had a murder."

"Murder?"

She cast me an irritated glance. "Look at her."

My gaze went to the standing woman, but contrary to most movies about them, ghosts don't walk around with the wound that killed them evident on their spectral bodies. No gaping brains. No holes in their heads, their chests, or anywhere else there shouldn't be. Even the massive amounts of blood on the reclining figure was nowhere in evidence upon the spectral one.

Jenn snapped her fingers in front of my face. "Not there." She pointed slightly to the left of the ghost. "There." She transferred her pointy nail south until it indicated the dead woman.

One of her arms was missing—that wasn't easy to do—and her body, from the chest down, was blackened. The scent of charred flesh reached us on a frigid breeze. Weird. When I'd left my apartment, I could have sworn it was Indian summer.

Jenn clapped a palm over her nose and fled, her itty-bitty Barbie feet and short legs moving so fast they appeared to blur. Jenn could move when she wanted to.

Chief Johnson stood next to the body, wringing his hands. He'd been the police chief since the last chief—his father, also Chief Johnson—had keeled over in his lutefisk.

I had to agree with him. I'd rather die than eat it too.

However, as long as the present Chief Johnson had been in charge, there hadn't been a murder in New Bergin. Had there ever been?

The funeral director was our medical examiner. The extent of our CSI was probably to put up yellow tape and hope for the best. It appeared that Chief Johnson had managed the first and was hip deep in the second.

Though I wanted to stay, I needed to get to school. If I wasn't in class when the bell rang it wouldn't be pretty. You think kindergartners are delightful? They are. But I learned not to turn my back on them. Or leave them alone long enough to trash the place.

I planned to cut through the alley between B and C—my shoes would get indescribable gunk on them, but I didn't have the time to care—and the ghost poured from the air, filling the space right in front of me. Her eyes were solid black. No whites left at all. I'd never seen anything like it before. I never wanted to again.

She had a burn, make that a brand, of a snarling wolf on her neck. I glanced at the body. Sure enough, there was the brand, though it was impossible to tell from here if it was a wolf. I probably wouldn't have seen it at all, beneath so much blood, unless I'd known where to look.

That I knew confused me. The wounds on the living did not transfer to the dead. Why had that one?

She grabbed my arm. I bit my lip to keep from screaming. Her fingers were fire and ice. Smoke poured from her mouth. In the center of her too-black eyes, a flame flickered. "He will burn us all."

Then she was gone. If it hadn't been for the trailing whiff of brimstone, and the blue-black imprint of her fingers just above my wrist, I'd have thought I imagined her.

"What the fuck?" I muttered, earning a glare from Mrs. Knudson, who stood in the doorway of her yarn shop, Knit Wits, contemplating the most excitement to hit New Bergin in a lifetime.

"I certainly hope you don't speak like that in front of the children."

"Children!" I resisted the urge to use the F-word again and ran, skidding through Lord knows what in the alley, then bursting out the other side, trailing the mystery muck behind me.

New Orleans Police Department

Detective Bobby Doucet stared at the photos spread across his desk. "Goddamn serial killer."

"Isn't that redundant?"

Bobby's partner, Conner Sullivan, lowered himself into the visitor's chair. The thing creaked then wobbled beneath his weight. Conner, used to such behavior in furniture, either didn't notice or pretended not to.

"A serial killer is, by nature, damned. And damned comes from God. Therefore . . . " Sullivan spread his quarterback-sized hands. "Redundant."

Bobby had joined the homicide division while Sullivan was on leave. The detective had been unwell, lost time, forgotten things. When he'd returned, no one had wanted to work with him.

Bobby, the new man, the low man, had been elected. He didn't mind. Though the two of them could not have been any more different in both appearance and background, Bobby had found the Yankee transplant from . . . Massachusetts? Maine? Maryland? Something with an *M*. It didn't matter. He'd found Sullivan to be thorough, fair, and an obscenely hard worker. As homicide in New Orleans was a busy, busy business, Bobby appreciated all three.

"'Tis a very Catholic view yer spoutin', Conner." Bobby's use of a thick Irish brogue brought a rare smile to his partner's face. "But then we are in the city of Saints."

Which made the man's annoying habit of rooting for the Patriots even more so. Bobby liked him anyway. They both had secrets in their pasts, shadows in their eyes, and chips on their shoulders.

Sullivan's was much wider than Bobby's but only because his shoulders were. The detective stood six five without shoes and ran about two fifty. He possessed sandy blond hair and oddly dark eyes considering the epic paleness of his skin and the potato-famine memories inherent in his last name. His habit of wearing amusing ties with his pristine dark suits—today's offering featured Fred Flintstone in full "yabba dabba doo" mode—had clued Bobby in to a lighter side of Sullivan that few bothered to uncover.

In contrast, Robert Alan Doucet came from a long line of Creoles—both French and Spanish, with a little Haitian thrown in. He topped out just above six feet and he weighed one seventy only after he'd fallen into the river fully clothed. His hair was black; his eyes were blue, and his skin appeared tan year round.

"Why are you staring at those?" The wave of Sullivan's huge hand created such a backwash of air that Bobby had to slap his palm atop two of the photos to keep them from sailing off the desk and across the floor. "Keep it up and they're gonna call you obsessed."

Sullivan should know. One of the reasons he'd been on leave was a tiny obsession of his own.

With another serial killer.

New Orleans seemed to attract them. Go figure. Large service population that worked on a cash basis meant very few records. The huge tourism industry caused folks to wander in and out hourly. Rampant alcohol—explanation unnecessary.

Costumes. Masks. Voodoo.

Then there was the fact that the city was surrounded on three sides by water, and water was a great place to hide bodies—or at the least make them damn hard to recover evidence from. In truth, Bobby was surprised New Orleans wasn't the serial-killer capital of the world. Although . . .

His gaze drifted over the photos on his desk. Maybe it was.

The killer Sullivan had been after had never been caught. Most folks in the department didn't believe there'd ever been one. The manner of death for each victim had been as different as the victims themselves. Which wasn't the usual serial killer MO.

Kind of like the case in front of Bobby now. Not only had his killer stopped killing—at least in New Orleans—but when he'd been doing so he'd offed his victims in all manner of ways. However, there was one thing they all had in common.

Bobby lifted the latest photo, a close up of a dead woman, where the brand of a snarling wolf was visible on her neck, despite all the blood. He offered it to Sullivan.

The big man accepted the picture, eyes narrowing on the image. "I never saw this one before."

"Just came in."

Sullivan stood. "Why aren't we at the crime scene?"

"Because it's in Podunk."

"Where?"

"Wisconsin."

"There's actually a Podunk, Wisconsin?"

"No." But Bobby thought that there should be. "It's . . . " He shuffled through the crap on his desk and found the information. "New Bergin."

Sullivan spread his hands. "Never heard of it."

"You are not alone."

The chair creaked a little closer to the floor when Sullivan sat back down. "When did it happen?"

"This morning."

"How'd you find out about it so fast?"

"FBI."

The detective's lips twisted. When he'd contacted the FBI about his case, they had been less than helpful. They hadn't been any more helpful when Bobby contacted them. However—

"The agent I spoke with about our cases was conveniently the one that . . . " Bobby glanced again at his cheat sheet. "Chief Johnson spoke with this morning."

"How many dead, branded bodies do they have in Podunk?"

"Just the one."

"Then why would they call the FBI?"

"Place hasn't had a murder since 1867."

"Good for them. Still don't see why they called the feds."

"They wanted help."

Sullivan rubbed his forehead. "Murder isn't a federal offense."

"This one might be."

The detective dropped his hand. "How?"

"The woman in that picture is the sister of a U.S. Marshal."

Understanding blossomed across Sullivan's face. "And the murder of an immediate family member of a law enforcement official jacks the charge into the big leagues."

"Retaliatory murder," Bobby corrected. "And this looks pretty retaliatory to me."

He tossed the rest of the crime scene photos—which weren't very good and made Bobby think they'd been taken with someone's outdated cell phone—to Sullivan. Despite his having seen the same, or worse, before, the man grimaced.

"Missing body parts are usually a good clue," Sullivan agreed.

Bobby had no idea why but gangsters—both the mob and the gangs—liked to hack people into pieces as a message. Usually they hacked them into more pieces than two, but the missing arm was both weird and worrisome.

"The police chief called the feds," Bobby continued, "and the feds forwarded his pictures to me to compare the brand on the Wisconsin victim to the brands on ours."

"And?"

"I think they match, but I want to take a closer look."

"Me too. When do we leave?"

"*We* don't."

"Goddamn budget cuts."

"Redundant," Bobby murmured, gathering the photos and information then stuffing them into the file. He had just enough time to pack a bag and catch his plane.

Sullivan shifted his linebacker shoulders. "I'd hoped this guy was gone for good."

They hadn't found a body in nearly a year. Bobby'd kind of hoped the guy was gone for good too. In prison. Dead. Lobotomized. He wasn't picky.

"I think he's back," Bobby said.

The spark of worry in his partner's gaze deepened. "I think you're right."

Chapter 2

I reached my classroom only a minute or two after my class did. Still, David had already painted himself turquoise and Susan had picked the lock on the scissors drawer.

I was really going to have to keep my eye on Susan.

Their excuse?

"Stafford told us to."

As Stafford was laughing his forever five-year-old butt off right behind them I believed it.

I'd hoped that working with children would lessen my exposure to ghosts, and it had, but not completely. Stafford was a case in point. The towheaded, blue-eyed imp was as dead as the scary lady on Avenue B. He liked to whisper naughty suggestions into the ears of my students then laugh and laugh at the chaos he caused.

When I was four, I stopped talking about the people no one saw but me. However, I never stopped seeing them. Most children do—right around the time they start to speak—but not all of them. Some see and hear spirits for a little while longer. These were the ones Stafford haunted.

I'd tried to discover how long the child had been walking through the walls of my school, but, predictably, no adult had ever seen him but me. The previous kindergarten teacher only stared at me blankly when I asked if any of her students had spoken of an invisible friend. Which made me think Stafford was newly dead. Except there was no record of a child of that name dying in New Bergin or anywhere close enough to warrant his presence.

Regardless of how devious my queries or how long I cajoled, he never gave me any information on himself whatsoever. No matter what I said, Stafford would not cross over. He liked causing trouble too much.

Today was no different. The kids behaved as if someone had slipped them chocolate-covered circus peanuts for breakfast. I felt like I was taming lions. When the last bell rang, I ushered them out, hoping for better tomorrows; then I locked my classroom door and had a conversation with Stafford.

"I'm starting to think you want to get someone killed so you won't be lonely."

Confusion flickered across his deceptively sweet face. "I'm not lonely. I have you."

"What about your mother?"

Wariness replaced the confusion. "What about her?"

"Is she still alive?"

It wasn't very nice of me to sic Stafford on his mother, but seriously, why me?

"If she is," I continued, "you could visit."

I doubted this would work—Stafford seemed attached to the school and therefore he probably couldn't leave to haunt—I mean "visit"—his mother. But I was desperate.

"If she isn't, you could still visit."

Once he was on the other side, I didn't think he could come back. At least none of the other ghosts I'd convinced to go into the light ever had.

"Stafford?" His eyes met mine. "Your mother?"

He looked away and didn't answer.

"How about your father?"

One of the fluorescent bulbs flickered.

"Stop that," I said.

"You stop that," he returned.

I had to bite my lip to keep myself from continuing the childish exchange. "I just want you to—"

The ghost child disappeared.

"Come back here!"

All the lights in the room went out. I didn't bother to check the fuse or the switch. Been there, done that. The only way they would go back on was if Stafford wanted them to. Which was usually after I'd called Mr. Jorgenson, head of maintenance—i.e., the janitor. He would arrive to investigate thirty seconds after all the lights went back on. Then he would point out that every bulb was fully functioning and shake his head at the foolish female who'd probably neglected to flip the switch in the first place. As he was unable to hear Stafford's laughter, I could hardly blame him.

I gathered my things and left. On the street, I glanced back. Every light in my room blazed, throwing Stafford's shape into stark relief beyond the window. Another one of his tricks. I could count on a note in my mailbox tomorrow from the principal admonishing me about wasting energy.

Stafford waved. I gave up and waved back.

I could have avoided the crime scene on the way home. New Bergin was small but not so small there wasn't an alternate route. However, I felt drawn there. Though I didn't want to see the dead woman again, I probably would. Ghosts revealed themselves to me for a reason, and until I knew that reason, she might turn up anywhere. There was no avoiding it, or her.

Yellow tape cordoned off the alleyway where she had died. The body was gone, but the asphalt still sported bloodstains and burn marks. I wasn't sure how they'd make those disappear beyond repaving the street. Until the murder was solved that was probably off the table.

I was surprised there weren't a few stragglers ogling the crime scene. Horrific as the murder was, it was the most excitement we'd seen in New Bergin since a deer had jumped through the front window of the Norseman Café during rut. He'd trashed the place pretty good before he'd rammed his rack into the drywall.

The sun was falling fast; the Indian summer warmth would disappear as quickly as Stafford had. The idea of standing on a dinnertime deserted street in the approaching twilight and coming face-to-face again with that ink-eyed specter had me hurrying in the direction of my apartment at the same pace I'd left it that morning.

Inside I slipped into my favorite yoga pants and a ratty tank top then studied the finger-shaped bruises on my arm. I was rarely without a bruise of some kind—shin, hip, thigh, chin—kids were rough.

I opened the medicine cabinet and took out the arnica cream. People could label the concoction hippy-dippy all they wanted, but it was the only thing I'd ever found that helped the bruises fade more quickly.

After squirting some onto my arm, I rubbed until the ointment disappeared. The marks still tingled like frozen toes immersed in warm water.

I watched television for a few hours. A day spent with children turned my brain to oatmeal and until I had some distance, I'd be no good for anything. Eventually I popped the cork on a new bottle of cabernet and took both it and the glass to my kitchen table where I proceeded to correct papers.

"You must run."

In the act of reaching for my wine, the voice nearly made me knock it over. My Puritan hugged the shadows of the living room. He had an accent—Irish? Scottish?—something with a brogue.

"I . . . uh . . . What?"

Not only had he never spoken, but he'd never come so close. At this range I could see he was nearer to my age than I'd thought—mid-twenties perhaps—and handsome despite the prudish, black clothes.

"Now, dear girl."

I glanced at my cell phone, which had been sitting on the table next to my papers, and it flew onto the floor then skidded toward the front door.

I stood. "Was that really necess—"

My Puritan disappeared.

Something moved within my darkened bedroom, and I took a step in that direction.

"Hey," I began.

The figure started toward me. Though I couldn't see a face, or even get a sense of male or female amid the swirling shadows, the meat cleaver was unmistakable. I threw open the door and tore down the stairs. "Help!"

Unfortunately it was ten P.M. In New Bergin. Everyone was safe at home, probably already asleep.

I was so dead.

I sprinted into the street, ignoring the chill of the pavement against my bare feet. Where I was going, I had no idea. The police department lay on the other side of town. Not that the town was that big, but it was dark. No streetlights. No need. No one drove around at this time of night, and if they did there was a lovely invention called headlights.

For an instant I believed my thoughts—or my wishes, hopes, and prayers—had conjured some. Then the car that was moving too fast for First Street hit the brakes and screeched to a halt about a foot from my knees. A man jumped out.

Talk about wishes, hopes, and prayers. He was the answer to all three.

Fury brightened his blue gaze. "Are you crazy?"

Despite the color of his eyes, he wasn't from around here. The Southern accent would have given him away even if I'd been too blind to register the deeper than sun-kissed shade of his skin.

"I . . . No."

Maybe, my brain corrected.

I pointed where I'd been, cringing when I realized the knife-wielding maniac could have caught up to me by now, but we were alone.

"There was someone in my apartment. With a meat clever."

I expected him to laugh and ask if I was high instead of crazy. Instead, those brilliant eyes hardened. "Get in the car." He reached inside and came out with a gun. "Lock the doors."

While I stood there gaping, he hurried toward my apartment. I glanced back and forth, torn between following him and doing as he'd ordered. Then the wind picked up, making the autumn leaves rattle like bones. The headlights blared down the street, creating shadows at the end that might be a dog, a cat, a murderer, or just shadows.

I got in the car.

Bobby climbed the steps to the second-story apartment. The door loomed open. No meat-cleaver-wielding maniac burst out. But there was still time.

On the landing he leaned right and left, able to see nearly the entire living area and kitchen through the open door. Both were empty.

"Police," he announced, and stepped inside. "Show yourself."

Nothing moved but the papers on the table, which ruffled in the breeze through the door. A few had drifted onto the floor next to a cell phone, which the woman must have dropped when she ran. A cell phone would have been a good item to take along, but people did strange things when they were frightened.

The papers appeared to be homework for the very young and proved an intriguing contrast to the nearly full glass of wine glistening like rubies in the lamplight.

On one side of the sheet were three fish, four cats, two bicycles, and so on. The other side listed the numbers. Wavy crayon lines connected the numbers to the pictures.

Bobby tilted his head, narrowed his eyes. Looked like Jacob needed some special help as he'd connected the cats to the three and the fish had been counted as two.

"Focus." The meat-cleaver maniac might still be through door number one or door number two.

The first loomed open on a shadowy bedroom. He flicked on the light, peeked behind the door, under the bed, in the closet. Nothing but brightly colored, casual clothes and more dust than she probably wanted anyone to see.

He backed out, flicked the next doorknob, and sent the closed door flying open.

Bathroom. Empty.

He lowered his weapon, stepped to the room's single window—painted shut—and glanced out. A dense forest began not more than fifty yards from the back of the building.

Bobby considered holstering the gun and didn't. Forests gave him the twitchies. Pretty much anything could be in there.

New Orleans had swamps—thick ones, with dripping Spanish moss and lots of alligators. Creepy in their own way, but also familiar. Bobby knew how to search a swamp. But a forest?

Not a clue.

He returned to the street. His car still sat in the center, the shadow of the woman shifted inside. Oddly no one had come out to see what was going on—as if shrieking women and cars idling in the middle of the road were commonplace. Then again, had she shrieked? Maybe not.

He crossed to the car, flicked his finger, indicating she should get out. Instead, she lowered the window a few inches. "Did you see anything?"

"No."

She frowned. "Nothing?"

"Was it a he? She?"

"Yes," she answered. "Definitely a he. Or a she."

Bobby's lips twitched. He shouldn't be amused, but

he was. "They didn't trash the place, unless you call knocking your phone on the floor along with a few of the 'One fish, blue fish' papers a mess."

She lifted dark brows toward hair as black as his own. The contrast of that ebony hair and milky skin made him think of Snow White. Too bad he wasn't any kind of prince.

Foolish thoughts. What was wrong with him? Probably nothing more than his having had no dates in the last year combined with the enticing sway of her ample breasts loose beneath that ancient tank top. Any man would want to be her prince the instant he saw breasts like that.

"Who are you?" she asked, her gaze on the gun in his hand.

He slid his weapon into the shoulder holster. "Bobby Doucet. I'm a detective with the New Orleans PD."

"You're a long way from New Orleans."

His gaze touched the trees again. "Don't I know it?"

"Why?"

As now was not the time for that explanation, he ignored the question. "I didn't find anyone in the apartment, Miss . . ."

"Larsen," she said. "Raye Larsen."

"The intruder could have come down the stairs on your heels, then hoofed it into the woods at the sight of my car."

"Maybe."

"The other option is that no one was there in the first place. Take your pick."

A police cruiser, lights flashing, slid to a stop behind Bobby's car. Apparently someone had noticed its presence after all and called 911. Or maybe the night watch had finally gotten back to this street. It wasn't as if there were that many streets to keep track of.

A sinewy fellow with tufts of white hair above his ears and none anywhere else stepped out. "What's goin' on here?"

"Chief!" Miss Larsen hit the locks and nearly smacked Bobby in the chest as she opened the car door. She was taller than he'd first thought, at least five seven in bare feet.

"Raye, what are you doin' out here?" He turned his scowl on Bobby. "Who are you?"

"Detective Bobby Doucet. Chief Johnson?"

The man nodded.

"I think you're expecting me."

"Not in the middle of the night," Johnson grumbled.

Bobby cast a glance at the numbers displayed on his dashboard. Since when was ten o'clock the middle of anything? In New Orleans ten was barely the beginning.

"Miss Larsen requested my assistance."

The chief's scowl deepened. "What kind of assistance?"

"I saw someone lurking around the crime scene," she blurted.

Bobby opened his mouth, then shut it again. What the—

Johnson's eyes moved to Raye's face, studiously avoiding parts lower than her chin. "Who?"

She shrugged.

"And then?"

"The detective arrived, and I flagged him down to tell him."

"You saw a strange man in a strange car and thought he could help you with the stranger?"

She nodded.

Bobby wasn't sure what to do. She was lying. Then again, he'd found no meat-cleaver-wielding maniac in her apartment, nor any sign of one. Perhaps she'd decided she'd had a vivid dream while drunk paper correcting and just wanted it all to go away. He could relate.

"Was there anyone there?" the chief asked.

"No," she answered. "Must have been a shadow."

Johnson grunted. He wasn't convinced. But what could he do beyond calling the woman a liar, and why would she lie about something so pointless? Bobby couldn't wait to find out.

"You have a place to stay, Detective?"

"Just point me to the nearest hotel."

"Forty miles that way." Raye's finger indicated the direction he'd just arrived from. Come to think of it, the only hotel he'd seen between here and the Dane County Regional Airport had given him *Psycho* flashbacks.

"There's no hotel in town?"

"We don't need one," she said. "Visitors stay with the relatives they came to visit."

"That's . . . " He wasn't sure what it was. Obviously not impossible.

"There's a bed-and-breakfast," the chief said. "You want to run him over to your dad's place, Raye?" Johnson lifted his eyebrows. "After you put on some clothes. If he sees you walking around like that he'll have a stroke."

If her attire was stroke inducing she better hope her father never came to New Orleans. Bobby didn't think he'd seen a bra—unless it was worn without a shirt—on Bourbon Street in years.

The chief paused with one foot inside his cruiser. "Let's meet at my office in the morning, Detective, and I'll bring you up to speed. Say seven?" The chief didn't wait for an answer, just climbed into his car, pulled around Bobby's and away.

"Talk about the middle of the night," Bobby muttered.

"I'll grab some shoes, a jacket." Raye turned, and he snatched her arm. She hissed as if in pain, and he released her. Her perfect white flesh was marred by finger-shaped bruises.

"You didn't say he touched you."

"He didn't." She continued toward the stairs. Bobby followed. There hadn't been anyone there before, but he still didn't feel comfortable letting her go back alone. He wasn't sure why.

"Who did?" He started up after her.

She paused, casting a glance back. "I don't need your help to dress."

She might not need it, but he wouldn't mind giving it.

"You really want to go up there alone?"

She shrugged, and the strap of her thin cotton tank slid to the edge of her shoulder. He held his breath, half hoping it would fall.

"I was imagining things."

He dragged his gaze to hers. "You do that a lot?"

"What's a lot?" She lifted her hand and shoved her hair from her face. The bruises shone black in the moonlight.

"Who hurt you?"

She dropped her arm. "I'm a kindergarten teacher." At his blank expression, she continued. "Kids run, and they can't stop. They fall. They slide. They bump themselves and their teacher. I've always got a bruise somewhere. I'm lucky I still have my front teeth." Her lips quirked upward. "Most of them don't."

She was lying again. Maybe not about the bruises in general, but about these, definitely. Bobby could smell it as clearly as that slight whiff of something burning on the breeze.

Chapter 3

I stomped up the steps and into the apartment before Detective Doucet could call me a liar. I tried to shut the door in his face, but he was too quick. I kind of liked that about him. Among other things.

Those blue eyes, the latte shade of his skin, cheekbones to die for, long legs, great arms, and a deep voice, with an accent that invited questions. He sounded both Southern and foreign. Although this far north, Southern *was* foreign.

He was beautiful and built. Not that we didn't see both in New Bergin. But not like this.

The most exotic being ever recorded in northern Wisconsin was Johnny Depp who had come here to make a movie about Dillinger. And while the grapevine had labeled him one helluva nice guy, local photo ops proved he was not as pretty as he appeared on screen—nor half as tall.

Bobby Doucet was about six one. I found it a welcome bonus to have to tilt my head to see into his face. Even scowling he was mouthwateringly gorgeous.

"I'll be right out." I pushed on the door.

"I'd rather you let me in." He pushed back.

"You said there was no one in the apartment."

"There wasn't." His gaze narrowed. "Why didn't you tell the chief about the intruder?"

I couldn't tell Doucet that I'd started to wonder if the figure I'd seen was just another ghost. Then he'd stare at me as if I were nuts. Wouldn't be the first time for me, but it would be the first time for me with him. And I liked the way he'd been looking at me. As if I were as exotic a being in his eyes as he was in mine.

"Maybe I imagined him. Her. It." I released my hold on the door.

I'd hoped my Puritan was hanging about inside, and I could ask why he'd suddenly chosen to speak to me tonight when he never had before. As he wasn't, no need to leave the detective out in the cold.

"It?" Doucet repeated, and I spread my hands.

"What else do you call a dream?"

"Nightmare?"

I'd been halfway to my bedroom but the word made me turn. His eyes were as haunted as my life. "I'm sorry."

"Why?" He glanced away. "Everyone has nightmares."

I didn't think everyone had the kind of nightmares we did, those that hung around in the light. But I didn't know him well enough to ask. Does anyone ever know anyone that well? I liked to think so, to hope so, otherwise what was the point of anything?

"True enough." I closed the bedroom door. If I was taking him to my father's bed-and-breakfast I needed more than a jacket and shoes. I yanked out jeans, socks, a real shirt, and a bra. I felt as if I were arming myself for battle. Because I was.

I knew in my head that I could no longer be sent "back," but in my heart I felt my father still kind of wanted to. I might have stopped talking to the specters in the presence of anyone but myself, but he remembered.

I think I'd freaked him out too much for him to ever forget.

Whenever he was around, I tiptoed. Not literally—much—but I was always afraid I might do something wrong. Even more afraid I wouldn't quite know that I had. No matter how hard I tried, I didn't fit in here because I wasn't being myself. I couldn't be.

As a kid I'd been uncomfortable in my own skin, forever awkward, and the vultures—I mean teenagers—sensed it and pounced. I didn't get picked on often, but I did get picked on well. The taunts of "Stray Raye" still drifted through my head more often than I liked.

I stepped into the living room, retrieved my cell phone and keys, took a fortifying chug of my wine then offered the glass to the detective.

"No, thanks."

We stepped onto the landing and I locked the place behind us.

"Should I follow you?" he asked.

"Don't have a car."

He laughed, then he saw I was serious. "Why wouldn't you have a car?"

"Everything I need is in walking distance."

"I heard it snows here."

"A lot. So?"

"Then what do you do?"

"Wear boots."

"But—"

"I don't melt in the rain, or freeze solid if the rain turns to snow. I know how to dress for the weather and a car would only sit on the street and rust. I'm a teacher. It's not like I have money to burn."

"You don't ever leave town?"

"Of course."

"How?"

"Other people have cars, and I have family. Friends." Make that *friend,* but Jenn had a car. I just had to really want to go somewhere badly to get in one with her. She drove a lot faster than she walked. "There's also this fabulous new invention called a bus. Lots of people can ride in it!"

"Very funny," he said, though he didn't appear amused. "Just point me in the right direction, and I'll drive myself. You don't have to come."

"I don't mind. It's not that far."

"Then I should definitely be able to find it."

"Maybe. However, you can't just walk up to the door and rent a room."

His forehead creased. "Why not?"

"It's my parents' house. A big house, which is why there are rooms to rent, but my father isn't going to let any nut job off the streets inside."

"Are there a lot of nut jobs on the streets?"

"Apparently more than we thought."

"Touché," he said, and I caught again that hint of France, which intrigued me far more than it should. Could he speak French? Would he?

I climbed into the passenger seat, and he got behind the wheel. "I'll bring you home as soon as you vouch for me."

"Not necessary."

He shifted into drive. "What about the maniac?"

"I imagined him. Her."

"It," he finished, taking the right turn I'd indicated. "There's a dead woman in town who begs to differ."

"Dead women don't beg," I said.

He cast me a quick glance. "You're lying again."

What could I say? He was right.

Raye's directions led into the damn forest. Did the place seem farther than far because of that? Or were distances different in a place so vast?

Bobby's low-slung mid-sized rent-a-car scraped along the dry, rutted trail between towering pines. He should have upgraded to the SUV, but he'd figured at this time of year that would be a waste of money.

He'd never seen trees this tall. They had to be older than God.

Something clanged against the undercarriage so loudly Bobby held his breath and waited for the car to die, but it didn't. Lights flickered ahead, materializing into the ground-floor windows of a very large house.

"Were your ancestors lumberjacks?" The place appeared big enough to house Paul Bunyan; the barn would have sheltered his blue ox.

"I don't know my ancestors." She got out of the car. "I'm adopted."

He bit back his automatic *I'm sorry*. Why would he be?

Because she'd sounded so sad. He thought again of those bruises on her arm and hustled after her, reaching the foot of the steps just as she knocked. Why was she knocking on her own front door?

The porch continued around both sides of the house. Several rocking chairs sat near handcrafted tables, perfect for holding a glass of iced tea or a chess set. Bobby could imagine relaxing here on a sunny afternoon. Except the woods were so thick and the trees so high the sun might only shine in this clearing for an hour at midday.

The door opened, and the silhouette of a man appeared; the lights at his back were so bright Bobby's eyes ached.

"Father."

Who called their father "Father" anymore?

"I brought you a guest."

Though Bobby still couldn't see a face, he sensed when the man's gaze turned in his direction. "Nice to meet you, sir. I'm Detective Bobby Doucet, from New Orleans."

Mr. Larsen continued to stand inside, his expression shrouded by the night.

"Chief Johnson sent him over," Raye added.

Her father pushed open the screen. Would Bobby have been invited in if not for Chief Johnson?

Raye reached for the door. Bobby's hand, already doing the same, connected with hers. Silvery blue sparks leaped through the silent night. They both pulled back, and the screen door banged.

"Sorry," Raye and Bobby blurted at the same time.

"Get a move on," Mr. Larsen said. "I was just about to head to bed."

Considering the barn and the early bedtime, Bobby wondered if the Larsens had once been farmers. Though if they had where were their fields? He doubted trees this big sprouted up like beanstalks.

Raye led him into a kitchen that appeared rustic. Butcher block. Large hand-crafted table with matching chairs. Frilly, seemingly handmade curtains. However, the appliances were state-of-the-art. The countertops and the floor covering might appear old, but they'd been made to.

"Detective Doucet, this is my father, John."

If Raye hadn't already told him she was adopted, he would have wondered. John Larsen was a short, squat man with silvery-blond hair, a florid complexion, and eyes of so light a blue Bobby thought it must hurt them to be exposed to the sun. Which might explain why he lived in shadow.

"Mr. Larsen." Bobby held out his hand. "Nice to meet you."

They shook. "I suspect you're here about the dead woman."

"I—" Bobby began.

"First murder in New Bergin in several lifetimes."

"You're very lucky," Bobby said. He had several lifetimes' worth of murder a week in New Orleans.

"And what are you?"

"Homicide detective." Bobby figured that was obvious but maybe not.

"No. I mean . . . " The man waved his hand, indicating Bobby's head, chest, feet.

Bobby glanced down. His fly was zipped; his shirt was buttoned. His shoes were a little scuffed, and he'd taken off his tie on the plane but—

He lifted his gaze to Raye, who was rubbing her head as if it ached. "I don't—"

"Thanks, Father. I'll show him his room." She grabbed Bobby's arm and practically dragged him through the door and toward the wooden staircase.

The steps gleamed with varnish, as did the hand-carved newel post and railing. Bobby ran his palm over them.

"Beautiful," he murmured. The craftsmanship was equal to some of the best restorations in New Orleans, and there were a lot of them.

"Father did all the work himself. Carved the tables and chairs too."

"He's a carpenter?"

"And a teacher."

"You followed in his footsteps."

"Didn't help."

He frowned. Help what?

"He was a high school shop teacher. Retired before he was phased out."

"Phased out?" Bobby echoed.

"Younger teachers cost less, and shop teachers aren't necessary."

"I enjoyed shop."

"Enjoy isn't on the program these days. Math. Science. Advanced placement." She held up a hand. "Don't get me started."

He understood the frustration in being a public servant. He'd gone into law enforcement to help people. Instead he spent a lot of time fighting the system instead of the bad guys.

"But my father's a lemonade maker." Her lips curved, though her expression was more melancholy than amused. "Turned what he taught into a second career, and he's doing pretty well."

"Your mom?"

"Gone," she said. "Cancer."

"I'm sorry." He resisted a bizarre urge to take her hands in his and warm them. "That's rough."

"It was."

They reached the landing. She opened the second

door on the right and flicked on the light. Every shade in the green spectrum appeared to live within—lime, pine, grass—there were more but Bobby had exhausted his color vocabulary.

"Let me guess." He shaded his eyes. "The green room?"

"There's also a blue room and a yellow room."

"No red room?" He ran the words together so they sounded like *redrum,* and she smiled. A Stephen King fan. He liked her even more.

"They considered it. Then I showed them the movie. My father's still traumatized."

"About your father . . . I'm not sure what he was trying to ask me."

"He didn't mean to be rude."

"He was being rude?" Now Bobby was really confused.

She bit her lip. "He might ask again."

"Whatever the hell he asked in the first place," Bobby muttered. "What am I?"

"He was asking where your ancestors came from."

The light dawned. "As in Africa?"

"Around here, the only nonwhite people are Indians."

He waited for her to laugh but she didn't.

In New Orleans a lot of folks were something as well as a little something else. The shades of skin varied widely and no one cared, or if they did, they didn't mention it.

"In New Bergin, most of the names end with some variation of *son* or *man,*" she continued.

Bobby spread his hands, clueless.

"Our ancestors are from Norway. Sweden. Germany."

"And Larsen?"

"Norwegian."

"You don't look Norwegian."

"I get that a lot." She didn't seem to care for it either. "As I'm adopted, I have no idea where I'm really from."

"Does it matter?"

"Seems to."

"Did you ever try to find out?"

She shook her head. He would have asked more but something in the way her lips tightened made him not.

"I'm Creole," he said.

Now she spread her hands and shrugged.

"Descendants of the French and Spanish, born in this country."

"No one's French around here. Or Spanish."

"Probably not Haitian either."

"Interesting."

"Not where I come from." He couldn't remember the last time he'd met someone who wasn't one, the other, or all three—unless it was Sullivan.

"The most exotic mixture in New Bergin is German and Norwegian, which isn't very exotic at all."

"There's something to be said for the nonexotic."

"That would be boring."

"You aren't."

For an instant he wished the words back. Then, her obvious surprise, followed by her equally obvious pleasure, made him glad they'd slipped out.

"Thanks," she said. "Everyone in New Bergin was born in New Bergin or near enough. People who move here from away are always from away. Once they figure that out, they don't stay."

"What about you?"

"What about me?"

He couldn't help it; he reached out and rubbed a piece of her inky black hair between his fingers. It was exactly as soft as it looked. "You stayed."

"Where would I go?"

"Anywhere that you wanted."

Interest sparked in her deep dark eyes. Maybe she'd like to—

"Raye?" Mr. Larsen called.

They stepped away from each other as if they'd been caught doing something they shouldn't.

"I'll be right down."

"You in his room?"

She stepped into the hall. "No."

Bobby snorted, and she cast him a wicked glance. Suddenly he wished they'd been caught doing everything.

His thoughts must have shown because she ducked her head and moved out of his sight.

"I'm getting his towels." She returned with an armload the shade of moss. "Bathroom is the first door at the top of the stairs."

"Tell me it isn't orange."

"All right."

"It isn't?"

"You said not to tell you."

He wasn't sure if she was kidding or not and that only intrigued him more.

"Breakfast is included," she continued. "Hence the name bed-and-breakfast."

"I'll be gone long before anyone's made breakfast."

"My father comes from a long line of farmers. Early to bed, early to rise. He'll be up before you are. And he cooks for threshers just like his mother did before him."

"I don't know what that means."

"There'll be more than doughnuts."

"I'm pretty much a coffee-for-breakfast man."

"Once you smell my father's food, you won't be."

"I'm from New Orleans."

"I don't know what that means."

They weren't communicating well, seemingly had nothing in common. And instead of being bored, annoyed, and frustrated, Bobby was intrigued and fascinated.

"The food in New Orleans is pretty hard to beat."

"We'll see."

He certainly wanted to. He made a valiant attempt not to let his gaze drop to her breasts, which were almost invisible now beneath a bulky, faded sweatshirt with a dancing cartoon Badger. The thing had a huge head. Didn't badgers have small heads? He wasn't sure. He'd never actually seen one. After seeing this one, he didn't think he wanted to.

"Will your father take you home, or should I?"

"I'll be fine."

"You're not walking."

"I'm not?"

The idea of her strolling through the dark, looming forest back to a town devoid of streetlights, even without the lurking murderer, gave him a twitch.

"You should stay here."

"Here?" She glanced pointedly around the room.

Yes, please, he thought.

"If only," he said.

She lifted her eyebrows. For a small-town girl who didn't even own a car, his suggestive banter didn't fluster her. He liked that about her too.

"Raye?" her father called again.

"Coming." She didn't move.

"Is *Raye* short for something?"

"Raymond."

"Your name is Raymond."

"My father's father's name was Raymond."

He found it interesting that she didn't use the word *grandfather.* But then he found everything about her interesting, which was . . . interesting.

"As I'm an only child they thought it would be nice to name me after him."

Bobby wasn't sure he'd call it nice. Maybe interesting.

He had to stifle a burst of derisive laughter. He appeared to have lost his mind.

She moved to the door, and he got a little panicked. What if he never saw her again? "You shouldn't stay alone."

"I won't." She smiled. "Don't leave town without saying good-bye. If I'm not at my apartment, I'll be at the elementary school."

His own smile froze.

One place he could never go.

A trapped expression shrouded the detective's face before he turned away. Why had I thought he was interested in me?

I'd never been good with men. Considering I'd known all the males in town from the cradle, you'd think I would be. But I fit in with them no better than I fit in with anyone. In New Bergin each kiss was cause for a bulletin. Which made me self-conscious on every date that I'd had. Not that there'd been all that many.

I'd had sex. Once. He who shall not be named—at

least the ass had gone off to college and never come back—had told everyone my breasts were even bigger than they looked. No one else got to discuss—or touch them—again. Except me.

I texted Jenn. *Need a ride from my parents' place.*

My phone buzzed with a return text before I'd reached the ground floor. *On my way.*

What would I do without her?

My father stood at the kitchen sink, staring out the window into the night. "Why would Chief Johnson bring in a homicide detective from New Orleans?"

A good question. One I hadn't thought to ask.

Bobby was a murder cop, and we'd had a murder, but why him? Just from the questions he'd asked he was unfamiliar with the area, its people. What possible help could he be?

Beyond improving the scenery.

"You'll have to ask Chief Johnson."

My father's lips pursed. "It's disturbing."

I wasn't sure what he was referring to, but since there was plenty to choose from I decided to nod.

Headlights flashed across the ceiling as Jenn arrived. My father reached for the pistol he kept in the cupboard. The back of my neck prickled. I'd never known him to be jumpy before.

"It's Jenn." I headed for the front door.

He followed, reaching for my hand. Surprised—my father wasn't much for PDAs—I reached for his too. He pressed the pistol into my palm. I tried to draw back, but he folded my fingers around the grip. "Take this."

"No, thanks." Guns gave me the wiggies.

"I've got another one."

Since when? Certainly firearms were commonplace

in the Big Woods, but as far as I knew he only owned the pistol in my hand and a shotgun for hunting. Maybe that's what he meant. If I had the pistol, he had the shotgun. Except I didn't want the pistol.

"I don't have anywhere to put it." I'd left with my keys not my purse. Although I wasn't sure the weapon—a forty-four Magnum—would fit in any handbag I had, and the idea of walking around with a gun in my handbag was so ludicrous I nearly dropped it.

"This is New Bergin," I said. "We have no streetlights and three cops for a reason."

"Which is probably the reason we also have a murderer." At my frown he continued. "It's dark and no one's watching."

Was he trying to be funny? He never had before.

"I'll be careful," I said, and tried to give back the pistol. He ignored me and went into the hall. Anyone who picked me up, girlfriend or boyfriend, came to the door. My father insisted.

He was probably right. He always knew that whomever I said I was leaving with was actually who I left with. In this town that went a long way toward avoiding trouble. If I left with Brandon Jensen, Brandon Jensen had damn straight better bring me back without a scratch, or John Larsen would be speaking to every Jensen he knew.

Jenn had just lifted her hand to knock when my father opened the door.

"How you be, Mr. Larsen?" She stepped inside, glanced up. "Holy fricking crap," she said.

Bobby Doucet stood at the top of the steps, shirt unbuttoned, hair a bit mussed, feet bare.

Holy, fricking crap indeed.

Chapter 4

Bobby had been getting undressed when he heard Raye and her father talking. Curious, he'd stepped into the hall. When the door opened, he'd moved closer to see who had come to pick her up, hoping more than he had any right to that it wasn't a guy.

Not a guy, but a tiny blond woman who looked right at him and smiled a smile that would launch a thousand ships. He was more interested in the gun in Raye's hand. The sight was so baffling he blinked a few times, but the weapon stayed right where it was.

"Button your shirt, Detective," Mr. Larsen snapped.

"Not on my account," Blondie murmured.

"Why do you have a gun?" Bobby descended to the foyer as he did what John Larsen had ordered.

Raye glanced down, frowning as if she'd forgotten she held the weapon, a forty-four Magnum revolver, which had to weigh two or three pounds. She shoved it at her father. "Take this."

The man pushed it back in her direction. "No."

Bobby took the Magnum away from both of them. "Whose is it?"

Raye pointed at her father.

"She's not going back to that apartment without protection," Larsen said.

"I'll stay with Jenn."

Bobby assumed the itty-bitty blond committee was Jenn. When he glanced at her she winked. He shifted his attention to Raye. "Do you know how to use a gun?"

"Nope."

Why did people think using a firearm was as simple as pointing and pulling? If you wanted to hit a can that wasn't moving, shouting, running toward you—often with a gun of its own—maybe it would be. However, that so rarely happened.

People also seemed to think that the bigger the gun the better, never considering how difficult it would be to hold the thing steady at all, let alone if it weighed close to three pounds, like this one. Dirty Harry might fire the weapon accurately, but he doubted anyone else could.

"I am not taking a gun home," Raye insisted.

"Yes you are," her father said.

"No I'm not!"

Bobby's head was starting to ache. "If you didn't want your father to worry, you shouldn't have told him there was someone in your apartment."

Silence fell.

"There was what?" Larsen asked. He didn't yell, yet still all three of them winced.

Raye shot Bobby a glare. He was glad he had the gun and she didn't. He took one step into the kitchen and set the weapon on the counter so it was far, far away from her, then returned to the front hall.

"You aren't going anywhere," Larsen began at the same time Raye said, "There was no one in my apartment."

"He just said—"

"He searched the place," Raye interrupted. "Tell him what you found."

"Nothing."

Larsen's gaze narrowed on his daughter. "What did you see?"

"A shadow. Something thumped. After this morning who wouldn't be spooked? But I had a trained detective search the place, and he found no indication of an intruder."

"The more important question," Jenn said, "is why you had a trained detective available to search."

Raye blinked. "What?"

"You saw a shadow, heard a noise, freaked out and . . . " She spread her perfectly manicured fingernails. "You rubbed a magic lamp and tall, dark, and well-armed swirled out?"

Raye made a disgusted sound. "Not now, Jenn."

"It's a legitimate question." Jenn shrugged. "Or close enough."

"I had just driven into town when Raye ran outside," Bobby explained. "She seemed upset; I asked if I could help, and it turned out that I could."

"And here I thought there was never a cop around when you needed one."

"Never mind her," Raye said. "She's always like this."

"Like what?" Jenn asked.

Raye didn't answer. She seemed a little pale, though it was hard to tell with her Snow White skin, a shade that could have been unappealing, especially with such dark hair and eyes, but instead reminded Bobby of smooth, thick cream. He wondered if it tasted as good as it looked. He wished he had the time to find out, but he doubted he'd be here that long, and considering the size of her dad's gun, that was probably for the best.

His neck suddenly felt cold, as if a winter wind had

swirled down his collar. But it wasn't winter, and there was no wind. He rubbed at his neck, shifted his shoulders, but that weird sense of a draft didn't go away.

Raye shivered, as if she'd felt it too, but before he could ask what was wrong, she pushed past her friend and out the door.

Jenn bussed Mr. Larsen on the tip of his chin. She cast Bobby a considering glance then followed Raye into the dark. No one but Bobby appeared to have noticed Raye's odd behavior or found her departure all that sudden.

The click of the door seemed loud in the silence they left behind. It felt as if all the light and air and movement had been sucked out of the place.

"She's always been like that," Mr. Larsen murmured.

"That's what Raye said."

"I meant Raye." Her father turned and walked away.

The night felt warm after the chill that had come over the house. Usually I was the only one who noticed it. But tonight, I thought Bobby Doucet had too.

He'd rubbed at his neck, twitched his shoulders, glanced over one with a frown. But he hadn't seen the man who stood right behind him. Only I had. As usual, I was the only one who heard him too.

"Tell him to look under the floor," the fellow had said. "Under the floor in the locker."

I'd tried to pretend I hadn't seen, or heard, him. Maybe then he would go away. It didn't work any better this time than any of the other times I'd tried it.

"Tell him!" the specter shouted, and I could have sworn my hair ruffled with the force of his icy breath.

I'd wanted to ask what floor? Which locker? Where?

Why? And what locker has a floor that could be looked under? But I didn't. Instead, I'd gotten out of there.

"Sheesh." Jenn caught up. "Why are you always in such a hurry?"

"I have to work tomorrow." I got into her car.

"You do realize it's not even eleven o'clock." She climbed behind the wheel.

I made the mistake of glancing at the house. In an upstairs window stood a man. I could tell right away from the shape of his silhouette that it wasn't Bobby Doucet. Both the shoulders and the shape of the head were too narrow to be Bobby, or even the spirit that had followed him downstairs. And it wasn't one of the few I'd encountered when I lived in the place, or even since. I knew each of them by both name and shadow-shape.

Ghosts attach themselves—some to a place, like Stafford—others to a person, for instance Bobby Doucet—for reasons known only to the ghosts. At least until they tell them to me.

I peered at the window again. The silhouette was now a woman's. How many ghosts did this guy have?

"Homicide detective," I said.

"Really?" Jenn threw her car into gear and drove down the dirt road as if she were Danica at Daytona. "From where?"

"New Orleans."

"Why?"

"I think he was born there."

She didn't bother with the eye roll. I heard it in her voice. "I got that much from the nummy accent—Southern and a little bit more." She made a purring, revving sound. "I meant why is he here?"

We still hadn't gotten to that. And, really, we should have. There'd just been so many other things to get to.

"I assume it has something to do with the murder."

We reached the main road, and Jenn turned toward her place. "Where are you going?"

She kept her gaze on the road. Despite her need for speed, she was a good driver. "You said you were staying with me."

"That was only so I could get out of there without a gun."

"It'll be fun."

"Take me home."

"No."

"I don't have any clothes for tomorrow."

"You can get some in the light of day. Right now it's too damn dark."

"You're afraid of the dark?"

"Only when I'm with you."

I cast her a quick glance. She never asked me how I knew things, why she sometimes caught me talking to the air. She pretended not to notice. But despite her party girl 'tude and her lighter-than-could-possibly-be-natural hair, she wasn't a fool.

"You don't have to be afraid."

Ghosts couldn't hurt you. They might startle you—make that me. And what they told me could be terrifying. But they were ghosts. Blasts of cold air and sound, no more corporeal than a wisp of smoke.

I glanced at the bruise on my forearm. Or at least they hadn't been until today.

"I know that too," Jenn said. "You're still staying with me." I opened my mouth to protest and she continued,

"Unless you want to leap out of a moving car, don't even bother."

My mouth shut. To be honest, I had no interest in staying in my apartment. Even if the meat-cleaver-wielding maniac had been a ghost, and at this point I was pretty sure he was, who wanted to see that coming at them in the dark?

The guy would be back. He might even turn up at Jenn's. Ghosts came to me for a reason, and they didn't leave until I'd helped them make the reason go away. Despite the meat cleaver he wouldn't, couldn't, hurt me. Permanently. However, I'd rather discover the purpose of his visit when it wasn't pitch-black dark and I was alone. If that makes me a coward, too bad.

Jenn lived at the opposite end of First Street from my apartment, in an adorable cottage set back from the road. The building would make a fantastic bookstore, café, or antiques shop, if New Bergin were the go-to vacation spot of west-central Wisconsin. Except the only tourists we saw were those on their way to La Crosse, Eau Claire, or Minneapolis who had a sudden need for gas and a restroom. Which meant we had no need for a quaint bookstore, café, or antiques store. Still, Jenn's place was much nicer than mine, even without factoring in the meat-cleaver maniac.

Jenn turned on all the lights. Like that would help.

I'd been trying to get the old woman in the corner rocking chair to cross over since Jenn had moved into the house. But she was attached to the cottage, and she wasn't going to leave until the building either burned to the ground or was razed—maybe not even then.

Instead I responded to her nod with one of my

own—when Jenn's back was turned—and went on with my business. Directly to the kitchen and the nearest bottle of red. I'd only had a swallow—large though it had been—of my nightly allotment. I was due.

Jenn held up two wineglasses. I snatched the one that was more of a brandy snifter and filled it with enough wine to be unfashionable then did the same for her. Whenever I went to a restaurant I had to fight not to laugh—or sometimes cry—at the splash of liquid considered a serving.

"TV?" Jenn asked.

I shook my head, sipped my wine.

"You wanna tell me about it?"

I wasn't certain which *it* she was talking about. The intruder? My father? The murder? Bobby Doucet? Didn't matter.

"Nope." I took a seat in the living room and continued to sip.

"You should take the plunge."

I frowned.

"With the detective."

I was still confused. It was October. Not a good time for swimming.

"Raye, sometimes I worry about you."

"Sometimes I worry about me too." I drank. The wine was nearly half gone. Damn.

"You're twenty-seven and still a virgin."

Suddenly I understood her reference to "the plunge," and I nearly complimented her clever euphemism. But that would only encourage her.

"I am not!"

"Once doesn't count," Jenn said.

"Technically, it does."

Even without the oversharing on the part of that eternal ass, Jordan Rosholt—whoops, guess I'd named him—the incident hadn't been intriguing enough to repeat. It had been awkward, uncomfortable, and other words I didn't want to think about let alone do. But, as Jenn had told me the single time I'd discussed it, we must not have been doing it right. I didn't know there was a wrong way, but then I didn't know much.

"The detective is into you," she continued. "Or . . . " She waggled her eyebrows. "He wants to be."

Apparently she needed no encouragement.

"Who says I'm into him?"

"You'd have to be blind, deaf, and dumbass not to be." She drained her glass. "And if you don't tap that, I will."

The idea of Jenn sleeping with Bobby Doucet bothered me more than it should. I had no claim on the man, even if I had seen him first.

Still, he *had* run straight toward danger at my request. Not that there'd been any danger, but he hadn't known that at the time.

Jenn set her glass on the coffee table. "You haven't had a date in nine months."

"Ten," I corrected.

"But who's counting?"

"It's not like one of the guys I've known all my life is suddenly going to become more appealing." Or learn how to keep his big mouth shut.

"But, Raye," Jenn said in a far too reasonable voice that set my teeth on edge, "the detective isn't from here."

She made an excellent point. One I considered further while I finished my wine.

It seemed a bit cold-blooded to sleep with a man just because he was from out of town.

Then again . . . I didn't think he'd mind.

The spirit of Henry Taggart hovered in the darkness outside Raye's childhood home.

He and Prudence had crumbled to ashes in Roland's witch pyre, then no doubt been scattered to the breeze. Who knew? Who cared?

Their spell had fanned the flames; the sacrifice of their lives had fueled their magic. Their daughters had been saved.

Centuries had passed in an instant. Henry had opened his eyes and seen the eldest of his three daughters, a baby in a crib, babbling to the corner. It hadn't taken him long to realize that she'd been babbling to him.

At first he'd wanted to speak to her, to tell her who he was, who she was. But she'd been too young to comprehend, and as time went on and he'd observed the world she was in, he'd decided that remaining silent was for the best. Perhaps, if they were very, very lucky, he'd never have need to speak to her at all.

For her sake, he probably should have remained invisible too, but there were times he just had to see her, and when he did she always saw him.

Seeing ghosts in this world wasn't nearly as much of a problem as it had been in his. She wouldn't burn for it. But it still marked her as strange in a place and time where no one wanted to be. Really, had there ever been a time when anyone wanted to be strange?

Leaves rustled, the foliage stirred, and a great, black wolf emerged from the forest to stand at his side.

"Darling," Henry murmured.

Sweetheart.

Pru, through virtue of her affinity with animals, had been reborn in this world as a wolf. Henry assumed his affinity with ghosts was the reason he was one.

His wife now communicated with him through some form of telepathy. He heard her thoughts, and despite her being a wolf, she understood everything he said.

When he'd first become aware that he'd traveled through time, he'd been afraid he had done so alone. But within days—maybe weeks or months, time was odd when one was a specter—Pru had joined him in her present form. They both bore the brand that Roland McHugh had left on them. Henry's was hidden by the high neck of his coat, Pru's by the thickness of hers.

She was still beautiful; he still loved her, he wouldn't, couldn't stop. However, Henry couldn't say he wasn't disappointed that they weren't the same, be they both ghosts or wolves. But when dealing with powerful witchcraft, time travel, life after death, one took what one was dealt and was thankful for it.

Pru had opened her eyes and seen their middle daughter—a child with an affinity for animals just like Pru. Henry, the ghost, had come to Raye. Neither one of them had any idea where their third daughter had landed, and it bothered them. Now that Raye was in danger it bothered them a lot.

"How is she?" he asked.

The same. Safe for now. And here?

"The same," he answered. "Safe no longer."

How did they find us?

"They didn't find *us,*" Henry said.

Pru growled, the sound rumbling against Henry's palm as he smoothed it over her sleek head.

"Hush, Mama Bear."

She growled louder.

"My apologies. Mama Wolf."

Do you think it's Roland?

His hand stilled. "Roland's dead."

So are you.

"But not in quite the same way."

Are you sure? Maybe Roland found a means to come back too.

"The man hated witches. He burned them. He burned us."

With all that blood on his hands, he could probably do just about anything.

Henry got a chill, which was an interesting trick considering he wasn't really . . . real. But he was a witch. Roland wasn't.

One doesn't have to be a witch to benefit from magic.

Sometimes Henry didn't even have to speak for Pru to hear him. He never had.

"Roland believed magic was evil, that witches were the tools of Satan."

Pru's lip lifted into a snarl. *He was tool.*

For an instant, Henry didn't know what she meant, then his seventeenth-century brain translated the word into twenty-first-century-speak and his lips curved. *Tool,* modern slang for arsehole, fool, and the like, was a perfect description for Roland McHugh.

He was obsessed. He would have done anything to have his vengeance.

"You don't think he had his vengeance? We burned, Pru."

And the girls disappeared. That had to have made him insane.

"He already was."

Precisely.

"The latest murder wasn't committed by Roland."

He always had minions.

"They should be as dead as he is by now."

Pru shook herself, and her sleek black fur shimmered brilliant blue in the silvery light of the moon, its only relief a ring of pure white fur that surrounded her own brand.

Someone has resurrected the Venatores Mali.

"It doesn't mean they've resurrected him."

The wolf that was his wife turned her all too human green eyes in Henry's direction.

It doesn't mean they haven't.

Chapter 5

Bobby dreamed of the dead.

Though he tried to put his cold cases behind him, only taking out those files and looking over them when he had no fresh murders to ponder—and how often did that happen in New Orleans?—nevertheless they were his failures and he would never rest easy until they were solved.

Two men and a woman—he remembered their faces, their names. He knew pretty much everything about them, except who had killed them. No wonder they haunted his nights.

He woke to the scent of coffee and the muffled clatter of a pan, the tink of silverware. The sun wasn't up, though the sky had lightened. The red numbers on the bedside clock read 6:15.

He was into and out of the shower in ten minutes flat. Bobby Doucet had never been one to waste time.

Coming downstairs, he considered heading straight out the door. There'd be coffee at the police station. There always was. However, the scents and sounds trailing from the kitchen revealed that John Larsen had taken the breakfast portion of *bed-and-breakfast* seriously, and as Bobby's stomach growled loudly—he hadn't eaten since leaving New Orleans—he decided he should too.

"Coffee's on the counter," the older man said, never lifting his gaze from the stove.

"Thank you." Bobby served himself. The brew wasn't as strong as he was used to, but considering the coffee in New Orleans, what was?

"Sit. It's almost done."

Whatever *it* was, it smelled too good to miss.

"I was going to make *pannukakku*," Larsen said. "But I took you for more of a *hoppel poppel* man."

"Sir?" Bobby asked. What language was he speaking?

"Call me John." Larsen turned with a cast-iron skillet in one hand and what appeared to be a hamburger turner for a very large hamburger in the other.

He crossed to the table and divided the heavenly smelling mass onto two plates. Bobby recognized potatoes, eggs, onions, salami. He took a bite and also tasted cheese, spices.

"Salt and pepper?"

"Shh," Bobby said, and let the mixture of flavors mix and melt on his tongue. He took another bite, chewed, swallowed, and did it again.

"I was right about the *hoppel poppel*."

"If that's what this is, then definitely."

"You've never had one?"

Bobby shook his head and kept eating. In every bite he found a different taste, each one better than the last.

"It's a German breakfast casserole. A lot of Germans in Wisconsin. More Scandinavians round here. Which is why I nearly made *pannukakku*." At Bobby's quizzical expression John continued. "Finnish oven pancake. They're good, but not as filling, and they take forty-five minutes to bake. I got up too late."

Bobby glanced at the window, through which shone a watery gray dawn. There'd been far too many days when he'd come *home* in light like that.

John refilled both their coffee cups. Bobby let him. He was still filling his face.

"Your daughter said I'd be impressed with your cooking." Bobby set his fork on an empty plate. "She was right."

"I'm glad you enjoyed it. My wife was a fantastic cook. When she got sick, I tried to entice her to eat with all of her favorites."

"I was sorry to hear of your loss."

John cast Bobby a quick, somewhat surprised glance. "Raye isn't usually so chatty."

"I wouldn't say she was chatty."

"She hasn't known you twelve hours and she's already told you her mother passed. Round here, that's considered at least third-date conversation."

"Around here there wouldn't be any need for the conversation, everyone would know about her mother's passing almost as soon as it happened."

John's brows lifted. "Pretty smart, aren't you?"

Bobby wasn't sure if he should agree or disagree. Depended what kind of smart John was talking about—book smart, street smart, or smart-ass. Bobby would admit to being at least two out of three, but maybe not right here, or right now, or to John Larsen.

Instead, he took his dishes to the sink. "I might be in town another night. Is that all right?"

John brought his own dishes over. "I don't have anyone waiting on your room."

Did that mean he could stay or not? Bobby decided

to assume that he could. It wasn't as if there was anywhere else to go.

"You never answered my question last night." John began to fill the sink with warm water, squirting in a healthy stream of dish soap. "Are you here because of the dead woman?"

Bobby nearly grabbed a dishtowel, then remembered he had an appointment.

"I am," he agreed, and moved toward the door.

"You came a long way. Why?"

"I really can't say."

Bobby had no idea what folks in the town had seen, what information the chief had released. Bizarrely, people confessed to all sorts of things they hadn't done for reasons beyond his understanding. Retaining a pertinent fact could prevent the wrong person from being convicted, no matter how much they might want to be.

"Did I get your back up last night with my question?"

"Which one?"

"About your people. Where you're from. We ask that around here. Didn't mean any insult by it."

"If I had a dau—" Bobby's voice cracked, and he discovered he couldn't finish that sentence. At least not the way he'd planned to. "I can understand your concern."

"I don't think you do. I don't care if you're . . . " He waved his hand in the general direction of Bobby's head.

"Black?" Bobby asked.

"You don't look black to me. More . . . tan."

"My people are French and Spanish."

"Doucet." John nodded. "Makes sense."

"Also Haitian, with a little *who knows* thrown in."

"Like Raye," John said.

Bobby doubted Raye was Haitian, but then again—who knew?

"Well," John went on as if they were talking about nothing more important than the weather, and maybe to him, they weren't. "Good luck."

Bobby paused with the door partway open. "Do I need a key?"

"I'll be here. If I'm not, the door's always open."

Which made Bobby wonder if he should stow his duffel in the rental car. On the other hand, if someone wanted to steal his toothbrush and dirty socks, let them. However . . .

"Maybe you should start locking the place."

"I'm not sure I have a key."

"Does anyone lock their doors in town?"

"Not many."

If Raye hadn't, maybe someone *had* been in her apartment. Though it still didn't explain where the man had gone, and so damn fast, leaving no trace behind.

I slept better than I expected. Probably because I'd stayed awake well past midnight hoping for a visit from my Puritan. But the only creature that stirred was the old lady in her chair—rocking, rocking, rocking. The creak of that chair eventually lulled me to sleep, and I did so without dreams—or at least any that I remembered.

As soon as I woke I dressed in the clothes I'd discarded on the floor, splashed water on my face, attempted to wake Jenn—twice—then hurried to my apartment, hoping I wouldn't run into too many people who wanted to know why I looked like I was taking the run-walk of shame down First Street.

Another reason not to sleep with anyone from here. That run-walk could become legendary. Ask Jenn.

I was in the shower before I remembered the maniac; by then it was too late. If he threw back the curtain and started to hack away with his ghostly meat cleaver I could ignore him just as well naked as not. Or at least that's what I told myself.

The memory of Bobby's blue eyes had me choosing a slightly newer, tighter pair of jeans and a sweater instead of a sweatshirt.

Which meant someone would throw up on me. It was a given.

I reached my classroom with very little time to spare, but it was still better than yesterday. The children filed in, and Susan ran toward me with such fervor I figured the winner in the barfing competition would be her.

"Stafford has a new friend," she said.

"New friends are always nice."

There'd been times in the past when the children had invented invisible friends for their friend who wasn't exactly invisible.

"Her name is Genevieve."

Interesting. Most invisible Stafford friends were named less exotically. Poopy Head came to mind.

I forgot about Stafford in the upheaval that began each new day. Getting fifteen five-year-olds into their seats long enough to count how many I had missing often took so long that I was missing one by the time I finished. But I managed. I always did. This wasn't my first rodeo.

We studied shapes, grouping quadrilaterals and circles and triangles. You could never get kids prepared for geometry too soon, or at least that's what the curriculum said. I handed out a worksheet; the children pulled out their crayons so they could color all the squares blue and so on. It wasn't until morning recess that I spared a thought for Stafford, and then only because I saw him.

And his new friend.

At first I wasn't sure if she was dead. Just because the child was hanging out with Stafford didn't mean she was a ghost. Didn't mean she wasn't either. More often than not, the specters I saw seemed very real. At least until they disappeared, walked through a wall, or walked through me. Talk about an ice bath.

I joined the two of them on the edge of the playground where they sat side by side on a bench.

"This is Genevieve." Stafford seemed so happy I almost liked him.

Genevieve had big blue eyes, short, curly chestnut hair, and skin just a shade darker than my own. The freckles on her nose were nearly as adorable as her frilly white skirt, black tights, ballet flats, and a pink T-shirt that spelled *PRINCESS* in bright, white sequins. No matter how far the women's movement came, really, who didn't want to be a princess?

"I'm Miss Larsen." I held out my hand, thankful I was on duty for recess, so the only people who might see me shaking hands with air would be children who'd seen me do such things before.

Genevieve's hand passed right through mine. She was dead all right.

Her lip trembled. She flexed her fingers. "Ouch," she whispered. "Hot."

"Sorry." I rubbed my own hand on my jeans. It burned too—like frostbite.

I'd met other ghost children. A curve of the interstate

bumped against the school property line. For some reason that meant elementary-school-age spirits killed on that highway often wound up here. They hung about to resolve fairly simple issues.

Kiss Mommy good-bye.

I want my dolly to go along.

Half the time I had them out of the building and into the light before the other children even knew they'd arrived. Which was why Susan had been so excited about Genevieve. I couldn't remember the last time there'd been more than Stafford on the ghost-o-meter.

I also couldn't remember anyone named Genevieve in New Bergin, and I hadn't heard about an accident on the interstate lately. So why was she here?

Genevieve probably wouldn't know. It often took ghosts a few days—months, years—to catch up. Nevertheless . . .

"Where are you from, honey?"

"Don't," Stafford ordered, though I wasn't sure if he was telling me not to ask or telling her not to answer.

I never got a chance to find out. He took her hand, and they went poof. My gaze drifted over the playground. If Stafford thought he could get a rousing game of run around in circles until you puke—one of his favorites—started, I'd put a stop to it and quiz Genevieve again. However, my kids, and everyone else's, were behaving the way kids do. Some playing nice, some not playing at all, and some not playing nicely.

"Drop it!" I pointed at the third-grade boy who had just picked up a worm and hauled back to toss it at a second-grade girl. I was in no mood for the high-pitched screaming that would ensue whether the thing landed in her hair or not.

He dropped it—whew!—and I headed for the door just as the bell rang. I took one final gander at the playground but caught no sign of Stafford or his friend.

He would be back. My luck was not that good. If Genevieve was with him, I'd try again. Maybe, by then, I'd know why she was here, and I could help her not to be.

Over my lunch period, I went to my computer. Google was no damn help at all. According to the search engine, the only death in New Bergin all week was that of a sister of a U.S. Marshal. The woman's photo revealed her to be the poor one-armed lady on First Street, Anne McKenna.

Anne's being the sister of a U.S. Marshal was interesting on several levels. Her brother had been assigned to the western district and stationed in Madison. She'd lived there too. Why was she in New Bergin in the first place?

Who would want to kill her? Obviously her brother had enemies, but she'd been a hospice worker. Because of my mother's illness, I'd dealt with them plenty. No one was calmer or friendlier; those people were saints. And there were far too few of them to throw away.

Last, but certainly far from least, what did a detective from New Orleans have to do with any of it?

All good questions, none of which I would find the answers to on the Internet, nor the reason I'd come to it in the first place.

Genevieve.

I'd need to discover her last name before I could do a more advanced search.

Bobby walked into the police station at 7:01. He was pretty proud of himself.

Chief Johnson wasn't. He scowled at the clock, but at least he didn't comment.

"Follow me."

Bobby cast a longing glance at the coffeepot. He doubted what was in there would do much beyond eat his stomach lining, but there were days he thought such eating was what kept him awake and functional. Right now he was barely either one. However, he'd been raised in the South where manners reigned and one did not take anything that wasn't offered. Even bad coffee.

He followed the chief down a corridor and through a door at the back of the station. It appeared he and Johnson were the only people in the place beyond the ancient dispatcher. Bobby couldn't tell if the officer was male or female—short gray hair, glasses, dumpy—the nameplate read *Jan Knutson*. Not helpful.

The door opened into a long, white corridor exactly the same as the first. But this one spilled into a funeral home, with an equally androgynous secretary. At least the nameplate read *Marion*. Then the person spoke—in a baritone—and Bobby remembered that John Wayne's real name had been the same.

"Morning." Marion pointed to yet another door, nodded to Bobby, then went back to his computer.

The smells beyond door number two identified the place even before they'd descended the stairs into the basement embalming area where a man—this time Bobby was certain—was hard at work on the single body in the room.

"Dr. Christiansen," Johnson said.

The fellow was tall and lean, he had to bend over fairly far to remove something pink from the corpse and set it on a scale. He was of an age with the police chief, but he still had all his fluffy blond hair.

"You must be the detective from New Orleans." Christiansen peered at the weight with eyes as blue as everyone else's in town but Raye's, then turned back to the body.

"Bobby Doucet."

Even though Bobby hadn't asked, Johnson explained the way things worked. "Dr. Christiansen is our funeral director and medical examiner."

"Thrifty."

"We don't have need for any more. There hasn't been a murder here in decades."

While that might be fabulous on the brochure, it did not give Bobby a good feeling about the state of the crime scene or the evidence.

"Forgive me, Doctor, but maybe the body should have been sent to . . . " Bobby paused, uncertain which city was the appropriate one.

He'd flown into Madison, the home of a well-respected university, a medical school, a teaching and research hospital—that had been on *their* brochure. Then again, maybe there was a closer place with adequate resources.

What did it matter? The doctor had already opened up the woman and started to dig around.

"If I'd felt I wasn't competent, I would have said so." Christiansen didn't seem offended. Like most funeral directors Bobby had encountered—and he'd encountered a lot of them—the man possessed a personality so laid-back as to be nearly asleep. Considering what he had to deal with, that was probably for the best.

"In this case, it wasn't difficult to determine a cause

of death." Christiansen lifted his gaze. "She's missing an arm."

"She died from that injury?"

"I've found nothing else that would have killed her."

Bobby moved forward. "I'm most interested in the brand."

"More than a missing arm?" Christiansen shrugged. "To each his own."

"We've discovered several bodies in New Orleans with a similar mark. May I see?"

Christiansen gently drew the woman's hair away from her neck. Branded into her flesh was the head of a snarling wolf.

"It's the same," Bobby said.

"Do you have any leads?" Chief Johnson asked.

"Haven't had a body in nearly a year."

"So, no," Christiansen murmured.

"No."

Johnson frowned. "How many bodies?"

"Five."

"And not a single damn clue?"

"I didn't say that."

Didn't mean they had a clue—literal or figurative—but he certainly hadn't said so.

"Different methods of death," he continued. "Young, old, male, female, white, not. The only thing they had in common was that brand."

"What did you find out about it?" Johnson asked.

"Nothing."

"It would seem," the doctor began, "that such a mark would be easily traceable. Especially in this day and age."

"Wouldn't it?" Bobby shoved his fingers through his hair. "We've been over hundreds of old books, examined ancient jewelry—amulets, rings—even family crests. Haven't found one that looks like that. You told her brother about the brand?"

"Did better than that." The doctor withdrew another organ, weighed that one too. "I showed him."

"He was here? When?" Bobby had gotten here pretty damn fast himself. How had he missed the man?

"Madison is only an hour away. He came immediately. Identified the body. Left."

"Did he have any idea why someone would off his sister?"

"None. She was a saint."

"I doubt she was killed because of who *she* was. Has he pissed off any Mexican drug lords? Mafia?" Bobby frowned. "Do you have mafia?"

"Doesn't everyone?" Christiansen asked.

Did that mean they did or they didn't?

"Marshal McKenna transports federal prisoners," Johnson said. "Might be drug dealers, or even mafia—ours are mostly boring old Italians from Milwaukee or Chicago." He lifted his eyebrows. "Remember Capone? But by the time he deals with 'em, they're convicted and sentenced. They've got no reason to retaliate at him or his family."

"Someone did."

"Mebe," Johnson allowed.

"If she wasn't killed because of her brother, then why?"

"I thought that's what you were here to find out."

"I'm just here to see if her killing is connected to any of mine."

"You think there are two psychos running around branding folks?" the chief asked.

Bobby rubbed his eyes. "I hope not."

"That makes two of us."

"Three," Christiansen said.

"What did the marshal say about the brand?"

"Never seen it either." Johnson shrugged. "But when he put it into the federal system—"

"My name popped up."

"Your cases did. But nothing on the brand."

Bobby already knew that. He'd put the damn brand into every system he could find. And gotten bupkis.

"What about the wound?" he asked.

"More of an amputation," Christiansen said. "Without anesthesia."

"She was alive?"

"It would be pretty hard to kill her with that wound if she was already dead."

Good point. Or bad point, Bobby wasn't sure.

"No one heard her?" he asked. At the chief's blank expression, Bobby continued. "She had to have screamed."

"She wasn't killed where we found her. Not enough blood."

"Could it have been an accident? Maybe she got her arm stuck in . . . " He waved his hands helplessly. "One of those big-ass farm machines."

"And flew into town on the wings of angels?" Johnson asked. "There'd be a blood trail."

"Not an accident," the doctor said.

"You're certain?"

"Her arm was hacked off, not pulled off, or even sliced with a decent blade."

"Do you know what kind of blade it was?"

Christiansen leaned down and peered at the wound. "From what I'm seeing here, my guess is . . . " He met Bobby's gaze. "A meat cleaver."

Chapter 6

Meat cleaver? That could not be a coincidence.

Raye *had* seen the murderer, and she'd thought she'd imagined it. Either she'd been lying—and for what reason, Bobby couldn't fathom—or she had issues with reality and fantasy. He wasn't one to throw stones, though he'd like to know why.

First he had to find her. Fast. Raye was walking around loose, and so was that maniac. If the man had come after her once, he'd do so again.

"Gotta go." Bobby started for the door.

"Back to New Orleans?" The chief followed.

"Not yet."

Bobby should tell the chief everything. But not until he knew just what *everything* might be.

"I have to make some calls," he said. Not a lie. He would—after he found Raye.

"Let me know what you need from me." Johnson held out a hand, and they shook. "And I'd be obliged if you kept me in the loop."

"Of course." Bobby shook and fled. He was driving back in the direction he'd come before he realized that he had no idea where he was going.

Raye was a kindergarten teacher. In a town this size, how hard could it be to find the grade school? He doubted there was more than one. He was a detective for crying out loud. He should act like one.

Bobby pulled into the gas station and asked for directions.

There was only one grade school, and it wasn't far. New Bergin Elementary stood on the nearest field to the town in a three-field parcel, with the junior high in the middle section and the high school in the northernmost plot. The athletic fields lay to the east, a parking lot flanked the west. He pulled in the space marked *VISITOR* directly in front of the entrance.

While the school itself had been built in the sixties, the security had been updated recently. Bobby stepped through the first set of doors and discovered he could not get beyond the next until he'd passed through a metal detector and then been buzzed in. At least no one with a meat cleaver could have gotten in ahead of him.

On the one hand, the need for such methods made him sick. On the other hand, so did the children. He hadn't been in a school since . . .

Bobby turned and walked right back out.

After lunch everyone retrieved their nap mats, blankets, sleeping bags. I turned down the lights and we had a quiet hour. I read a story; everyone rested, or at least pretended to.

The first weeks of a new school year I often had to sit next to one or two of the kids, keep my hand on their backs until they got the idea that they would stay on their mat until the hour was up. But by this time of year, over six weeks in, everyone knew the rules. I think most of them even enjoyed that bit of downtime. It recharged them enough to rev right through dinner. I'm sure their parents were thrilled.

I opened Stafford's favorite book, guaranteed to get him to come out, come out, wherever he was, and began to read. " 'I went to sleep with gum in my mouth and now there's gum in my hair.' "

You can see why Stafford might enjoy the tale of Alexander's terrible, horrible, no-good, very bad day.

Because I'd read it so many times I could recite most of the story without even looking at the book, I spent half my time glancing around the room. Stafford didn't materialize, but Genevieve did. As it was her I wanted to talk to, I didn't mind. I did wonder where Stafford had gotten to. I should have wondered harder.

I read the last lines just above a whisper. Then I got up and walked to the back of the room—with no fast, loud, or too interesting movements, otherwise everyone's head would be up and my peace would be over.

Genevieve sat in the alcove of cubbies where my kids kept their coats, boots, sleep mats. "My daddy used to read that to me," she said.

Curses! Alexander had been published in 1972. While it was helpful for getting Stafford to come out, it was not very helpful for deciphering much of anything else. If I'd chosen a more recent release, it would have given me a smaller window to determine when Genevieve might have died. But I'd been a kindergarten teacher long enough to become crafty. In truth, it had taken about a week.

"You love your daddy?"

Genevieve's lips curved in the kind of smile reserved for the most beloved—Mommy, Daddy, Granny, depending on the kid.

"More than anyone," she said.

"What's his name?"

She took a breath. Her mouth pursed. I leaned forward, expectantly.

And the fire alarm went off.

My entire class popped up like jack-in-the-boxes. Genevieve vanished. For the rest of the afternoon, the children were so jazzed I wished I had a whip and a chair.

Or an industrial-sized bottle of Benadryl.

By the time school let out, I was fantasizing about an industrial-sized bottle of something dry and red for myself. As it was Friday, I could even drink one.

I'd almost forgotten about Bobby Doucet. Almost.

I considered calling my father, asking if the detective was still in town, and if he was, suggesting he and I get together for a fish fry.

Friday night in Wisconsin meant that every place serving food served fish. Fried. Certainly you could get your fish baked. In butter. Sides of potatoes—pancakes, French fries, boiled in butter. Rye bread, with pats of butter. Cole slaw—mayo base, never vinegar.

Sense a theme?

However, I'd never asked out a man, and as I found my key and opened my front door I decided against making the call. One didn't dive into the deep end of the pool after the very first swimming lesson, and a woman like me shouldn't ask out the hottest man she'd ever seen the first time she asked anyone out at all.

Instead, I did what I did every day. I went into my bedroom and took off my school clothes, grimacing as I drew what had once been my best sweater over my head.

I'd been right about the barf. The fire alarm had riled everyone up so high that not only had Susan urped on me, but so had Troy.

After kicking off my shoes—they'd been christened too—I took the sweater into the bathroom and filled the sink. The garment was in desperate need of a presoak. It appeared Susan—or maybe Troy—had enjoyed grape jelly for lunch.

I stepped into the bedroom and felt a draft. Ghost or . . .

I glanced toward the front door. "Damn."

Unless I locked the door, and usually I did—I could almost swear I had—the thing blew open in any stray breeze.

I moved toward it in nothing but my bra and jeans, hoping the UPS man wouldn't suddenly appear on the landing—it had happened before—and got a chill the instant I stepped into the living room. I turned my head.

Ghost this time. Meat-cleaver maniac. Big guy. Ugly. Bald. Looked like a member of the Hell's Angels. Did they still have those? I'd be scared if he were real.

"Take a hike," I said, and continued on my way.

The blade splintered the doorjamb I'd just passed.

I stared—blinking, stunned. Ghosts couldn't splinter wood.

Thankfully, he'd sunk the cleaver in so deeply he was having a hard time yanking it back out. Then, suddenly, he did.

It was going to be a shame that I hadn't taken the time to pull on a sweatshirt, although the UPS man seeing my tacky, worn bra would soon be the least of my worries.

"Get down!"

I kissed carpet.

The report was louder than today's fire alarm, but staccato—*bang, bang, bang*—and over more quickly, yet my ears rang just the same. A current that smelled of smoke swirled past, then something thudded next to my head.

The meat cleaver had missed me by an inch, slicing into the carpet and not my brain. The maniac fell right next to me, his weight causing the floorboards to jump beneath my cheek. I stared into his dead eyes.

Talk about a terrible, horrible, no-good, very bad day.

Bobby kicked the weapon away from the intruder's hand. He'd seen enough dead men to know that this one was. Still, he was taking no chances.

He'd left the school in a rush, thinking Raye would be safe inside. He was nearly an hour away, driving past fields dotted with pumpkins, before it occurred to him that the kids were not imprisoned inside all day. They imbibed in that dangerous activity known as "recess," and their teachers probably did too.

He'd turned around, then gotten stuck in a bumper-to-bumper jam when an eighteen-wheeler had jackknifed on the expressway. After taking the next exit, he had become horribly lost—the GPS on both his phone and the rental car telling him his destination lay on the other side of a field dotted with massive windmills. Unfortunately the road it instructed him to take through that field, in an annoyingly robotic voice he wanted to reach into the machine and rip out by the throat, did not exist.

He'd arrived at New Bergin Elementary after school let out. Seeing a janitor dumping garbage, Bobby flashed his badge, and determined that nothing worse than an unscheduled fire alarm had broken up the day. As it was Friday, all of the teachers had already gone home.

Terrified he would find Raye bleeding and branded in an alley, he sped to her apartment, relieved to pass no commotion on the streets. He parked in front of her building and ran up the stairs. He arrived just in time.

His chest hurt. He couldn't decide if his fear had been worse upon seeing the maniac so close, huge blade lifted to plunge into her back, or seeing the knife tumble from the man's hand toward her head.

He had no idea how the thing had missed her. Halfway down it had shifted, as if a sudden breeze, or invisible hand, had pushed it just enough.

"Are you all right?" Bobby went onto one knee, laid a finger to the man's neck. As expected, the maniac had no pulse.

Raye continued to hug the carpet. He began to worry that the intruder had done something more than sink his cleaver into the wall. She *was* missing a shirt.

Bobby tried not to be distracted by the long, smooth expanse of her back—so pale it shimmered—but for just an instant he was.

Then a chill current of air that smelled strongly of wood smoke stirred his hair, and he lifted his head to make certain the fool had not started a fire somewhere. There was nothing in the room but the two of them and the dead man.

"Raye." Bobby touched her shoulder. "You're scaring me."

She made a strangled sound—half sob, half laugh. "I'm scaring you? Can you move the huge knife that almost gave me a lobotomy?"

"Sorry, no." She tilted her head, so she could meet

his eyes, but she remained on the ground. "This is a crime scene."

She muttered a word she could never use in school.

"Can you stand?"

"I can, but I'm not going to." She let out an annoyed huff. "Didn't your mother ever tell you to always wear clean underwear in case you were in an accident?"

His mother had been a cop, as had his father. The only noncop in their family was Bobby's brother, Aaron, who'd gone to the dark side and become a lawyer.

Their parents had met on the job, stayed on it until they couldn't anymore, then opened a private security firm, which they operated to this day. His mother had never once mentioned underwear to Bobby that he could recall.

"Did you hit your head when you fell?" he asked.

"If only. Then I wouldn't know, or maybe I wouldn't care, that I'm lying here in my oldest, grayest, most worn bra."

"Oh." He'd lived in New Orleans all his life. Folks danced on tables in fewer clothes than she wore now, and a lot of those clothes looked worse for the wear than what he could see of hers.

He stepped into her room and retrieved a green and gold sweatshirt from the end of the bed, thankful he wouldn't have to rifle drawers to find her something to wear. People kept odd—read scary—things there. He should know. And he didn't want to know that about her.

Bobby returned, dropped the shirt next to Raye's hand, turned, and pulled out his cell.

"Someone already called."

Bobby paused, finger poised over the nine. "What?"

"Gunshots in the city limits? Several people called. Maybe all of them."

He crossed to the door. She was right. Chief Johnson had just reached the bottom of the stairs; another officer followed close behind.

"We're clear, Chief," Bobby called.

The man frowned at the sight of him, but nodded and put away his gun before he motioned for the other guy to do the same. The kid—young and blond—hesitated. Bobby knew the type. Brand-new on the force and just dying to use his gun. In other words, trouble. But after sending an annoyed glance in Bobby's direction, he did put up the gun.

"You can turn around."

Bobby glanced over his shoulder as Raye stood then swayed. He dived forward, hands outstretched. He didn't need her toppling on top of the dead man. Not only would that compromise the crime scene, but she appeared shook up enough already. Falling onto a dead body just might send her over the edge.

"Sit." He urged her to the sofa, and she let him. When she clung to his hand, he sat at her side.

"He's dead now," she said. "He wasn't before."

Bobby didn't know what to say to that. Both statements seemed fairly obvious. But people in shock said strange things.

Chief Johnson came into the apartment. "What happened?"

"I came home," Raye said before Bobby could even open his mouth. If she'd been in shock, she'd come out of it pretty fast. She sounded completely lucid as she continued her recitation.

She'd started to change, saw the door was open, thought it was the wind, discovered it was a maniac. He'd tried to kill her. Bobby had shot him. She left out only one thing.

The guy had tried to kill her once already. Bobby couldn't figure out how to tell the chief about it now when he hadn't before.

"Do you know him?" Johnson asked.

Raye shook her head.

"Chief?" They all looked up. A third officer held out an evidence bag. "Found it in his pocket."

Johnson took the bag, glanced at the contents then handed it to Bobby. Inside was a ring emblazoned with the head of a snarling wolf.

"You'll need to test this for blood," Bobby said.

"Ya think?" the chief snapped, then sighed. "Sorry. I'm not . . . " He shoved his thick fingers through the remaining white tufts of his hair. "Before yesterday, the worst thing I'd had to investigate was a hunting accident."

"Same principles apply. Work the scene. Connect the dots."

"I can connect one," Raye said. "The dead woman in the alley was branded with that ring."

"How do you know about the brand?" Bobby asked.

"I saw her."

His frown deepened.

"She was lying in the middle of town. It was kind of hard not to."

Bobby lifted his gaze to the chief, who shrugged. "A lot of people saw."

"He planned to kill, then brand me."

Raye was catching on faster than Johnson, but Bobby wasn't surprised.

"Why?" she asked.

"That's what I'm going to find out."

"You?" both Raye and Johnson asked at the same time.

Bobby sighed, nodded.

Someone had to.

Chapter 7

Dr. Christiansen arrived, and the chief moved off to talk to him. I could tell Bobby wanted to join them.

As my Puritan stood in the corner, scowling at the dead man as if he'd like to kill him again, I encouraged him to. "Go on. I'll—"

"You'll stay right here," Bobby said. "Crime scene, remember?"

Even though the idea of my apartment as such was nearly impossible to get my mind around despite the dead guy in the living room, I nodded.

"As soon as I finish, I'll take you . . . " he paused, then shrugged. "Away from here."

I doubted he'd take me as far away as I wanted to go, which was Nebraska. But anywhere would be fine. I certainly couldn't sleep in my apartment tonight, even if they'd let me. I might never sleep in it again.

Bobby joined the others. Low-voiced murmurs commenced. I did my best to ignore them. They only made my head ache. Or maybe that was just phantom pain from a narrowly averted meat cleaver to the brain. Considering where the maniac had been standing and where I'd been lying, I couldn't figure out how I was still breathing.

My eyes met those of my Puritan, who continued to hover in the corner, gaze steady on me.

Then again, maybe I could.

I wanted to talk to him. But he'd no doubt disappear as soon as I tried. As if I could talk to the empty corner with all these people around.

My cell phone began to ring from somewhere in my bedroom—my father's ring tone, "If I Had a Hammer." I wasn't surprised he'd heard already there was trouble, what surprised me was that it had taken this long.

I started to rise, and Bobby lifted a hand, pointed a finger at the couch, then went into the other room himself. He came out with my purse, which he handed to me before returning to the meeting near the dead body.

My fingers brushed the phone just as the ring tone switched to the *Friends* theme. Jenn. She'd have to wait. I sent her to voice mail and answered the summons of Peter, Paul, and Mary.

"Father," I said instead of hello. Why waste time?

His breath rushed out. Was he worried? He so rarely showed emotion, I wasn't sure.

"Mrs. Knudson called. Said that young man from away ran up your steps, burst inside, and then there were shots. I didn't like the way he looked at you. Did you have to shoot him?"

Since I'd refused to take the gun he pressed on me that would have been a neat trick. A burble of hysterical laughter threatened to burst free. I slapped my hand over my mouth until the urge went away.

"Raye? Raye! I'm coming over there."

"No!"

I did not need another person in this apartment. I did not want my father here at all. I was uncertain of what to say to him under normal circumstances. This would be a nightmare.

Wait, it already was.

"I'm fine. Bobby saved my life."

Silence came over the line. I wanted to ask just how Bobby Doucet had looked at me, but the man in question appeared directly in front of me. I glanced up; he smiled. I forgot I still had my father on the phone.

"Raye?"

I blinked, came back to the earth. "I'm here."

"What happened?"

Quickly I told him.

"Why would someone want to kill you?"

"I wish I knew." Would knowing make me less shaky, or more?

"You can't stay there."

"I don't want to stay here."

"You won't be able to," Bobby said. "I'll take you home, but tell your father it'll be a while. You're a vic—" I must have flinched because he paused. "A witness. You have to give a statement."

"Father, I—"

"I heard," he interrupted, and then he was gone. Typical. No words of love or concern—never his strong suit—although perhaps him calling at all meant both.

My phone beeped. Three messages. All from Jenn. She wouldn't stop until I answered. Or worse, she'd show up. I called her back without listening to the messages.

"Shit, Raye! Every cop in the land is at your house."

As that meant three, it wasn't exactly a convention, though the EMTs and the fire department had come too. In New Bergin, they always did. I never had been sure why. Perhaps boredom.

"I'm there, Jenn. I know."

"What happened?

I seemed doomed to answer that question, but I answered it again.

"I'll come over."

"Don't. It's a madhouse. And a crime scene. I have to give a statement, then Bobby—"

"Bobby is it?" She made a purring, revving sound that was Jenn-speak for *hubba-hubba* and phrases less fifties and more R-rated.

"He'll take me to my father's."

"Convenient."

"It is."

"Don't do anything I wouldn't do."

As there wasn't much she wouldn't do, I wasn't worried.

Over the next hour and a half I learned a lot. For instance, Bobby was in New Bergin because the brand on the dead woman matched that of several victims in New Orleans, which equaled *serial killer.* Ain't life grand?

Bobby had come here only to compare the marks, ask a few questions. But he hadn't figured on the killer still being in town, and really, really wanting to kill me.

I answered the same question in a variety of different ways, from a variety of people, including Bobby. But he never did voice a query as to why I'd lied about the maniac the first time. At least while we were in the hearing of any of the others.

Once I'd been released, packed a bag, and gotten into his rental car, which was parked sideways in front of my building, that was his second question, right after, "Where's the closest decent restaurant?"

As he'd qualified *closest* with *decent* we had to head

out of town. I gave him directions, and a few minutes outside the city limits, he cast me a sidelong glance. "Why did you lie?"

"Why did you let me?"

He returned his gaze to the road. "Are you going to answer my question?"

"As soon as you answer mine." I was stalling; we both knew it.

He let out a long breath. "I figured you must have had a good reason to lie. You don't seem the type to do it just for fun."

"People lie for fun?" It had always made me twitch. Although I'd gotten better at it. I'd had to.

He flicked another glance toward me, then away. I was still stalling. He still knew it.

"You checked my apartment that night. No maniac. No sign of one. What was I supposed to think?"

"That the guy was fast, not invisible."

"I didn't say he was invisible." I'd only thought that. "I said I'd imagined him."

"There's a difference?"

"Technically, yes. *Invisible* means someone or something is there but can't be seen. *Imagined* means they weren't there at all, except in my head."

"Potato. Po-ta-toe," he said. "You still lied."

"If you consider my *not* telling the chief I'd imagined a man in my apartment lying, then I guess I did."

"A lie of omission is still a lie."

"I can't omit what wasn't there in the first place."

He took one hand off the steering wheel to rub between his eyes. "But he was there."

"I didn't know that until today."

"What was different about today?"

"I told him to take a hike, and he stuck the meat clever into the wall."

"You talk to imaginary folks a lot?"

"He wasn't imaginary."

"You didn't know that when you talked to him."

Now I rubbed my head. "What do you want me to say?"

"The truth?"

I considered it, but only for a second. I knew better than to tell anyone about the ghosts. I hadn't even told Jenn. I wasn't going to start with Bobby Doucet.

"Why are you questioning me like I did something wrong? I was attacked in my own home by a man who already killed someone."

"And if I could question him about it I would. You're all I got."

"I'm not going to be much help. I don't know him. I have no idea why he tried to kill me."

"Twice."

"Twice," I agreed. "Though his failing the first time probably explains the second."

Bobby gave a half snort, half laugh. "You don't seem very concerned."

"Should I be?"

"Someone tried to kill you."

"Twice. But he's dead. I'm not. All done." I frowned. "Isn't it?"

"Depends on why he was doing it."

"What difference does it make? He isn't going to be able to try again from a grave." Though he might come back and ghost-try it and wouldn't that be swell?

I'd researched all types of hauntings. Considering my life, wouldn't you?

In a residual haunting great trauma caused negative energy to be blasted into the aura, air, atmosphere—whatever—and the event imprinted itself on that location, then was reenacted over and over. In those cases the specters are not aware the event is being reenacted, and they have no interaction with the living. Think of it like a short video that plays over and over and over.

Residuals are considered harmless hauntings. Though having that huge, scary guy become a ghost and try to kill me again and again would be as creepy as he was. Even knowing that he couldn't hurt me, that the loop would never change, that the result—me safe, him dead—would only repeat itself wasn't as soothing as it should be.

There was always the chance that the maniac would become an interactive haunting, which meant he would be able to speak with me, perhaps even touch me like the lady on Avenue B. I wasn't in the mood. Therefore I needed to discover why the man had tried to cleave my head, if only to be able to put him to rest if he wasn't.

"I suppose he *can't* kill you from the grave," Bobby said, but he didn't sound convinced. "How far is this place?"

"Not much farther. You think he *will* try it again from the grave?"

Did Bobby Doucet believe in ghosts? He was from New Orleans, which I'd heard tell was the most haunted city in America. One of the reasons I'd never visited. What kind of vacation would a place like that be for a woman like me?

"What?" He glanced at me. "No. The dead don't come back."

I managed not to snort. But he was a detective. He

heard it anyway. Though he peered through the windshield, it felt as though he were peering at me.

We'd turned onto a two-lane highway, which had once been asphalt but due to too many years, too many winters, and too many trucks was now closer to gravel. His rental wasn't built for it and fishtailed if he went too fast. Which meant anything over forty-five.

"You're sure there's a restaurant down this road?"

"Why else would we be on it?"

His lips quirked, and my cheeks heated. The curse of being fair skinned. I had long envied those with darker complexions—not that there were any in New Bergin—but we did have television. Women with lovely olive skin did not go red and blotchy over a smirk and the hint of a make-out session at the end of a deserted forest path. Luckily it was dark, and I doubted he could see my blush.

"Do you believe in ghosts?" he asked.

"I keep an open mind."

Very open. The ghosts waltzed in and out and back in again.

His face hardened. He looked almost angry, his reaction completely out of line with the subject. "The dead don't come back," he repeated. "Anyone who says so is a liar. Probably a thief and a charlatan too."

"Thief and charlatan?" I repeated. "I don't follow."

"Preying on the grief of the living, taking money for it. Telling people that their departed loved ones have a message for them." His fingers tightened on the wheel. "Charlatans, thieves, and liars."

I'd read about those who used their gift for gain. Some were charlatans, but others weren't. As I couldn't admit to what I heard, what I knew, who I was, that made me a charlatan of sorts too.

A two-story building sprang from the gloom. The ground-floor windows of the restaurant spread golden squares of light into the gloaming. Cars were parked four deep already.

Bobby hit the brakes, cursed when the rental slid a bit, then parked in the last space available. We got out and started for the door.

Considering what he'd just said, I probably shouldn't tell him the place was haunted.

Bobby was grouchy. He had good reason to be.

For one thing, he was going to be stuck in Podunk longer than he'd planned. Of course he hadn't figured on not only finding his killer, but shooting him too.

Second grumpy reason—the discussion of ghosts. He hated anything that smelled of the supernatural. Sure, he lived in the land of voodoo. According to family legend one of his grandmothers—many greats removed—had been a priestess. But the religion of the slaves was one thing, woo-woo was another. Too many had had their hopes lifted and their pockets picked by people saying they could do things they couldn't. Like talk to ghosts.

He growled.

"Hungry?" Raye asked.

Reason number three. He hadn't eaten since the *hoppel poppel*. His head was starting to pound. Though that might just be because of the day he'd had.

He opened the door on what appeared to be a well-preserved two-story farmhouse—again in the middle of the forest, which made the entire farm thing iffy.

"What's the name of this place?" he asked.

"Thore's Farm."

"Thor," he repeated. "The god?"

"No. Thore, the Swedish farmer."

Was she being sarcastic? He didn't think so.

She lifted two fingers in the direction of the hostess. The woman—blond, who wasn't around here, it was starting to freak him out—nodded. "Ten minutes."

"We'll wait at the bar," Raye said.

Inside was as rustic as the outside. Weathered wood walls, tables, chairs. There were two empty seats at the far corner of the bar, and they took them. The bartender—another blonde—gave Bobby the once-over then smiled at Raye as if she'd just brought her the top prize in the local scavenger hunt. Bobby pointed at Raye, who ordered Cabernet.

"You have a specialty?" he asked.

The bartender's smile widened, and Raye muttered, "Sheesh."

"A house drink," he blurted. Didn't most bars have them?

"Old-fashioned," the woman said. "We make our own mix."

"All right." The woman continued to stand in front of them expectantly. "Please?" he prompted, and she glanced at Raye, brows lifted.

"Brandy, whiskey, or Southern Comfort?" Raye recited.

"Whiskey," he chose.

The bartender continued to wait.

"Jack, Jim, Evan, Knob Creek, Maker's Mark?" It wasn't until Raye uttered the fourth choice that he realized she was listing whiskeys and not people. He usually drank beer. Maybe he should . . .

He glanced at the taps. There were at least ten, several of them variations of *Leinenkugel*. He didn't even want to try and pronounce that.

"Jim," he said.

She still didn't move. He spread his hands.

"Sour or sweet?" she asked.

"Dear God."

"Sweet," Raye answered for him, and at last the woman went away. "Don't they make an old-fashioned in New Orleans?"

"They make everything in New Orleans. I just don't drink them." He shrugged. "I've never been much of a drinker."

Except for that one time, which was more than one time, although he hadn't sobered up for months, so maybe it was "one time." But he certainly hadn't been drinking top-shelf-whiskey old-fashioneds.

Their drinks came. They tapped glasses, sipped. Bobby's was surprisingly good, the glass pleasingly large. He twirled it this way and that in his palm, admiring the swirl of amber and ice. "How fast do trees grow?"

She'd been about to take another sip of wine and instead set her glass down. "That was random."

"Not in my head. I've been wondering how this place could be Thore's Farm when it's surrounded by a forest."

"Ah." This time she did take a sip. "Reforestation."

He lifted his glass to indicate the bar taps. "Is that like *Leinenkugel's*?"

Her smile made the tight angry knot that still pressed against his throat loosen. He might enjoy himself if he didn't try too hard not to.

"You mangled that pretty badly. Leinenkugel's is a

brewery in Chippewa Falls. I'm not sure if they give great deals to all the taverns in a two-hundred-mile radius so that they carry their product on tap, or if folks just like that one of our small businesses has done so well and want to show it off." She shrugged. "We call it Leinie's around here."

He could see why.

"Reforestation is replacing trees lost through deforestation. There are several government programs. A big one is CRP—Conservation Reserve Program—where farmers are paid a fee not to plant crops but instead plant things that will improve the environment."

"Like trees?" he asked, and she nodded. "Why?"

"Too many empty fields, overabundance of crops, erosion, soil problems. Take your pick. This farm became part of the program before World War Two."

"And your dad's place?"

"More recently but yes. His father was a farmer. Mine was an eldest son who wanted no more to do with it than any of his siblings. Instead of selling the place, they put it in the program, planted trees, and watched them grow."

"Sounds peaceful."

"Or boring," she said.

"Potato, po-ta-toe," he repeated.

She laughed, just as the hostess appeared with menus. "Follow me."

The woman seated them at a cozy table for two just past a shadowed staircase. The restaurant had attempted to keep the feel of a farmhouse—with open doorways into several smaller rooms. The main room—living, sitting?—was now the reception/bar area. Antique furniture decorated the corners, tin pots and farm implements hung on the walls. Here and there Bobby caught a glimpse of a modern convenience—a Bunn coffee maker tucked behind an antique folding screen, electrical outlets painted the same color as the rough-hewn walls. Somewhere out of sight, a grill hissed.

Bobby opened the menu. Steaks. Pork chops. Chicken. A Thore burger, which was a half-pound ground chuck, stuffed with jalapeños, topped with ham and bleu cheese. His chest hurt just reading about it.

"Every appetizer is deep-fried," he observed.

"What isn't better when deep-fried?"

"I'm sure there's something."

"Don't tell it to the Wisconsin State Fair. They pride themselves on deep-frying everything. Wait!" She reached over and pointed to the fourth item in the appetizer section. "This isn't deep-fried."

"The cheese and sausage plate?"

"I'm sure they could deep-fry that if you'd like."

He took a big gulp of his drink. At home he might have ordered shrimp. They had shrimp here.

But it was deep-fried.

"What are you going to order?" he asked.

"Fish fry." He winced. She tapped his menu. "Broiled perch."

He perked up. "Is there catfish?"

"I'm sure there's a catfish somewhere, but not here. Walleye pike, perch, bluegill."

He squinted at the menu again. "What is *lefse*?"

"Norwegian tortilla."

"You're making that up."

She lifted her hand as if she were in court. "I swear."

Bobby felt as if he'd stepped into a jumbled fairy-tale land. Raye resembled Snow White. They'd gone into the woods like Hansel and Gretel. Was the wolf he kept hearing in the distance someone's grandmother?

"Would you like another old-fashioned?" Their waitress had appeared. She was blond. Big shock.

Something tumbled down the stairs on the other side of the wall their table was tucked against. Raye frowned. The waitress did too. Several customers glanced that way, but no one seemed overly concerned.

Bobby waited for a worker to come around the corner, but none did. Maybe it had just been a box set too close to the top of the steps that had eventually teetered free and fallen down.

But if that were the case, where was the box?

Chapter 8

We ordered—perch for me, pike for him. *Lefse* for me, rye bread for him. Potato pancakes for both. I had more wine. Bobby ordered coffee.

He pretended he hadn't heard the thumps on the stairs, which continued across the ceiling and sounded like footsteps. I guess if one didn't know the history of the place, one might conclude that real people were up there.

Sometimes they were. The restaurant kept dry goods on that floor—paper towels, napkins, things that didn't need refrigeration and were not subject to rodent infestation. An employee might be sent to get them. Always a new employee. Because it usually only took them one trip to decide never to go up there again.

"This place was a stop on the Underground Railroad," I said.

"Really?"

He offered me first dibs on the relish tray—olives, coleslaw, cottage cheese, pickles—I declined.

"There's a story on the back of the menu."

He glanced up in the middle of scooping a smorgasbord onto his plate. "You tell me."

"Slaves on their way to Canada stopped here. Probably one of the last stops, considering."

"Considering what?"

"How close we are to Canada."

"We're close?"

"Three hundred and fifty miles, give or take."

"Still a pretty long walk."

"They didn't walk much. Kind of obvious."

"In what way?"

"Not a lot of black people in the Big Woods even now. Then, there were none. Why do you think people are staring at you?"

He glanced around. Several people quickly looked at their plates. "I'm not that black."

"Up here there aren't levels of different. There's just different. You've noticed the abundance of blond?"

He nodded.

"Anything darker than light stands out." I ran my fingers through my black hair. "I should know. The Thores hid runaways . . . " I pointed upstairs. He paused with a forkful of slaw nearly to his mouth. "Some died, some survived."

Bobby set his fork on his appetizer plate and the coleslaw slid off. He didn't notice. He flipped over his menu, which the waitress had neglected to take with her, read the few short paragraphs. The story didn't mention the ghosts either.

I'd tried to work here as a teen, had to quit. Some people saw the specters; some only felt them. I heard everything they said, and once they knew that they just wouldn't shut up.

The ghosts of Thore's Farm were attached to the house—more specifically the second floor—just as they'd been when they were alive. This meant I could have dinner here and be bothered no more than anyone else by the thumps. I caught an occasional, distant whisper. However, if I went upstairs, I got an earful.

Probably best to avoid the place, except Thore's was a decent restaurant, and it wasn't as if we had a lot of them.

We finished our meal, ordered dessert. I could never resist their apple kuchen. Bobby had strawberry schaum torte. Too sweet for me, but he seemed to enjoy it.

I tried to pay; he wouldn't let me. Not even Dutch treat.

"Why is it *Dutch* treat?" he asked as he doled out twenties.

"We each pay our own."

"I know *what* it is. I just don't know why they call it that. Considering the area, I thought you might have a clue."

"I've heard it explained that the Dutch built their doors with two equal halves." I shrugged. "We did a unit on the Dutch in my class. Another explanation is that the term came about because the English and the Dutch fought over the East Indies and the English weren't doing too well. They took every opportunity to put down the enemy by coining derogatory terms. For instance, *Dutch uncle* is someone who isn't your uncle but yells at you like one."

He indicated I should precede him toward the exit. "My uncle never yelled at me."

"My uncles were gone before I was born."

"Too bad. Uncles are fun. It's a shame you never got to meet yours."

I *had* met them. But not in a way I could share. Uncle Jim showed up now and then. He liked to have a cigarette just outside the open kitchen window. Drove my father bonkers. He couldn't see Jim, but sometimes he could smell the cigarette. I'd told my dead uncle to knock it off, but he didn't listen any better now than he had while alive. If he had, he might not have expired at thirty-two from lung cancer.

Uncle Charley was even more fun. He liked to drive the Dodge Charger he'd died in across the field and into the same damn tree. Over and over into eternity.

Men. They never learned.

Bobby slid behind the wheel. The meal had been excellent, but the place had been . . .

He shifted his shoulders. He'd felt watched the entire time. Probably because he had been. As long as he was here, he probably would be. In New Orleans he did not stand out. He was in no way different. In New Bergin he was in no way the same. But neither was Raye.

After he'd heard those thumps upstairs no one had ever come down. And he'd watched. He had a perfect view from his seat.

He started the car. "What's upstairs?"

Raye cast him a glance, but he kept his gaze on the windshield. "Storage."

That explained why someone had been up there, it even explained the thumps. A worker searching for "whatever" had dropped it down the stairs. However, it didn't explain why the worker had never followed. What it really didn't explain was why nothing had actually fallen down the stairs in the first place.

Which only meant the house had weird acoustics. Something had fallen elsewhere, but sounded like it was on the other side of the wall. Made more sense than any of the alternatives.

"Penny for your thoughts," Raye murmured. "Though from the way you're scowling, they're worth a lot more."

"Cold cases," he blurted, though he wasn't sure why. "Sometimes I think about them." Just not right now.

"Is there one that bothers you in particular?"

No one had ever asked him that before, and it was a pretty good question.

Bobby rubbed the back of his neck, which often tingled whenever he thought about this particular case. He figured there was something he was missing, which was why it so often came to mind. "There's an old hotel in the quarter."

"French Quarter?"

"Only one there is, *cher*."

She lifted her brows at the endearment but he could tell she liked it. He'd used the term a thousand times before. In New Orleans *cher* tumbled from nearly everyone's lips, especially the Creole. Technically it meant dear, though it had the connotation of *sweetie, cutie, honey, baby*. Most folks used it to avoid keeping track of names. In his profession, considering how many names he heard, how few were real, how often he forgot, *cher* was helpful. But right now, here, with her, he actually meant it.

"Aren't most of the hotels old in the quarter?" she asked.

He reached the main road and turned toward New Bergin. *"Oui,"* he agreed, and became captured for an instant by her smile.

At home he peppered his English with French and Spanish. He always had because his mother had, his father had, nearly everyone did. Except for his Yankee transplant partner, Conner Sullivan.

"This hotel wasn't too bad," he continued. "But it wasn't too good either."

"Hence the murder."

"Who said anything about murder?"

"You're a homicide detective, and we were talking cold case."

"Right. Have you ever heard of a locked-room mystery?"

"Impossible crime."

"Not impossible, since the guy was killed. But the body was in a room locked from the inside. Windows painted shut."

"Suicide?"

"Gunshot wound to the head. No residue on his hands. No damn gun in the room."

She frowned. "How big of a room?"

"What difference does that make?"

"Just trying to get a picture. Sometimes it helps."

"One room. Queen bed. Small bath. Old place. Had a locker—"

She tensed. If she weren't already so pale, he'd think she'd gone paler. But why?

"I suppose lockers are the equivalent of safes in newer hotels?" she asked.

"A locker is a New Orleans term for closet."

"With a lock?"

"No. It's just something we say. Not sure why. We call regular old closets a locker."

She seemed to be thinking overly deep and long about that.

"All places have their quirks," he continued. "New Orleans has a lot of them."

"In Milwaukee they call a water fountain a bubbler. No idea why. What about the floor?"

"Wall-to-wall, nailed-down carpet, no holes. We checked the ceiling too. Nothing."

"What about the closet? Any holes in that floor?"

Bobby tried to remember, couldn't. He should probably check.

"How close was the body to the closet?"

That he did remember, and the answer was . . .

Close enough.

After I delivered the ghost man's message regarding the locker/closet, Bobby became very quiet. I hoped the information was useful. I didn't see how it couldn't be. Ghosts didn't bother to hang about to deliver news that wasn't.

I'd called earlier and told my father we were going for fish and not to wait up. He had anyway. I would have been surprised if he hadn't.

"You should have gone to bed."

"It's nine o'clock," he said.

I checked the time. "Huh." It only felt like it was past midnight.

"I talked to Chief Johnson."

"What did he tell you?" Bobby asked.

"The man who killed that poor woman tried to kill my daughter."

"We don't know that for certain."

"There's more than one maniac with a meat cleaver running around?"

At my father's words, my earlier calm disappeared.

"I doubt it. But until we have confirmation from the . . ." Bobby paused. "Christiansen. You should be careful."

"Why would anyone want to hurt Raye?" my father asked.

"That was a question I had for you, sir."

"Me?"

"Raye said she was adopted."

My father cast me a curious glance. I didn't usually share. But, around here, I didn't have to.

"She was," he agreed.

"What can you tell me about her birth parents?"

"Nothing."

"Closed adoption?"

My father let out a long breath and didn't answer. He knew I didn't like to talk about the way I'd been discarded like garbage.

"I was dumped," I said. "Side of the road. No note, no nothing. Newborn."

"Assholes," he muttered, and my lips twitched as he echoed my opinion.

"To have survived you must have been found pretty quickly."

"That was the consensus."

"No one's ever come looking for you until now?"

"Wait—" My father stopped, glancing back and forth between the two of us. "You think he was looking for her?"

If the man had been in my apartment once we could call it random. Twice? He'd been looking for me.

"I'm just following routine lines of questioning," Bobby said. "Everything I eliminate—however far-fetched—is one less question on the list."

"All ri-i-ght." My father didn't sound convinced.

"I've gotta go to bed." I started up the steps.

"Maybe you should sleep down here."

I glanced over my shoulder. "My room's up there."

My father's eyes flicked to Bobby Doucet then to me.

Ah. So was his.

Even if Detective Doucet was interested, and so far I'd seen no indication of that, I wasn't going to do him in the room directly above my parents'. The *ew* factor on that was so high I nearly said "Ew!" out loud.

"I'll be fine." I climbed the rest of the stairs, shut the door, and flicked the lock. Then I hurried to the heating vent at the front of the room and fell to my knees. Everything that was said in the hall, as well as the living room, drifted upward. As a kid, I'd found out a lot from chatty ghosts; the rest I'd found out right here.

"Is she safe?"

My father sounded really worried, and while that concerned me—did he know something I didn't about why the maniac had wanted me dead?—it also made me happy to know that he cared. He wasn't much for hugs or the sharing of feelings. Everything I knew about his opinion of me, I'd heard right here, and I'd never heard any of it said in a voice like that.

"I'll protect her."

"That isn't an answer."

"It's the best one I have, sir. I'll stay until I'm sure the case is closed. I need to know who this guy was and why he's killed who he has. Usually murder victims are connected in some way."

"Unless it's a moron with an automatic weapon in a movie theater, or worse."

"Even then the victims are connected by location."

"But there's no reason behind it," my father said.

"There's always a reason. Though it might not make sense to anyone but the reasoner."

"You think this man came after Raye for a reason, not just because she was there."

"Yeah," Bobby said, "I do."

"Why?"

I waited for him to tell my father that I'd lied, but he didn't.

"A hunch."

Silence stretched so long I would have caved, but Bobby was made of sterner stuff, or perhaps, he just didn't want to please John Larsen as badly as I always had. As badly as I still did.

For the first time in a lifetime of interrogations, my father broke first. "How can you possibly connect Raye to the dead woman? She wasn't from here. They didn't know each other. They weren't even close to the same age."

"I'll do my best to find out why this happened in your town."

"You think it has something to do with the town?"

"No."

My father sighed. "Too bad."

I had to agree. Because if it didn't have anything to do with New Bergin then it had something to do with me. I just didn't know what.

Murmurs of good night were followed by footsteps retreating toward my parents' room, then Bobby's came up the stairs. I returned to the door and quietly opened it. By the time he reached the landing, I stood in the hall and beckoned.

He cast a quick glance at his room, and I shook my

head, beckoned again. "Your room is right over his. He'll hear everything we say."

And do.

He joined me. "What are we going to say?"

Nothing half as interesting as what I'd like to do.

"You didn't tell him I lied."

"I didn't tell the chief of police, why would I tell your father?"

"I suppose you'll have to tell Johnson. It's relevant now."

"Only if we can figure out 'why you' in relation to 'why her.' "

"Good luck with that," I said. "No one's been able to connect me with anyone on the planet so far."

Might that be why I felt so damn lonely? I had friends—well, Jenn. Parents—well, Father. A job. Students. Stafford and assorted ghosts. But there always seemed to be something missing.

Bobby stepped closer and brushed a strand of hair from my cheek. His fingertips trailed across my skin, and that part of me that felt so empty . . . felt emptier.

"Who's tried?" he asked.

I blinked, managed, barely, not to gape and say, "Huh?" But he must have seen it on my face because he continued. "Who tried to find your family? How did they do it?"

"Police, social services. I think my father hired a detective."

"DNA?"

"Over twenty years ago? No."

"Even now." He shrugged. "Unless one of your relatives is in the system it isn't going to help, but . . . I could see what the protocol is if you're willing."

"Why wouldn't I be?"

"They dumped you. From what you told me, they might have been trying to kill you."

"That appears to be a new favorite pastime."

"And why is that? You're a kindergarten teacher. Who could you piss off?"

"You'd be surprised."

"No doubt," he agreed. "The other victim was a hospice worker."

"Guy has a problem with saints."

Bobby stepped closer still. "Maybe you should sin a little."

"I wouldn't know how."

His eyes shone cool blue, but his gaze had gone as hot as the hand he placed on my hip. "I can help."

I kissed him. Why not? He wouldn't stay; I couldn't go. What could one kiss hurt?

Questions like that were always trouble. Because one taste of his mouth, and I forgot everything. My job. This town. The ghosts. My name.

He tasted of coffee and strawberries, sugar, heat, the night. Something howled—the wind, a wolf, me?

My hair stirred in an impossible breeze. No, wait. Those were his fingers tangling in the strands, tilting my head so he could delve with his tongue. My hands on his biceps flexed, my thumbs stroked; I licked his teeth. I wanted to lick a whole lot more.

I lifted my arms, wrapped them around his neck, pressed my entire body to his. He wanted to lick a whole lot more too.

The door of my room slammed. We leaped apart like two teenagers caught in the back seat of a car. I half expected to find my father, outraged, holding the shotgun.

Instead Genevieve stood halfway between us and the door.

"Holy hell," Bobby muttered.

I had to agree. What was she doing here?

I let my gaze wander the room, searching for Stafford. He'd never left the school grounds; I hadn't thought he could. I hoped he hadn't decided to start. All I needed was a freely roving Stafford.

"I shouldn't have done that," Bobby said. "But . . . " He rubbed the back of his head as if it ached. "Wow."

Genevieve scowled. I scowled back. I wanted to order her out, but I didn't dare.

Bobby took a step toward me; I took a step back. "I can't."

Genevieve shimmered. Maybe I could. If she'd get out. But how to make her stay out? I had no idea.

"Your dad. Right." He turned toward the window. "Sorry."

"Crap." I'd forgotten my father, which showed how far gone I was.

I could see Bobby reflected in the endless night beyond the glass. I could see Genevieve too. They wore identical frowns.

"The window's shut," Bobby said.

"It's forty degrees." More like thirty, but I didn't want to scare him. "It better not be open."

He spun. "I mean . . . " He shifted his shoulders. "Why did the door slam?"

A book fell from my nightstand and clapped against the floor like thunder.

"Old house." I shot Genevieve a glare. "Drafty."

He grunted, unconvinced. I didn't blame him. That

had to be some draft if it could both slam a door and drop a book.

None of my ghosts had ever done anything like this before. Stafford usually instigated trouble in the living, rather than perpetrating the trouble himself. Although there had been the incident with the fire alarm today. I'd thought Stafford had done it.

I considered Genevieve. But maybe not.

"I'd better go." Bobby started for the door.

Genevieve reached out as if to hug him, and he walked right through her. The expression on the child's face made my heart kick up even faster than it had from his kiss.

"Daddy," she whispered, and I understood.

She wasn't my ghost. She was his.

Chapter 9

Bobby hurried across the hall. Honestly? He nearly ran. He told himself it was because he wanted to kiss Raye again. Kiss her and a whole lot more.

And he did want to. Badly. But that wasn't what had him shutting his own door, locking it too. No, that was the strange cold spot and the whiff of . . .

Sunshine in the depths of the night, cinnamon on toast, and the rain that came at dawn. All mingled together into a scent he hadn't smelled since—

He never should have gone to the school today. That was the only reason he was reacting the way he was now. The kids had devastated him. But he'd forgotten about it in the heat of pursuing the maniac.

He should go to bed, start fresh tomorrow. But even if it hadn't been nine-thirty, he wasn't going to be able to sleep now. He dug out his cell phone and called his partner.

"You on your way back?" Sullivan demanded.

Ah, the magic—and rudeness—of caller ID.

"Hello, to you too." Bobby moved to his window, which gave him a bird's-eye view of the forest. Except clouds had drifted over the moon, and he couldn't see a single tree past the dark pane; he could only see himself. He didn't look too good.

"Hello," Sullivan said. "You on your way back?"

"Miss me?"

"I'm getting slammed here."

"I'll take that as a yes."

"What are you doing up there?"

Bobby had an image of Raye Larsen, lips still wet from his. He'd almost been doing her.

The erection he'd lost when he'd walked away came right back. He ground his teeth.

"Sounds like you're chewing gravel."

Bobby relaxed his jaw, wiggled it about so he could talk, then told his partner everything. Almost. He left out the taste of Raye Larsen's lips. He also left out the scent that had made him run from them.

"Huh," Sullivan said. "Seems too easy."

"You come on up here and shoot a moving maniac, then tell me how easy it is."

"I just meant we've been searching for this creep for a while, then you go to Podunk, and a few hours later he's dead. That never happens."

He was right. But—

"Shouldn't something work out once in blue moon?"

"Don't talk to me about the moon," Sullivan said. "Makes me twitchy."

Full moons always caused cops to twitch—as well as nurses, waitresses, and psych ward workers. That big round orb made the crazies crazier. Maybe it had something to do with the tides and their magnetic pull. Who knew? But if one full moon caused people to go bat shit, what would two in one month—known as a blue moon—do? Bobby didn't even want to think about that.

"If the blood on the guy's ring matches your victim," Sullivan continued, "the case is closed, and you can get back here before I lose my ever-lovin' mind. Again."

"Not so fast. Who's to say he didn't find the ring on the ground."

"Really?"

"I'm just talking like a defense attorney."

"Guy's dead," Sullivan said. "Does he get a defense attorney?"

"True. But we can't stamp closed on something until we're sure."

"What would make you sure?"

"If the meat cleaver is the murder weapon, I'd say we're in business."

"Not so fast." Sullivan repeated Bobby's words. "No meat-cleaver killings here."

Man had a point. He often did, which was why they worked so well together.

"Although, since we seem to have hit an uncommon streak of luck, maybe he was stupid enough not to wash the branding ring between victims and there'll be DNA from all of them all over the place."

"What are the chances of that?" Bobby wondered.

"Slim to none."

The usual odds.

"Remember that case in the Hotel St. Germain?" he asked.

Silence came over the line. Bobby could almost see his partner's face crease in thought. The hotel was in a seedy section of town; therefore they'd had more than one case there. Bobby gave him a hint. "Locked-room mystery."

"Hated that thing."

"Did we ever check the floor in the locker?"

"Not following."

"Seemed like the guy could have been shot through the door of the room, but no hole in the door, and it was still locked, bolted, chained."

"Hence my hatred. What about the closet?" Despite years spent in New Orleans, to a man from Maine—or was it Massachusetts?—a closet was always and forever a closet.

"Not sure. But the door to the locker and the door to the outside were right next to each other. One was open; one wasn't. I had a . . . " Bobby shifted his shoulders. "Hunch. Check the floor in the locker of that room and let me know what you find."

" 'Cause I got nothin' better to do? There were four murders last night. One of them was another one of those damn wild-animal killings that just makes my head pound."

Sullivan's leave of absence had followed a spate of wild-animal attacks in New Orleans. Some by wolves, a creature that had not been seen in Louisiana for at least a century. Others by a big cat larger than any bobcat found in the swamps. Folks had whispered of a loup-garou, a werewolf legend of the Crescent City, whereby the beast attacked beneath a sickle-shaped moon and not the full.

Sullivan—born and bred Yankee that he was—hadn't believed any of it. He'd figured serial killer, even called the FBI. They had not agreed. The killings had continued. He'd snapped. Then, the killings had stopped. But, apparently, not forever.

Bobby had been briefed about his partner's issues. *Brief* being the operative word. He didn't really know what had happened or why, and he hadn't asked. Sullivan was the best partner he'd ever had, and he wasn't going to fuck it up by sticking his nose into things that were over. Except . . .

What if they weren't over?

"You okay?" Bobby asked.

"Yeah." Sullivan let out a long sigh. "I'm not going to jibber in the corner."

"You say that like you've done it before."

"Haven't we all?"

Bobby certainly had.

"What's wrong, Genevieve?"

Tears shimmered in the ghost child's eyes. "He never sees me."

"I know, baby." She had Bobby's eyes. I saw that now.

"Where's your mom?" I asked.

"She couldn't see me either." Her face scrunched into an expression I first thought was confusion and then, when she stomped her foot, realized was anger. "She should have been able to!"

I was confused. Should her mom have been able to see her because she was also dead? Or just because the child thought a mother should always have that connection? I could relate. I still looked for my mother everywhere.

Of course she wasn't really my mother. But not being blood relations didn't keep every other specter in the township from appearing to me.

"Why are you here?" I asked.

Genevieve hadn't moved on for a reason, one I needed to discover so that she could. She didn't belong in this world. I glanced at the closed door across the hall.

No matter how much the living might long for her.

"My daddy is sad."

He was, and now I understood why.

"Tell him . . . "

I leaned forward, but she trailed off, her gaze flicking to his closed door.

"What should I tell him?" I pressed, even though the idea of talking to Bobby Doucet about his dead daughter made me cringe. But who else was going to?

"Tell him it wasn't his fault," she said. Then she disappeared.

I stared at the empty space where she'd been, then glanced at the closed door across the hall and back at the empty space.

I couldn't just knock on his door and tell him I had a message from his dead daughter. I'd learned the hard way that I needed to impart info from beyond with a little more tact. Therefore, I had to get him to tell me about Genevieve and what had happened to her before I could ever tell him "it" wasn't his fault.

Whatever "it" was.

Curious, I dug my laptop from my overnight bag and Googled. *Genevieve Doucet* brought many returns, none of them a child, which made me even more reluctant to mention her to Bobby.

Still, I'd never known a ghost to lie. She had to be his daughter.

Was he unaware of her? I didn't think the child would attach herself so strongly to someone she hadn't spent time with during her life, but one never knew. There was information missing, and though I had no idea where to hunt for it, I kept trying.

I searched on *Bobby Doucet,* got a ton of hits, the *Times Picayune* mostly. His cases exclusively. No marriage announcement, no birth announcement either, but that didn't mean much. Perhaps he'd gotten married elsewhere. Perhaps they were just private people. Newspapers only printed the announcements they were given, and, in some cases, were paid for.

At a loss, I moved to the window. My Puritan and his wolf stood in the yard.

I was out of my room and down the stairs before I considered that they'd only be gone by the time I got there. Nevertheless, I opened the door and went outside. The two remained, though they'd moved closer to the trees.

I glanced over my shoulder, at what I have no idea. My father was in bed, or at least in his room. Bobby too. No one here but me and my shadows.

The Puritan beckoned. I sprinted across the distance between us. I didn't need to be asked twice.

Up close, the wolf was huge, the top of its head level with my waist. The man laid his hand on the beast's back. The two nearly blended into the night—he all in black, the wolf too. Only their eyes shone like jewels—onyx and emerald.

I wished, not for the first time, that I could paint. Their image, here in the dark, with the trees at their backs and the moon just coming out, would be exquisite. However, my artistic skills ran toward stick folks and primary-colored collages. Not a surprise considering my occupation.

"Is there something you need?" I asked.

The wolf snorted. The man's lips and his fingers curved—a smile for me, a calming stroke for the wolf. "I'm here to help you, child."

"Usually ghosts come to me for help."

"Most do, aye."

His accent beguiled. I'd never realized what a sucker I was for accents. How could I? In New Bergin, there weren't any.

"Where are you from?"

"Is that what you want to ask after so very long?"

He had a point, but his not going poof the instant I approached after so many years of doing just that seemed to have frazzled my brain.

"It's as good a place to start as any."

"I suspect it is. Well, then . . . " His fingers continued to stroke the wolf as he lifted his gaze to the night. "I was born in Scotland."

"When?"

"A forgotten time."

"I doubt that."

He lowered his gaze to mine. "Perhaps I only wish it was forgotten, as it appears to have returned. You must beware of the hunters."

Living in the woods, I'd been taught young to have a care during the hunting time of the year. But it was bow season not gun—the latter being far more dangerous by virtue of bullets instead of arrows, and more morons per square mile. While killing with a bow required some skill, blasting a rifle did not. Either way . . .

"There's no deer hunting after dark." Of course morons were often unclear about what constituted darkness—as well as hunters' blaze orange. Hence the accidental shootings of the many.

"That is not the kind of hunter of which I speak." The wolf gave a very feminine yip, and he nodded as if he understood. "You must beware the *Venatores Mali*."

"My Latin is . . . nonexistent."

"Hunters of evil," he translated.

"Evil what?"

"Witches."

I laughed. "Right."

"You are talking to a ghost yet you laugh at the concept of witches?"

I stopped laughing. "Isn't the time for the persecution of religions past?" Except for Muslims, Jews . . . maybe he had a point.

"Though the burning of witches was couched in religion, it had nothing to do with God."

Had to agree there.

"I wasn't referring to the burners' religion, but the burnees'."

"I do not understand."

"Wicca is a religion."

"What is Wicca?"

"The religion of witchcraft."

The wolf snorted again.

His gaze sharpened. "Are you of this religion?"

"Me? No." I stifled a nervous giggle at the idea of telling my father I was Wiccan. His head might explode.

The discussion of fire reminded me of something. "The black-eyed ghost from the alley said, 'He will burn us all.' "

The wolf snarled.

"Hush, Pru."

"Your wolf is named Pru?"

"Prudence."

I should probably find a wolf named Prudence amusing, but right now so little was.

"And your name?" It would be too weird, now that I

knew her name was Prudence, to continue thinking of him as the Puritan. "Prudence and the Puritan"—sounded a little kinky.

Now *that* was amusing.

"Henry," he said absently. "Who is *he*?" At my confused expression he continued, "He who will burn us all?"

"The maniac?" It was his turn to appear confused. "Big knife. Tried to kill me."

"Ah. I don't think he'll be killing, or burning, any of us again."

"Who's *us*?"

"Witches."

I glanced at the wolf, frowned. He had said *us,* but how could a wolf be a witch? For that matter, how could he? Not only was he a *he*—and wasn't that a warlock?—but *they* were ghosts.

"You lost me," I admitted.

"I am a witch; Pru is a witch." He spread his hands. "Have I found you?"

"Not really. How can you burn?"

Prudence yipped. The sound, or perhaps my words, made the ghost appear even ghostlier.

"How do you think we became what we are?"

"You were burned as witches?"

His shudder was answer enough.

"When?"

"Sixteen twelve."

"That explains the hat."

Henry lifted his hand and touched the brim.

"Why are you here?" I asked. "You're talking over four hundred years. Why me? Why now?"

"The hunters are back." His lips tightened, and he

stroked the wolf again, though I think this time more for his own comfort than hers. "For you."

"Me?" I didn't realize I'd spoken more loudly until he repeated, "Hush," as he had to Pru. "I'm not a witch."

"Then why did the hunter try to kill you?"

"He was crazy?"

Henry shook his head.

"I don't know anything about witches or witchcraft. I haven't studied. I don't own a cat. No eye of newt."

"Being a witch has nothing to do with any of that. You are born a witch; you die a witch." He swept his hand down his black-clad form. "Even after you die, a witch you remain."

"I can't be."

"You see me."

I didn't bother to answer what wasn't a question. I was talking to him, obviously I saw him. Didn't mean he was actually there.

"You see others."

"I don't want to."

"Want has nothing to do with it."

"Got that right."

"You have innate supernatural abilities."

"Plural?" I asked, and he nodded. "Hell."

"Hell has nothing to do with it either. Abilities are from God."

Considering how he'd died and when . . .

"I bet the witch hunters *loved* you."

"They did not. Hence the burning."

Sarcasm appeared lost on him. Had they had it back then?

"What else do you think I can do?" I asked.

"Move objects with your mind."

"No way!"

"Thus far only when you are upset, frightened, or under some stress, but with practice . . . "

I remembered the phone flying off the table the first time I'd seen the maniac. I'd thought Henry had done it. I still kind of did.

"Seeing ghosts and flinging things doesn't seem very witchy to me."

"What does?"

"Broomsticks. Familiars." I eyed the wolf. "Is she yours?"

"My familiar?" Pru growled as he laughed. "She's my wife."

"How—" I began, and Henry's gaze flicked past me.

I spun. Bobby Doucet stood on the porch.

"Who are you talking to?" he asked.

I glanced over my shoulder. Prudence and the Puritan were gone. Even if they'd been there, it wasn't as if he could see them.

"Myself." Only when I started for the house did I realize how cold I was. How long had I been out here?

"Okay." His gaze remained fixed on the trees. "Because for a minute there I thought you were talking to the wolf."

I stumbled, righting myself before I ate dirt. "I . . . uh . . . " I looked at the trees again, then back. "What?"

"The huge black wolf. Is it someone's pet?"

"No." He'd seen the wolf. I wasn't sure what to make of that.

"If it isn't a pet, then what were you doing anywhere near it?"

"Wait." I held up my hand. "You saw a wolf?"

"Wasn't hard. It was right there. Within biting distance of your . . . " He waved in my direction. "Everything."

"What else did you see?"

"What else was there?"

Nothing that he should have seen. Including that wolf. That he had seen Pru and not Henry meant . . .

I wasn't sure. She was real? Bobby was special? I was nuts? I needed Henry back.

"Raye?"

I tried to remember what he'd asked me.

What else was there?

"Nothing," I said. I couldn't exactly explain that I'd been talking to the ghost and not the wolf. But what was I going to say about the wolf?

I considered denying its existence. Telling him he'd been dreaming or imagining things, but I couldn't. My lying had improved, but I'd never enjoyed it. And I liked him, which was going to be more trouble than he was probably worth. Although, after that kiss earlier, he might be worth just about anything.

Still, I couldn't tell him he was crazy when he wasn't. I'd been there, and it sucked.

"I couldn't sleep," I blurted.

He tilted his head. "So you decided to take a walk on the wild side?"

"Yes. I mean . . . What?" I was so thrown by his seeing Pru, I couldn't seem to focus, and I needed to. The more holes I dug, the harder it would be to avoid falling into one.

"You often stroll through the wilderness when you can't sleep?"

"This isn't the wilderness. This is my yard."

He cast what I could only call a nervous glance at the trees. I guess, after he'd seen a huge, black wolf melt into them, I could understand that. If I'd thought Pru had been anything other than ethereal, I might have been more nervous myself.

"No wolves in New Orleans?" I asked.

"Depends on who you talk to." He let out a short, sharp breath at my frown. "Wolves have been absent from Louisiana for about a century, but that doesn't mean folks don't see them. It's New Orleans. During Mardi Gras people see dragons."

"Like Oktoberfest."

"I doubt it."

"Lots of alcohol, tons of people, more weird shit than the cops can handle."

"Okay, maybe it is like Oktoberfest," he admitted. "You don't seem concerned that there was a wolf on your property."

"I don't have any small animals to worry about." At his blank expression I continued. "A wolf might run off with a cat or a yippy dog, maybe a lamb or a chicken or a new calf. But not a person."

"You've seen wolves before?"

I'd seen Pru before. As I wasn't sure how to phrase that, I went with a general statement that sounded like an answer. "There are wolves in Wisconsin. A lot of them."

"They don't usually come near people, unless they're rabid."

"You seem to know an awful lot about wolves for someone from a place that doesn't have any."

"I surf the Web a lot." Which smelled like a statement that wasn't an answer too. "Did that wolf seem wrong to you?"

More wrong than I could say, but I wasn't going to. He was right. Lone wolves that hung around populated areas were usually rabid. If he called the Department of Natural Resources, they would come and shoot her, and that I couldn't allow, even if I wasn't quite certain that shooting Pru by usual methods would even draw blood.

"There was nothing wrong with her that I could see."

"Her?"

"I can tell the difference between him and her."

"You were close enough."

"I was in the yard. She happened by. We startled each other. I spoke calmly and quietly." I'd been a kindergarten teacher for years and I'd learned straight off that with wild beasts . . . sometimes it helps. "You came. She left. End of story."

He stared at me a while. "I doubt that's the end of the story."

Unfortunately, so did I.

Chapter 10

Raye was lying about the wolf. But why?

"Why did you come out here?" she asked.

Bobby wasn't sure. After talking to Sullivan, he should have gone to bed. But he'd been restless. Unable to sit, let alone lie down.

"I had to move and my room isn't exactly huge. Not to mention that your father's is right below mine and pacing probably wasn't any better of an idea than—" He broke off. Probably best not to mention other ideas. He was the one who'd walked away from them.

This house, this town, those trees made him twitchy. He'd thought because everything here was so different from home. But, really, a lot of things were the same. For instance, that constant feeling that he wasn't alone, even when he was, remained.

"Listen, Raye . . . " he began, moving closer, meaning to share at least a little of his past. Perhaps it was too soon, but she deserved to know how very fucked up he was before he lost his mind and kissed her again.

She held up a hand—to stop him from talking, or keep him from touching—he didn't know, then scooted by him and disappeared inside.

Bobby stayed on the porch for a few moments longer, staring into the darkness, fingers on his gun. He doubted the wolf would come back. Until Raye had said she'd seen it too, he'd doubted the thing had been there in the first place. When he realized it had, that she'd been talking to it and not herself, he was both concerned and intrigued. But there was little about Raye Larsen that didn't intrigue him.

She was different from anyone he'd ever known—both sweet and sexy, funny and serious, down to earth and a little mysterious. He was captivated as he hadn't been since . . .

He rubbed a hand over his face.

Since he'd arrested Audrey. His first mistake in a litany of them.

The instant he'd felt that ridiculous pull he should have uncuffed Audrey Larue and let her go. Instead, he'd followed his cock and wound up sorry for it. What man didn't?

Back then he'd still been on patrol. Audrey had been selling jewelry in Jackson Square. He'd arrested her for carrying concealed. In Louisiana, one could carry openly without a permit. However, as Audrey had pointed out—

"Tourists get hinky if they see a gun."

When he'd asked why, then, she had one, her reply made sense too. "Too many hinky tourists."

He'd had to take her in; there'd been a complaint. But the charge wasn't serious. In a city like New Orleans where most crimes were, a concealed weapon on a street vendor just wasn't. He advised her to get that permit. They got talking about how and the next thing he knew, he was driving her home.

Audrey had been stunning. Tall and built, with long red hair and ridiculously green eyes. Not a freckle on her face, but elsewhere . . . there'd been a lot of them.

He'd found out just how many the very first night. He moved in a week later. Moved out a year after that.

The problem with Audrey was she lied. She was selling a lot more than jewelry in her stall. And what she was selling, she also smoked, shot, snorted, and swallowed.

Because of her, he'd developed a sixth sense for untruths. Sometimes he thought he could almost smell them, like a distant, raging fire. That sense had helped him become a detective. But it hadn't helped him become a better father.

Because of him, his daughter had died.

Bobby went inside, fell on his bed, and watched the spindly shadows of tree branches play across the ceiling. He dozed on and off; however, thoughts of Audrey and their little girl had never made a good bedtime story. He finally gave up trying to sleep as dawn seeped into the sky. He checked his e-mail and found one from Dr. Christiansen asking both him and the chief to meet in his office first thing.

As Bobby had learned, first thing in New Bergin meant *Oh God thirty,* so he showered, shaved, and left before either of the Larsens stirred.

His breath streamed out as white as the frost sprinkling the grass. An October dawn in northern Wisconsin was freaking cold. Luckily his rental car had a fabulous invention called heated seats, something he'd never had a need for at home and therefore had not known existed. With a toasty backside, his shivering stopped before he reached the main road back to town.

He bought coffee at the Perk-o-Latte, three doors from the funeral home, and walked in the front door as the chief came in from the station. A nod was all they exchanged as they descended to the doctor's lair.

"Whaddya got, Doc?" the chief asked.

The maniac lay on the table, all of the holes Bobby had put in him, as well as the ones Christiansen had, sewn or plugged. Bobby did not want to know with what.

The dead man was big enough that he could have doubled for Frankenstein's monster. The jagged scars and the Cro Magnon brow only added to the image. Even lying there dead, he gave Bobby the creepies.

"Cause of death, bullet to the heart." Christiansen glanced at Bobby. "Nice shot."

"I do my best." He'd learned long ago that if he needed to shoot, he'd better make it count or not bother at all. "Tell me something good."

"I think you're gonna like this. Anne McKenna's blood is on the blade."

No big surprise there. Two meat-cleaver maniacs in one small town would be something out of a horror novel. Though lately Bobby had started to wonder if he'd stepped into one. To get out, he needed answers.

"Any idea who he is?"

"No ID." The chief took over. "But most murderers avoid carrying their wallets. However, it's difficult to walk around without their fingerprints."

Bobby perked up. "He's got a record?"

"He hauls hazardous waste." The chief shrugged. "A lot of jobs require fingerprints now and that's one of them."

"What does hazardous waste have to do with anything?"

"No idea." The chief removed a small notebook from his pocket, flipped it open. "Karl Wellsprung, from Ohio.

As far as I know he's never been to Wisconsin, though we don't check folks at the border. The feds are interviewing his wife. Maybe they'll uncover something, but right now it appears as though he slipped a gear and went on a killing spree."

"Randomly choosing New Bergin by pinning the tail on the donkey map?" Bobby asked.

"You got a better explanation?"

"The ring brought me here, linked this murder to others." He glanced at the doctor. "I don't suppose you got anything off that."

"The FBI wanted it." Bobby cursed, and Christiansen lifted his hands in surrender. "I took a gander at it before I sent it to them. Seemed to me like the guy had cleaned it pretty well. Smelled like bleach. Feds will have a better chance of getting something off it than I would."

"No connection between this guy and the marshal's sister?"

"None." The chief shut his notebook.

"Any idea what she was doing here?"

"Visiting her aunt."

Bobby rubbed his head. This whole thing smelled more random by the minute.

He fucking hated random.

"Look at it this way," the chief continued. "If the murders stop, then you got your guy."

"They already stopped for a year, then they started again here."

Johnson scowled. "Are you sure?"

"What do you mean, am I sure?"

"From what you told me, the murders are only connected by that ring, by the brand. But this guy tried to burn the body."

"So did our guy. But burning a body isn't as easy as they make it seem on TV."

"Damn right," Christiansen muttered. "Why do they think I have a huge oven?" He gestured in the oven's direction. The thing did take up a lot of space. "It isn't like they're setting fire to kindling."

"If there were other murders in other places where the body was burned, that would make the brand . . . " The chief searched for a word, shrugged and went with, "Invisible, then—"

"The year of inactivity wasn't inactive. We were looking for the wrong MO," Bobby finished. "I should talk to the FBI."

"They're on it," the chief said. "Questioning the widow, requesting his travel schedule from his employer. Checking the airlines."

If Bobby was lucky, the maniac—Karl, Bobby amended—had flown to New Orleans the day before every one of the other murders, then flown home afterward. Or perhaps he'd driven a load of hazardous waste there, as well as to towns across the country where people had died then been burned.

Although, if the man had hazardous waste, why burn a body? Why not just dump it wherever they dumped such waste these days? Then again, nothing about this perpetrator had made any sense from the beginning.

Most likely the man had driven not flown on his own time, paying cash at dive motels or sleeping in his serial-killer white panel van. A hazardous waste truck would be as conspicuous as a credit card with his name on it.

Just because he was a maniac that didn't make him stupid.

* * *

When my alarm went off, I groaned. Saturdays should be about sleeping in, doing nothing, and they usually were. However, today was the New Bergin Elementary School Carnival.

Torture at its finest.

Bobby's door was open, the room empty. I panicked for a minute, until I saw that all his stuff was still there.

"You're an idiot." I headed for the bathroom. I cared too much, too soon. Bobby wasn't going to stay now that he'd killed the maniac. He had places to go, other people to arrest. When he left so would Genevieve. And while one less ghost in my life would be fan-fricking-tastic, a heartbroken Stafford would not be.

I turned on the shower, stepped beneath the stream. Henry had said the *Venatores Mali* were back. Plural. That meant there were more out there like the maniac. Would they come here? How did they know I was a witch when I hadn't even known it myself? And how would I tell Bobby about them without appearing to be a lunatic?

"Aargh!" I scrubbed my scalp, wishing I could wash all these crazy thoughts out of my head. I needed to talk to Henry.

Would I be able to summon him? I'd never tried. I wasn't going to try now. I shut off the water. At least until I put on some clothes and got out of sight and hearing range of anyone with a pulse.

A half hour later, dried, dressed, and waiting outside for Jenn—she'd been due here five minutes ago, which meant I had about fifteen minutes to spare—I whispered, "Henry?"

Nothing.

"Henry!" I said a little louder. "I have some questions. I'm alone." As if he couldn't see that.

"Pruuuu-dence!" I called, and received the same result. Although what I would have done with a wolf, I had no idea. While she'd seemed to understand us, she certainly hadn't been able to talk. At least to me.

"Ghosts. Never around when you need 'em." Always right there when you didn't.

I called a few more times. Closed my eyes and thought of Henry's face. I'd seen it enough. I conjured nothing but a slight headache. Which was just what I needed for a day with elementary school children on a sugar high, playing with sticks and balls and water.

Jenn's tires kicked up gravel as she fishtailed out of the trees and into the yard. I glanced at my phone. Ten minutes late. Which, for Jenn, was pretty damn early.

"Are you okay?" she asked, turning the car in a circle so fast, I nearly tumbled out the door right after I'd gotten in.

"If you wouldn't drive this thing like a go-cart, I might be." I fastened my seat belt with a sharp click.

She glanced at me, then back at the road. "I meant after last night."

"Last night," I repeated, images tumbling through my mind. Bobby's kiss. Genevieve's tears. Henry. Prudence.

Jenn huffed, exasperated. "Someone tried to kill you."

Ah, that.

"I'm fine. Not a scratch."

"You thought someone was in your house the other night too."

"There wasn't."

"It seems odd that you thought there was, and then a few days later . . . there was."

It was worse than odd, but I didn't say so, and when I didn't, Jenn moved on. One of the things I liked about her—she didn't dwell.

"I heard Detective Hot Stuff shot the guy. Bang, bang, straight through the heart."

"Where'd you hear that?"

"Where do you think?"

Dumb question. There'd been more people at the scene than emergency services. Pretty much anyone in town who could come out to watch, had. They'd have heard things; they'd have shared them.

"What was it like?" Jenn asked.

I remembered the fear, the shots, the huge knife just missing my head.

"Huh." Had Henry done that or had I?

"All you can say is *huh*? This is the most exciting stuff to happen in this town in years."

"I'd rather our excitement didn't involve murder."

"Attempted murder."

"Tell it to Anne McKenna."

"Dead lady in the alley?"

"Yeah."

"I heard she was the witch's niece."

I'd been reaching over to change the radio station, which was yammering some advertisement for a hayride and pumpkin festival, but let my hand fall to my lap. My fingers suddenly felt as cold as the ones Anne McKenna's ghost had wrapped around my wrist. Had that only been yesterday? I still had the bruises.

"What witch?"

"Oh, that's just what me and my brothers called Mrs. Noita."

Jenn had two brothers—big bruisers, who'd played offensive line for New Bergin High, then gone on to Wisconsin, where they'd cracked heads for the Badgers and been paid with a full ride. A lot of people believed that football players were stupid—and I had to say that some who got hit in the head a few too many times—Brett Favre—did stupid things.

However, attending the University of Wisconsin Madison in any form meant you weren't an idiot. The academic requirements were extremely high. To stay in school, and keep up the ridiculous schedule that went along with a Big Ten sport, meant that the athletes didn't just excel on the field. Jenn's older brother was an electrical engineer and the younger one had just been admitted to law school.

"Your parents' neighbor is the dead woman's aunt?"

"That's the word on the street."

"And she's a witch." Why hadn't I heard of it?

"She was nasty. To be fair, when we were little we probably drove her nuts. Baseballs smacking against her house. Footballs in her herb garden. Tom once threw my favorite Barbie on her roof, then threw Ken, as well as the back porch of the Barbie Dream House, up there too. When she'd come screaming out the front door her hair seemed to stand on end. My mom called her a witch after the Barbie incident, and it stuck."

"You never told me this."

"It was a family joke, not a community-wide opinion. Although she did keep to herself and everyone thought she was strange. Didn't you?"

To be honest, I'd never thought of the woman at all.

I could count on two hands the times I'd seen her in my lifetime. Which was odd right there.

Jenn turned into the parking lot, already half full with teachers' cars. "I asked her for help once."

"What kind of help?"

"Remember *The Sixth Sense*?"

As I was still living it . . .

"How could I forget?"

We'd been too young to see it at the theater, but there'd been one rainy Friday evening in high school when we'd indulged in the DVD.

"I couldn't go to the bathroom alone in the night after that." Jenn shuddered. "Kept seeing my breath. Was afraid to turn around. Didn't it bother you?"

I shrugged. I was always afraid to turn around. You got used to it. "Why did you ask Mrs. Noita for help?"

"If she was a witch I figured she knew a way to get rid of the ghosts or at least keep them at a distance."

"Since when are witches and ghosts in any way related?"

Since last night? my mind whispered. *When you met a ghostly witch?*

"I figured weird calls to weird," she said. "It wasn't as if I had anyone else to ask."

"What about the Internet?"

"Because I was going to buy something funky off the Internet? And give out my address to the nut who was selling it? That's how kids disappear."

"Well, at least you had the sense to know that." I was kind of annoyed she hadn't confided in me. Though what would I have done? Confessed that I saw ghosts too?

She cast me a narrow glare. "Don't you understand? I was scared shitless."

I did understand. More than I could, or would, ever say.

"Did she help?"

"She did."

I straightened, intrigued. I'd read every book, searched every Web site, tried a lot of things. None of them helped.

"How?"

"She gave me some rosemary and slammed the door in my face."

Something as simple as rosemary was something I hadn't tried. "And that worked?"

She cast me a wry glance. "We're talking ghosts, Raye. They weren't real in the first place, so it worked pretty damn good."

It had never occurred to me to go to a witch and ask for a way to ward off ghosts. Probably because it hadn't occurred to me that we had a witch in town. Until last night, witches had never entered my head at all.

My head had been too full of ghosts.

Chapter 11

The three men went across the street for breakfast, where they mulled the case and the autopsy results in between visits from the locals, who liked to shoot the breeze with both the doctor and the chief, as well as take the opportunity to meet the stranger in town.

The food wasn't half as good as what John Larsen had served Bobby the day before, but the coffee was hot and plentiful. A few hours later, they returned to the basement of the funeral home as Bobby's cell phone rang.

The FBI agent assigned to the case was different from the one who'd taken Chief Johnson's call, then contacted Bobby. At least Nic Franklin appeared to know his job. He'd already interviewed the maniac's widow and discovered no connection to the murders in New Orleans.

"Guy has an alibi for all your dates," Franklin said.

"Have you checked similar murders elsewhere?" Bobby asked.

"Similar how? Where else?"

"Burned bodies? Anywhere?"

"That's a wide net, Detective."

"And the FBI's just the one to cast it."

Agent Franklin sighed. "I'll get back to you."

Bobby informed the chief and Christiansen of the maniac's alibis for the New Orleans murders.

"That means there's more than one of them," Johnson said.

"More than one of what?"

"Murderers with the same damn ring."

"A murder club?" Christiansen asked.

"There's gotta be a connection somewhere," the chief continued. "If not with the murderers then with the murderees." He glanced at Bobby. "You wanna go with me to talk to Mrs. Noita?"

"Who?"

Johnson's cell began to ring. "Dead woman's aunt." He lifted a finger in a "hold that thought" gesture and answered his phone.

Bobby needed a lead—something, anything. Although what connection there could be between Anne McKenna, a never-married hospice worker from Madison, and Raye Larsen he had no idea. Probably even less of one between Anne, Raye, and the dead people in New Orleans.

"Godammit." Larsen shoved his cell phone into his pocket.

"What's wrong?" Bobby feared another body.

"Cows," the chief snapped.

Was that a local curse word, similar to *bull hockey* or *H-E-double toothpicks*? Although he hadn't noticed the chief was too concerned about watching his language so far.

"They're all over the highway. I gotta get out there."

"You—uh—need help?"

"You any good at it?"

"I know how to use a shovel."

Johnson's face creased. "We don't hit 'em, son, we herd 'em."

"Hit?" Bobby echoed.

"With the shovel."

They were speaking the same language, and then again they weren't.

"When you said 'all over the highway' I assumed . . . " He let his voice trail off.

"Roadkill?" The chief shook his head. "Ever hit a cow with your car?"

Now Bobby shook his head. What kind of question was that?

"Like hittin' a brick shithouse."

Bobby opened his mouth, shut it again. He was lost.

Johnson saw it and chuckled. "A cow will total your car. My father-in-law hit one in the dark once. Thing was lyin' right in the road. They do that sometimes when they get out of the pasture. Lie on the blacktop, try to soak in the heat. Angus cows, blend right in. Come over the hill and wham!" He smacked his palms together, the resulting *crack* so loud Bobby could have sworn even the maniac jumped. "But there ain't gonna be a bunch dead on the road. Hittin' one is a wake-up call."

"Unless you wake up dead," Christiansen said, gaze on his paperwork. "It's happened before."

Bobby eyed the maniac, then shook his head. *He'd* jumped, not the dead man. Dead men couldn't jump any more than white men could. "So when you said they were all over the road, you meant—"

"Wandered through a hole in the fence and are now meandering across the highway stoppin' traffic."

"And you want me to help herd them back through the fence? Cows are huge."

"That's why we need them off the road. A few cows

in traffic and there's no more traffic. You got a traffic jam."

The closest Bobby had ever been to a cow was on his plate. He wasn't sure he wanted to change that.

Johnson slapped him on the back. "Cows won't hurt you." His smile turned upside down. "A bull is another story." He pulled out his cell. "I should probably make sure there isn't a bull."

"What do bulls do?" Bobby asked the doctor, who was still fussing with his paperwork.

"Besides the cows?" Christiansen looked up. "A lot of damage. Basically a bull is pissed off in a huge package. With horns."

Bobby started to get nervous. Maniacs with knives, druggies with guns, no problem—but a ton of pissed off, with horns—

"No bull." The chief snapped his phone shut. "I was thinking that since you're not familiar with livestock you might spook 'em."

Bobby was spooked all right. However, he couldn't let the chief go off on his own to herd a herd. "I'll manage."

"Maybe you could interview Mrs. Noita instead."

"Sure!"

Christiansen snorted. Bobby had sounded pathetically eager.

Ten minutes later he was knocking on Mrs. Noita's door. He'd already rung the bell twice. If she was still sleeping, she shouldn't be anymore. He listened for signs of movement—heard none. He should have called first.

The house was nondescript—wood plank painted white, gray shingles. The trees, on the other hand, were odd. Not only were they birch, willow, oak, walnut, and a couple others he couldn't identify, instead of the usual maples and pine he'd seen everywhere else, but items had been tied in the branches. Mostly paper, some metal—he could swear one of them was a spoon—and on many of the leaves symbols had been drawn.

The wind stirred, causing the papers to rustle and the spoon to clank and jangle. Bobby rubbed the back of his neck and knocked again.

After a few more minutes on the front porch, he walked around to the rear—more trees, more stuff swaying in them. He tried knocking on that door with the same results. He bent to glance in the window stationed about gut high in the door, straightened, turned, froze as his brain caught up to his eyes.

Then he yanked off his jacket, wrapped it around his hand, and punched his fist through the glass.

We were doing pretty well at the carnival until the fire alarm went off.

Not our fire alarm. We were outside. Even if the school alarm had blown, it wouldn't have mattered except to our eardrums.

However, when the New Bergin fire alarm sounds, every last male on the staff responds. Not that there are very many in an elementary school. How many first-grade teachers do you know who are guys?

But all emergency services in New Bergin, except for the police, were volunteer and belonging was a status thing. Personally I just think they liked to run away from whatever they were doing whenever they could—and wear the T-shirt.

When the alarm blared we lost six people from carnival duty, and the crowd went wild.

"I'm volunteering for the fire department tomorrow," Jenn said.

We were working the goldfish game. An ocean of tiny fishbowls filled with water, a bucket of Ping-Pong balls, toss one of the latter into one of the former and Nemo is yours. For the few days until he goes belly up and is consigned to burial at sea—i.e., the sewer system.

"I think there's a height requirement." I transferred another Nemo from the huge cooler beneath the table where the extras swam, into an empty fishbowl. I'd just dumped the previous contents into a plastic bag for another lucky winner.

"Bite me." Jenn glared at the taillights of the volunteers' cars as they raced toward town.

"I don't know what you're complaining about." I checked the bowls to make certain we had no floaters. I'd had kids point and shriek at the sight of one. It made for bad business. "You're handing out Ping-Pong balls. I'm trolling for dead guppies."

It was that or do everything myself. Jenn did not touch fish—even when sautéed with capers and butter. Anything slimy or scaly was my department. Always had been.

With the loss of six workers, several game booths had closed, along with the popcorn machine. This meant that those who'd wanted popcorn bought cotton candy or snow cones or Raisinets, increasing the sugar quotient at the worst possible time.

Because there were fewer game booths available, that meant longer lines at the ones still open. When combined with the excess sugar . . . disaster.

Shoving and pushing, pinching and crying. Someone dropped their Nemo, someone else stepped on it, slid, banged into someone else. A punch was thrown, a shirt was torn, several bodies landed in the grass and began to roll around.

And those were the adults.

"Watch out for the—" Jenn shouted, then ran shrieking as the table holding our game toppled over, followed by the cooler, releasing Nemo upon Nemo to flop and flip and die in plain view of everyone.

We'd thought there'd been crying before . . . that was nothing compared to now. The wailing competed in volume with the still shrill sirens. What was going on in town?

In the midst of trying to salvage as many Nemos as I could—it wasn't easy. I only had one net, and no water—I froze at the scent of smoke.

My Puritan, or any other ghost for that matter, was nowhere around. No wolf—thank God with all these kids—at the edge of the trees either. Come to think of it, I hadn't seen Stafford all day, and that was unusual. Not to mention troublesome. The only thing worse than a present Stafford was a missing one. Bad stuff happened when he was too long on his own.

I frowned in the direction of town. The fire couldn't be his fault; he was attached to the school. But what about Genevieve? She seemed to be able to travel farther afield than any ghosts I'd encountered before. She'd obviously come to New Bergin with Bobby, but didn't seem confined to his immediate radius. I'd never seen that before.

Then again, I rarely *left* town, and folks rarely stayed *in* town long enough for me to analyze any ghost they might have brought along. Despite having seen spirits all of my life, I'd spent most of my time avoiding them, or trying to ignore them, rather than understand them. Wouldn't you?

"So many ghosts, so little time," I murmured.

"Here, Miss Larsen, you can put them in my bag." Troy held open his plastic Ziploc. I dumped the contents within. Too small for five fish, they all began bumping into one another, twirling, swishing. Troy giggled and zipped the lock.

"Take them home and put them in a larger container," I ordered.

His mom arrived, and he held up the bag for her inspection. She cast me a glance.

"Sorry," I said. "They're discounting fish food and bowls at Ben Franklin." They always did on carnival weekend.

We wound up losing money on the fish game, which was close to impossible considering the outlay on goldfish and the income on Ping-Pong balls. However, when three quarters of the inventory winds up part of an alfresco Picasso painting . . .

Genevieve materialized, and I dropped the handful of quarters I'd been trying to roll. They bounced all over the fish-strewn ground.

"I'm not picking those up," Jenn said. "They've got fish cooties."

"Like you'd pick them up regardless," I muttered. Even if she hadn't been wearing a skirt too short for such acrobatics, Jenn did not squat.

"Daddy!" Genevieve shouted.

No sign of Bobby anywhere.

Her lip trembled; her gaze turned toward town. "He's going to get hurt."

"Where is he?" I asked.

"Where is who?" Jenn worked the calculator. I wasn't sure what she was adding, since I wasn't done counting. She also didn't touch money. It was "icky."

"There's going to be a fire," Genevieve said.

Going to be? Wasn't there one already?

I bit my tongue to keep from quizzing the invisible child. "Did you ever hear what was on fire?" I asked Jenn.

She pulled out her phone, scrolled through her texts. "Apparently nothing."

Genevieve spread her hands in a "told you so" gesture far too mature for her years. Most little girls were.

"They needed EMTs," Jenn continued.

As one emergency service brought all emergency services this made sense. Though the damn siren was usually reserved for fire only.

Genevieve wrung her hands then hopped back and forth as if she had to pee.

"Where?" I asked, a question for both of them.

"The witch's house," they said at the exact same time.

Bobby reached through the broken window and flipped the lock on the back door. He stepped inside, crunching glass beneath his shoes as he hurried through the kitchen to the hallway where he'd seen the feet.

They were attached to a woman. She was very white. Hair, athletic shoes, skin. Everything else was very red—clothes, hands, walls.

"Mrs. Noita?" He hunkered next to her, trying not to screw up the crime scene. He could swear she was still breathing, though with that much blood outside instead of in, he couldn't see how. The woman's eyes opened.

"Mrs. Noita?" he repeated.

She blinked then lifted a trembling hand toward the gaping wound in her neck, obviously the source of all the blood. A wolf snarled—fresh, red, and raw—from the back of that hand.

Bobby cursed. Dead maniacs could not brand anyone, which meant . . .

They had a live one.

He dialed 911 without even glancing at the numbers. He had no idea what he said, but sirens wailed almost immediately. At least, in a place like this, help wasn't very far away.

Considering the scope of this injury, he wasn't sure their resources would be sufficient. He wasn't sure anything short of a miracle would be.

Her eyelashes fluttered.

"Ma'am! Stay with me. Look at me."

She did.

"Who did this?"

Her mouth opened, her teeth pushed against her bottom lip. At first he thought it was the pain, then he heard a slight outrush of air and a word, "Vena."

"Vena did this?" Odd name, but this was an odd place.

"N— Na." She was getting agitated. Blood bubbled from her mouth.

"Vena," he said. "I got it."

"Venatores," she blurted, and now blood sprayed.

"Shh," he soothed, sorry he'd even asked her the question, though he'd had to.

"Mali!" More blood.

A siren wailed to a stop outside. A door slammed, footsteps followed. Seconds later the pretty blond officer—Bobby thought his name was Brad—skidded through the glass. He took one glimpse of the blood and promptly lost his breakfast in the sink. Why was it this guy always seemed to be wherever there was trouble? Then again, there were only three officers in the entire town.

"Stay," Bobby told him. He heard more sirens on the way.

The second arrival was Christiansen. Thanks be to God.

The man hurried in, then froze when the woman opened her eyes again.

"She isn't dead." He sounded as horrified as Bobby felt.

"Yet. Do something."

"I don't work on the living."

"I thought you were a doctor."

"Not that kind."

"Get your ass over here and pretend."

Christiansen glanced out the door. Sirens still wailed. "The EMTs should be right behind me."

"Then you won't have to pretend for very long."

The man took a breath, squared his shoulders, and approached—slowly as if afraid the nearly dead woman might bite. He paused, still several feet away.

"Now, Doc. She's—"

"Gone," Christiansen interrupted.

Bobby glanced down. He was right.

The doctor moved forward, no longer hesitant. He snapped on gloves, handed Bobby a pair too.

"What the hell?" the doctor muttered, gaze on her branded hand. It was kind of hard to miss, even with the mess, since she'd laid it right below her wound. "That's fresh, and the ring is—"

"Forget that for now," Bobby ordered. He indicated Mrs. Noita's neck. "How old?"

"She's lived here as long as I can remember, and I don't recall her ever being anything but ancient."

"I didn't mean how old is she, I meant how old is the wound?"

"Oh. Right. Not very." Christiansen plucked at her clothing. "Strange."

"What?"

"Some of the blood is dried. That takes more than a few minutes. Wounds like this the victim bleeds out pretty fast. I'll have to get her on my table to find out for sure but from the amount of blood I'd say the carotid artery was nicked. She should have been dead in minutes, certainly unconscious."

"Minutes?" Bobby repeated. "That's not possible."

He'd been farting around outside her door longer than that. If anyone had been inside he'd have heard them. At the least he'd have heard her screaming. The back door had been locked, and no one had come out the front.

"I've discovered that possible is a much wider area than we know." Christiansen brushed one gloved finger over Mrs. Noita's branded hand as another siren-blaring vehicle arrived outside.

"She was still conscious when I got here," Bobby said. "She was conscious when *you* got here. How?"

"Either a miracle or magic."

Bobby didn't believe in either one.

"Where's the fire?" Christiansen asked.

They were both still hunkered on either side of the dead woman. Bobby wasn't in a hurry, hadn't even made a move to leave. "Huh?"

"The last body was burned. You're here because so

were yours. The brand and that burning connected the deaths."

"But not the killers since the maniac is dead. He had nothing to do with this, and his alibis proved he had nothing to do with my victims either."

"Which means we're back to the murder club," Christiansen said. "Except this guy screwed up. No fire."

"Unless I interrupted him before he could finish. Although where he would have gone—" Bobby straightened. "Get out."

Christiansen glanced up. "Excuse me?"

Bobby lowered his voice. "I didn't clear the place."

The doctor frowned, his gaze darting to the basement door, then the bedrooms down the hall, before returning to Bobby's.

"She was still awake. She spoke to me." Gibberish, but he hadn't known that at the time.

The EMTs crowded in the back door. Their steps faltered. Bobby jerked his head at Christiansen. "Take them with you." He glanced toward Brad, who still hovered near the sink looking peaked. "Keep everyone out until I say they can come back in. Can you manage that?"

The kid drew himself up, nodded, then herded everyone ahead of him and closed the door.

Bobby drew his weapon and crept down the hall.

Chapter 12

For the first time ever, I was glad for Jenn's need for speed. She got us to the witch's house in record time, even for her.

Unfortunately everyone else in the universe—or at least in New Bergin—was there ahead of us. Everyone except the man I was searching for.

"Where's Bobby?"

"Don't see him," Jenn answered, at the same time Genevieve—who'd accompanied us in the back seat; it hadn't been easy not to talk to her, let alone look at her—said, "In the basement. You have to hurry."

I tried, but Brad stopped me. Why did it have to be him?

He'd treated Jenn badly; she'd responded in kind. I hadn't been friendly either. As a result, I didn't expect much help from him, and I was right.

"No one in until the all clear." His voice and his face were far too smug.

"I need to talk to Detective Doucet."

"When he comes out."

"Now."

"Why?"

I couldn't mention the dead kid, who thought the house was going to self-combust.

"Isn't it dangerous for him to be in there alone?"

"He's a cop, Raye. One who deals with a lot more dangerous things where he's from than we've ever seen here. He'll be fine."

I could try and scoot around Brad, make a run for it, but he'd won a medal at State in the two-hundred-meter dash. He'd catch me, and then I'd never get inside.

I hurried to Jenn, who sat on the hood of her car, playing with her phone. "Distract him."

"Who?" She didn't even glance up.

"Brad."

"No." Still no eye contact.

"Now, Jenn, or someone's going to die."

That got her attention. She lifted her gaze, saw I was serious, and put away her phone. She'd known me long enough to believe what I said. She was Jenn enough not to ask questions.

She slithered off the car with a long-suffering sigh, fluffed her hair, hiked up the girls, and moved off. Unfortunately, Brad was familiar with Jenn. The instant she came near him, his gaze went to me and stuck there.

"Son of a bitch." Brad had never been as dumb as he looked. He knew that Jenn would not have come near him unless I sent her.

Genevieve gasped. I'd forgotten about her.

"Sorry!" I needed to watch my language around kids—both dead and alive.

She cast me a disgusted glance. "Run," she said, then she ran straight at Jenn.

My mouth fell open. I had no idea what she was going to do. Possess her? The idea made me squeamish for more than one reason. A child in Jenn's head—talk about trauma. For both of them.

"Wait!" I shouted.

Jenn turned to scowl in my direction, and Genevieve shoved her in the chest. The child was spirit not form, that shouldn't have worked. Although Stafford had been around long enough to learn how to do a lot more than any other ghost I'd ever encountered. Why was it that the good children never managed to teach the bad ones their behavior, it was always the other way around?

Jenn tumbled backward; Brad caught her; I scooted around the side of the house and ran.

The back door gaped. Mrs. Noita hunkered beside her own body. I hated when that happened. Not only was it creepy to see the dead and the living right next to each other, but the ghosts were always confused and as upset about seeing their own dead selves as I was. However, I didn't have time to soothe or explain. I stepped over one and through the other, ignoring both the chill and the scent of too much blood.

"Bobby!" I shouted from the top of the steps.

My response was a muffled curse and a faint: "Stay there."

Instead, I hurried downstairs.

"I'm going to kill that pretty blond kid," Bobby muttered. "Get out."

"Only if you come too." My gaze flitted around the basement, which was remarkably empty, dry, and clean for a basement. It still had nooks and crannies where all sorts of nasty things might hide.

"I have to make sure whoever killed Mrs. Noita isn't still down here." He held his gun pointed toward the ground, but his body was tense, and he appeared ready to lift it at any time.

"She isn't." Mrs. Noita no longer hunkered next to Mrs. Noita but stood in her own basement.

"Who?" I asked.

"Never saw her before in my life," she said.

"If I knew that," Bobby answered, "I wouldn't even be here."

"You shouldn't be."

Genevieve appeared at his side. She tugged on his belt. "Daddy, come on! Daddy!"

He frowned and glanced down. When he stepped forward her fingers went through his side, and he shuddered.

"Raye." Henry stood next to the furnace. It was a convention down here.

I scowled at him. Now he showed up? He pointed at something on the side that I couldn't see.

"You need to get out." His gaze followed his own finger. "Quickly."

I hurried over, ignoring another curse from Bobby, as well as Henry.

"Goddammit, Raye. Anyone could be—"

"Shit," I said, when I saw what Henry was pointing at.

Bobby's gun came up, and he joined us, hesitating when he walked through Henry. Bobby Doucet might not believe in ghosts, but he felt them, and I had to wonder why.

His gaze lit on the timer, ticking down to doomsday. We had about a minute left.

"Shit," he echoed. "Run."

I wished people would stop saying that to me. I wished even harder that I didn't have to listen,

Our footsteps thundered up the stairs. I leaped over Mrs. Noita a second time.

"Front door," Bobby shouted, and I cut in that direction. It was closer.

I glanced back, saw him hesitate near the body, knew

exactly what he was thinking: He shouldn't leave her behind. But the clock in my head was thumping to the same beat as the one downstairs.

"No." I snatched his hand, and after a sharp yank on my part, and a shove from Genevieve, he followed.

We tumbled out the front door. Everyone in the yard faced us, eyes widening as he shouted, "Get back!" and I added, "It's gonna blow!"

The crowd scattered; the house erupted upward and outward. I don't know if Bobby dived and landed on top of me on purpose, or if he was propelled by the blast. Nevertheless, every last bit of air was driven from my lungs as his weight slammed me to the ground.

Silence blanketed the world, along with a fiery heat. Bobby rolled free. Only when he kept rolling did I realize he was trying to put out the tiny flames in his clothes.

He sat up, his gaze first going to me then the house. I was pretty sure it looked worse than I did.

"He will burn us all."

Mrs. Noita stared at what was left of her place. I opened my mouth to ask about her pronoun confusion—she'd identified her attacker as a she, but he was going to burn us? Before I could say anything—and considering Bobby's gaze had already returned to me that was probably for the best—Mrs. Noita behaved just like her niece. Her pure black eyes had a hint of flame at the center, smoke poured from her mouth in a stream, and then she was gone.

Bobby got to his feet, held out a hand. All around us, ash swirled like dirty snow, and the heat of the still-blazing house made my face feel as if I'd gotten my first sunburn of the summer. He helped me up, kept hold of my hand. "How did you know about this?"

"It's New Bergin." I indicated the crowd, which had swelled considerably since I'd gone inside. "The instant the sirens went off, everyone knew."

He was still a little dazed; so was I. "I meant the bomb." Suspicion flickered in his eyes. "You knew."

"Did not." My denial was automatic, and actually the truth for a change. I hadn't known about the bomb until Henry had pointed to it.

Bobby rubbed his head. It probably hurt as badly as mine did. He was just about to question me further, and make both our heads ache even more, when Chief Johnson pulled up—where had he been before now?—and beckoned him.

"I have to go. I'll talk to you later."

"Okay."

"I mean it," he said, but he was already moving off to join the chief.

By then maybe I'd have a better explanation than . . .

I didn't have an explanation.

"Raye!" Jenn threw her arms around my waist. Color me surprised; she wasn't cuddly. Then I felt her shaking.

I set my hands on her shoulders. "What's wrong?"

She stepped back and punched me in the arm. "You almost got yourself killed."

"I didn't."

"Not for lack of trying." She hit me again. "What is wrong with you?"

More than I could ever say.

Bobby glanced back just as Raye's friend punched her in the arm. He agreed with the sentiment if not the execution. What *had* she been thinking?

"Holy hell." The chief stared at the pile of charcoal that had once been a very nice house. Oddly the trees that had spooked Bobby before swayed and jingled, virtually unharmed, despite the grass around them being severely overcooked. "What did you do?"

"Me?" Bobby asked.

"Christiansen said you ordered everyone out."

"Because I thought the guy was still in there."

"Was he?"

"If he was"—Bobby eyed what was now mostly a crater—"he isn't anymore."

The chief snorted.

"I'd nearly checked the whole place when Raye—"

"Raye was in there?" Johnson scowled, first at Bobby, then at Raye, who still had her hands full with her little pal.

When Jenn wasn't punching Raye's arm, and yammering at her like a yappy minidog, she had her arms around Raye's waist, clinging to her like . . .

Bobby rubbed his side, which still ached as if a bullet had glanced off the skin. Genevieve used to cling to him like that when she was really scared.

Bobby shoved thoughts of his child from his mind the same way he always did whenever they came. He couldn't function and think of her, so he refused to think of her at all.

He'd probably have to eventually—the thoughts were coming more often; the memories had invaded his dreams. He could swear he'd even smelled her a few times, and that was just—

"Doucet!"

Bobby blinked.

The chief glared. "Am I keeping you awake? We got a situation here."

Bobby ran a hand over his face, grimacing at the soot that crunched between his palm and his skin. "What did you say?"

"You ordered everyone out?"

"I did."

"But you let Raye stay?"

"She came in after."

"Why?"

"She found the bomb."

"There was a bomb?"

Bobby indicated the smoldering ruin. "You think that happens without one?"

"Looks"—the chief sniffed—"and smells, like a gas leak."

"Which is no doubt what they wanted it to look and smell like since the bomb was on the furnace. If I hadn't seen the body and the bomb . . . " He spread his hands.

"You didn't see the perp?"

"Two out of three ain't bad," Bobby said, causing the chief to snort again.

Dr. Christiansen arrived. "I wish I'd had that body removed right away."

"We all do," Johnson agreed. "What did you find before you ran?"

Christiansen cast him an evil glare then recited his short list of findings.

"How did she manage to stay conscious with her throat slit?"

"Without the body, we'll never know," Christiansen said.

"Swell," Bobby muttered. They weren't going to discover much about anything without evidence, which was probably the point.

"You were here first," Johnson continued. "What did you see?"

It seemed so very long ago but . . . Bobby glanced at his phone—saw he'd missed a summons from Sullivan; he'd have to call his partner back—and figured the entire incident had taken place in under an hour.

"Doucet," the chief said again. "Did you hit your head?"

"Probably." It hurt enough.

"You need an EMT?"

He shook that head, flinched. He'd had concussions before, knew exactly what to do—ibuprofen, rest, go to the hospital if he started to puke or forgot who he was—he did not need anyone poking and prodding him. However . . . Raye should probably be examined.

He took a step in her direction and saw that one of the EMTs was doing just that—checking her pupils, asking her questions, in between barks from her still-furious best friend.

"Hello?" the chief called.

If Bobby weren't careful he'd wind up in the ambulance on the way to the hospital. Did they have a hospital? He resisted the urge to rub his head again. One of the symptoms of a concussion, as he recalled, was slow thinking, along with inability to recall both what had happened right before the injury as well as after.

"She didn't answer the door," he blurted.

There. No problem remembering what had happened before the world went boom. All good.

"Probably a little hard for her to move," Christiansen said. "Considering."

The wind stirred, flinging ash everywhere and causing the tree ornaments to jingle.

"What's up with her trees?" Bobby asked.

Both Christiansen and Johnson frowned. "You sure you're all right?"

Bobby narrowed his gaze; it helped with the headache. "I'm fine."

The chief jerked his head at the doc, and the latter moved in close enough to peer at Bobby's pupils. "You know where you are?"

"Podunk."

Christiansen lifted his eyebrows. "Not the time for ha-ha, Detective."

The man was right. "New Bergin, Wisconsin. My name is Bobby Doucet. I am twenty-eight years old. I came to this house to talk to Mrs. Noita. Okay?"

The doctor stared at him for a few seconds, then stepped back and nodded to the chief.

"The trees?" Bobby repeated.

"Mrs. Noita was flaky," Johnson said. "A bit hippie."

"She looked pretty skinny to me."

"Not big hips." Christiansen gave the peace sign. "Hippie."

"A lot of herbs," Johnson continued. "Voodoo."

Bobby glanced at the trees. "That's not voodoo." Voodoo, he knew.

"Whatever." The chief's lip curled. "She was a vegan."

"Last time I checked, that wasn't a crime."

"Around here." Johnson's gaze went to a distant but still visible farm to the east. Cows peppered the landscape like black and white polka dots. "It's damn close."

"She practiced herbal medicine," Christiansen put in, then lifted his hand. "Not a crime, I know. In truth, some of that works pretty good. No clue why."

Bobby still wasn't hearing why she'd decorated her trees. Maybe they didn't know. Mostly, it didn't matter.

"I broke the window on her back door," Bobby continued. He seemed to be having a difficult time staying on point and finishing a thought—definitely mild to moderate concussion. "I called her name. She lifted her hand, and I saw she'd been branded."

Johnson cursed. "You're sure?"

Bobby nodded, glanced at Christiansen, who nodded too. At least he hadn't imagined it.

"Did she say anything?" the chief asked.

"I asked her who had done it. Her answer was pretty much gibberish. Understandable, considering."

"You wanna relate that gibberish, son? One never can tell what might be useful down the road."

"She said, '*Venatores Mali.*' " He spread his hands. "I don't—"

"That isn't gibberish," Christiansen interrupted. "That's Latin."

"You speak Latin?" Johnson asked.

"No one *speaks* Latin. Dead language."

Bobby'd never understood what that meant. How could a language be dead? But bringing that up would only be another pointless point.

"I'm a doctor. Latin is a daily pain in my behind."

"What does it mean?" Bobby asked.

"*Venatores Mali* translates to 'hunters of evil.' "

"Evil what?"

"Unfortunately," Christiansen murmured, "we aren't going to be able to ask her."

Chapter 13

I managed to escape before anyone beyond Greg Gustafsson, emergency services, tried to question me. Greg offered me a ride to the clinic in town; I refused.

I had a few scrapes. I'd live. I just wanted to get out of there.

The scene was chaos. It wasn't every day something blew up in New Bergin. That it had blown up after yet another murder . . .

Like I said, chaos.

I wouldn't be able to escape questioning indefinitely, but for now I took the opportunity and ran with it.

Jenn was more hysterical than I'd ever seen her—hysteria gave her hives—and that was before a piece of Mrs. Noita fell out of a tree.

My father arrived on the scene right after Mrs. Noita's arm. His gaze went to the house, before scanning the crowd. When it reached me, his lips tightened and he strode over.

I wanted to apologize; I always did. That incessant need to please and appease. He let out a sigh that sounded more like a huff, then ran his finger down my cheek. Not a caress, more of an indictment. His finger came away black. I had been a little close to the action.

"Not a scratch on me," I said brightly. I did have a

scratch, probably more than one, but I lifted my hand anyway. "I swear."

He didn't believe me, but he didn't say so. Instead he lifted his chin to indicate Jenn. "What's wrong with her?"

I'd always thought Jenn was making up the connection between hives and hysteria but apparently not. One look in her direction, and I steered her toward her car. "She needs calamine, Benadryl, Epsom salts—maybe all three." I could probably do with some myself. "I'll call you later."

I tried to put Jenn in the passenger seat. That woke her up pretty fast. "Are you nuts?"

"She's baaack," I said as she tore free and got behind the wheel.

We reached my apartment a few minutes later. "Oh," she said. "Forgot. You're staying at your father's."

"No." I laid my hand on hers. Her skin was like ice, or maybe mine was on fire. "I had an e-mail that my apartment was cleared for me to go back."

"Is it safe?"

I knew there was another killer, but she didn't, and considering her condition, I wasn't going to tell her. She'd have hives on top of hives.

I'd be safer here than in the forest at my father's. He wouldn't be back for a while anyway. Almost everyone in town was at the scene, and there was a lot to see. But mostly I didn't want Jenn staying with me. Because there *was* another killer, and I did not plan to allow Jenn anywhere near her. Him.

"It," I said. In my book, murderers were definitely *it*.

"What?"

"It's safe." I'd always been good at making my often

random statements less random, and lately I was getting even better at it.

Bright red spots bloomed on Jenn's cheeks; several bumps littered her neck and chest. I thought her lip might be starting to swell. "Are you gonna be okay?"

She flicked a glance into the rearview mirror. "I gotta go."

"Jenn," I started. Though I didn't want her insisting on staying with me—too dangerous—I also didn't want her alone if there was any chance her being alone was equally dangerous. What if her throat swelled up like a puffer fish and she couldn't breathe?

"I need to down some pills before I look like Angelina Jolie. So either get out, or come along. Your choice, but make it fast."

I hesitated, and she started to pull away. "Wait." She'd had hives before; she had pills. My cursed presence was going to be more of a threat than bumps and splotches. There wasn't a pill that could cure death by *Venatores Mali*.

"Call me," I said. "I can always—" She took off with the door still open. I managed to shut it before she flattened a mailbox.

She raced down First Street far above the legal speed limit. What else was new? At least everyone was still at Mrs. Noita's, so there was no one for her to run into or over, and no police presence to issue yet another ticket. She was getting close to losing her license.

Again.

I climbed the stairs to my apartment. Even though I'd only been gone a few days, the place smelled musty—closed in and old. I cracked a few windows.

At first I thought the scent of smoke was coming

through those windows, and I nearly closed them. Then I got a glimpse of my hands, my clothes. That smell was coming from me.

I locked the doors—both outside and bathroom—then turned on the shower full blast, lost the clothes—I wasn't even going to bother trying to wash them, they were toast—and stepped in. Dirty water swirled down the drain for quite a while. Eventually I pulled back the curtain, reached for a towel and managed—barely—not to scream when my hand went right through Henry.

I had the presence of mind to grab that towel as I whirled, pulling it tightly around me. "Get out!"

"We must talk."

"I wanted to talk this morning and no you."

"I had another . . . never mind."

"Get out," I repeated. I should have bought rosemary before I came home. Did I have some in a jar? Would it work? I hoped so.

"Raye, I've been with you since you were born."

"Point?" I climbed out of the tub and strode into my room, pulling clothes out of the drawers, uncaring what they were just that they were.

"I've seen you naked."

I fumbled, and half the clothes hit the floor. "I didn't need to know that."

"It means nothing to me."

"It does to me. Get out."

He sighed, turned his back. I figured it was the best I could hope for and got dressed. More slowly than I would have if I wasn't required to hold on to the towel with one hand and yank on jeans and a T-shirt with the other, but I managed.

"Done."

He faced me.

"What do you want?"

"All I've ever wanted was to keep you safe."

"How are you going to do that when you can't even come when I call you?"

"I am not a dog."

"Speaking of . . . where's Pru?"

"She's not a dog either."

"Nor a ghost."

"I never said that she was."

"You said she was your wife."

"Aye. Always has been."

"You married a wolf?"

"I know the world has come a long way since my passing, but one cannot yet marry a wolf." He frowned. "Can they?"

I ignored that, walking out of my bedroom and into the living room. I obsessive-compulsively checked the lock on the door—one maniac had been one too many—then moved into the kitchen where I palmed the jar of rosemary, tucking it into my pocket, just in case.

"You've been dead over four hundred years."

Henry stood near the window, keeping watch. "And yet it seems like only three hundred."

"Ha," I deadpanned. "You and Pru, who I assume was human at the time, were burned as witches."

"Aye," he agreed, still staring at the window. "I have always had an affinity for ghosts, my wife had one for animals. She could not only talk to them, but understand them too."

"And they burned you for it?"

He turned. "Among other things."

I opened my mouth to ask, *What other things,* and

Henry waved a hand. "My past is not important except in how it shapes your present and your future."

"What does any of it have to do with me? What do you have to do with me?"

Something flickered in his eyes—there and then gone—like a wisp of smoke. In fact, I smelled smoke. And I'd washed and rinsed twice. I sniffed my wrist. Wasn't me. Which meant that lingering scent of smoke was him. I guess I'd always known that.

"I am here to protect you."

And he had. I should be more grateful. "I appreciate that. I do."

He lowered his head then faced the window again.

"Mrs. Noita said her attacker was a she. Then she told me he would burn us all."

Henry's shoulders tensed.

"Can you explain that?"

"Not yet." He tore his gaze from whatever was out there—hopefully not her. Or even him. Or it. "You need to discover what you can about the *Venatores Mali*."

"How?"

He pointed to my laptop. I resisted the urge to smack myself in the head and mutter, *Duh!*

I jiggled my mouse, and the computer awoke. A few strokes of the keys and information poured onto the screen. I became immersed.

The backstory of the cult would have made a good HBO series. They'd have to sex it up—when didn't they?—but the violence was there. Hell, it was everywhere.

The Tudors had been a hit. I was surprised they hadn't continued with the Stuarts. King James was a real hoot. Not only had he rewritten the Bible and gotten away with it, but he'd composed *Daemonologie,* a treatise detailing his beliefs on witchcraft.

After his ascension to the English throne in 1603, he expanded previous legislation on witchcraft, making the raising of, and communication with, spirits punishable by execution.

As most of the English had seen enough burning, hanging, and beheading during the reign of Bloody Queen Mary, they had no desire to see any more. Add to that the prevalent English belief that the Scots were a backward, superstitious race and James found himself unable to enforce those laws without appearing ignorant.

Not a fool by any means, His Majesty had commissioned a secret society, the *Venatores Mali,* to do his bidding. He'd put Roland McHugh at its helm.

According to his Wikipedia entry Roland had burned more witches than anyone in history. Of course Wikipedia was often wrong, but even if I cut the number in half, he was still a peach.

"Roland burned you and Pru?"

"Yes. He hated witches."

"And here I thought he burned them for fun."

"That too," Henry said dryly. "At least he is dead."

"So are you. Yet here you are."

"And I'm not exactly sure why." He flicked a hand at the computer. "Does it say anything about his ring?"

I clicked about a bit. While there were no drawings or photos of it, there was a bit of text about the brandings.

"McHugh used his ring to brand suspected witches before their burning. The mark would cleanse their souls, banish their demons, and purify them for their imminent entry to heaven." I lifted my gaze from the laptop. "I guess he was just trying to help."

"My soul was clean, and I've never met a demon. Except for McHugh."

"Got that right." I lost myself in the process of surfing, reading, and surfing some more. Once in a while, I read parts of what I found to Henry. I thought he listened, but it was hard to tell as he kept staring out the window. This must have gone on a few hours, because eventually when I looked up, Henry was gone.

I turned back to the computer just as someone tried to open the door.

Bobby finally got a chance to return Sullivan's call several hours later. By then his partner had called a few more times.

"Asshole," Sullivan said by way of greeting.

"I almost got incinerated today. Be nice."

Silence followed. "You what?"

"I went to interview a witness, and her house exploded."

"Really?"

"Do I often make things up?"

"That's usually me."

Conner Sullivan was the least likely person to make things up that Bobby had ever met. Which was why he'd always wondered about the whole loup-garou thing. Of course anyone could snap. He had. And while Bobby hadn't seen werewolves, he had felt, seen, heard, smelled . . . something. Usually when he was tired, sad, alone.

And drunk.

He shook off those memories. He didn't need to dwell on that time in his life. He had too many other things to dwell on.

"You and the witness get out okay?"

"I did. She was already dead when I got there." Or close enough.

"How many bodies does that make?"

"Two. Well, three if you count the perp. The first perp. Not the second. Who's still at large."

"And here I thought you were getting the sweet deal."

"I'd trade you but—" Bobby paused. He wouldn't trade. He was staying until he solved this case and made sure Raye was safe.

"No, thanks," Sullivan said. "I don't like big trees."

Which only made two of them.

"You'd really have hated the wolf that came out of them last night."

"Wolf?" His partner cleared his throat. "What did it look like?"

"Like a big dog with spindly legs. What was it supposed to look like?"

"Was there something weird about its eyes?"

Bobby'd been too far away to see much beyond the fact that it had eyes. "Weird how?"

"Never mind. Just . . . " Sullivan took a breath, let it out. "You got any silver bullets?"

"Funny guy."

"I've never been funny in my life."

"Except for your ties."

"What's wrong with my ties?"

"Besides that you're always wearing them?" Bobby had tossed his ties after one summer as a New Orleans detective.

"Bobby," Conner said, so softly Bobby leaned forward, even though he wouldn't be able to hear any better across the thousand-plus miles separating them if he leaned over so far he fell on his face. "Silver kills same as lead."

"Then why do I need it?"

"Because lead doesn't kill the same as silver."

"You're starting to worry me."

"Only starting?"

"I doubt there's a silver bullet shop here anyway." Although Bobby could easily see there being one in New Orleans.

"You'd be surprised."

Bobby let the subject drop. "Why did you call me . . . "—he glanced at his phone log—"four times?"

"First because the boss wanted to know when you were coming back."

He should have known that question was coming. He'd only been authorized to stay for a day. "Not until things are settled here."

"He ain't gonna like that."

"He doesn't like much. I'll take some of my vacation time if I need to, but I'm staying."

"All right," Sullivan said. "Just . . . be careful."

"It's a lot less dangerous here than it is there, pal."

Bobby wasn't really so sure about that, and from the way Sullivan snorted, he wasn't either, but his partner moved on. "I finally got a chance to go to the Hotel St. Germain."

It took a second for Bobby to place the name. Cold case. "What did you find?"

"Like most hotels, every room on every floor has the same floor plan. Which means that if someone on the floor below goes into their closet and cuts a hole in the ceiling . . . "

"They come out in the locker upstairs. How could no one see a hole in the floor?"

"It was under the carpet."

"Then how could anyone get shot? Carpet would not only prevent the shooter from seeing, but leave a bullet hole."

"Not if the stuff lies loose and isn't tacked or glued down. The rest of the room was, but not the closet, which is probably why no one thought of it. The shooter cut a hole—very well I might add, only cut through the ceiling and not the floor covering. He tosses it back, waits for victim to open the closet, bang, pulls the carpet in place and glues in the ceiling hole."

"Pretty smart."

"And he might have gotten away with it too—"

"If not for those pesky kids," Bobby finished.

"Scooby-Doo," Sullivan said. "Love that show. Bought the tie."

"Of course you did. Did you catch the guy?"

"Yep. Typical perp. Smart about some things, not so much about most of them. He registered for the room under his own name."

Bobby was constantly amazed, and by now he really shouldn't be, at how dumb some people were.

"You wanna tell me why you had a hunch about a case that is so cold I got shivers just thinking about it?"

Bobby had a shiver right now. He'd had a lot of them since coming to New Bergin. He blamed the autumn chill, which had settled over the crime scene like an icy fog as the sun fell toward the trees.

"We solved the case. Does it matter why?"

"Suppose not."

"Out of curiosity, why did he do it?"

"A woman."

"Figures." When a murder wasn't about the opposite sex, it was about money. And a lot of times it was about both.

Which made him wonder about his current murder. Sex or money? Both or neither? Bobby no longer thought these murders were random, but if not, then what were they about?

His head ached again. Probably time for more aspirin. Or a new job.

"I'll be in touch."

"I can't wait," his partner replied.

"Asshole," Bobby said, which rounded the conversation nicely.

The local police were still working the scene, because the scene was all over the place.

"You need help?" he asked Johnson.

"Not from you." The chief rolled his eyes. "Don't get your knickers in a twist. You look horrible. Go home."

"Happy to." Bobby headed for his car.

"Not home, home," Johnson shouted. "Don't leave town."

"Hadn't planned to." Bobby drove toward his current home away from home, which led him on the same path he'd taken the first night he'd come. And like that night, he stopped in front of Raye's apartment. Not because she ran in front of his car, but because he happened to notice that the crime scene tape was gone. Raye hadn't mentioned that her apartment had been cleared and neither had Johnson.

Then he saw a flicker of yellow over the edge of the

landing. As if someone had yanked off the tape and gone inside.

The window was open. Flickers of light played on the ceiling. Not gold, like a lamp. Not blue, like a television. If Raye were there, wouldn't she have turned on both?

He got out of the car and climbed the stairs, hoping none of them creaked. To avoid an overworked area, he crept along the guardrail, careful not to jiggle it too. He made it to the landing without a sound—you'd think he'd done this before. Once there, he listened, thought he heard a voice inside, but he couldn't be sure.

Was Raye on the phone? Talking to herself? She seemed to make a habit of that, but really, who didn't? He listened again, but he couldn't tell if the voice was hers.

He was tempted to call her name, but what if it wasn't her? What if it was another maniac? Right now surprise was on his side.

He drew his gun with one hand and turned the doorknob with the other.

Chapter 14

As I'd obsessively checked the lock on the door, it didn't open. Still, I was stuck in here, with someone out there trying to get in. I could call a cop, but by the time any arrived I'd be dead. In that moment, I really wished I had my father's gun.

The door rattled. My breath caught, and the butcher knife from the block on the counter flew toward me. I snatched it out of the air. Startling, a little frightening, but also very handy. I might be bringing a knife to a gun-fight, but better than bringing nothing at all.

My heart pounded so loudly I was afraid whoever was out there would hear it. If not that, then definitely my rasping attempts not to hyperventilate. I considered calling out, *Who's there?* Or perhaps, *I'm armed!* But maybe, just maybe, if they thought I was gone they'd go away too. So I bit my lip and remained silent.

The door rattled again, harder this time. I needed to know who was out there. What if he or she *did* go away? I'd never know who'd been there, and that was probably something I needed to.

I crept closer, fingers grasping the hilt of the knife so tightly they hurt. I'd never had a curtain on the window next to the door. Unless my guest was a Wallenda, it was too far over for anyone to peer into from the landing. Now I had to hope that whoever was out there was peering the other way, or that I could take a peek quickly enough for them not to notice. Why had I never had a new door installed? One that possessed one of those fancy, newfangled peepholes?

Because in New Bergin we didn't have strangers. Until recently—yesterday—I'd probably been one of the few who locked the door that I had. And that was only because mine was inclined to blow open.

"Raye?" Bobby said from the other side.

Could a person have a heart attack from relief? I yanked open the door, and then I just stood there trying to breathe. He looked like I felt—overworked, underpaid, and desperate for an adult beverage.

"Expecting someone?" He cast a pointed glance at my right hand.

I still held the knife. I set it on the coffee table. "It's been kind of a rough day."

"Kind of," he agreed.

"And you?" I cast an equally pointed glance at his gun.

He shrugged and put it back in the holster. "Everyone's jumpy."

He was still covered in soot, the dirt on his face making his eyes shine bright blue. He had shadows beneath them—he had shadows *in* them—but shadows called to me. *He* called to me. Reaching out, I pulled him inside. He kicked shut the door and kissed me. I fisted my hands in his filthy shirt and held on.

His heart beat hard and fast like mine. I suppose he'd been as concerned about what was on the other side of the door as I had. Hence the gun.

I let my fingers stroke, along with my tongue. He grasped my hips, pulled me close, tilted his head and delved. His teeth grazed my lips, his thumbs grazed the heavy fullness of my loose breasts, and I shuddered, opening, swelling, groaning.

When he lowered his head and took both my nipple and my shirt into his mouth, my body bowed. My hands went from his chest to his head, my fingers clenching in his hair. I both didn't want him to stop and I wanted him to move on, to take that clever mouth and show me all that I'd missed.

Then he used his teeth, and I thought I would explode like Mrs. Noita's house. The sound I made was none I'd ever made before. When he lifted his head, I lifted mine. He frowned at my chest, then let me go so abruptly he had to catch me again before I fell. He cursed.

"I'm sorry," I said. Had he been able to tell just by touching me that I hadn't been touched in so long it barely counted?

"What do you have to be sorry about? I grabbed you. I put my filthy hands all over you. I'm sorry."

Filthy hands? He had more issues than I did. Then I glanced down and saw what he meant. Black, finger-shaped marks marred my shirt; a gray circlet haloed my nipple. I twisted and sure enough, handprints clutched my ass. It was too ridiculous; I giggled.

His lips twitched. "You think it's funny?"

"Right now," I managed between gasping, half-hysterical breaths. "Everything is."

"Maybe I should take you to the doctor."

"I'd rather we played doctor." I clapped my hand over my mouth. Had I said that?

Now he laughed. "You're crazy."

About you, I thought. I managed, barely, not to say it.

"I . . . " He lifted a hand to his hair, grimaced, and

lowered it, rubbing his palm on equally soiled jeans. "I need a shower."

I indicated the bathroom. "Be my guest."

"I don't have any clean clothes."

With what I had planned, he wouldn't need them.

"I'll put yours in the wash."

For a minute I thought he'd refuse, then what would I do? Beg? I wanted him. But I also didn't want to be alone. The idea of him walking out, of me staying here . . .

No, thanks.

Nevertheless, I'd have to remain. Being near me was dangerous.

"I can't go back to my father's," I said.

Instead of asking why, he merely nodded. Another thing I liked about him. He connected the dots often and without help. Or at least those dots that ran in a fairly straight line.

Bobby unbuckled his belt, removed it and his gun, laid them on the end table near the couch. Then he reached for the hem of his shirt. He drew it upward, revealing bronzed, rippling flesh. I ran a fingertip along his stomach, just above the waistband of his jeans. Muscles danced.

"Keep that up," he said, "and you'll get a lot dirtier."

"I don't mind."

He cocked his head. His fingers toyed with the top button of his jeans. I licked my lips, and he stilled. "I should probably take that shower."

"Like hell," I said, and opened the button myself.

He sprang free, hard and hot. I took him in my hand and squeezed. French curses erupted, perhaps a few in Spanish. I didn't know, didn't care. He felt more than good, better than great. He felt right. And that was such a strange thought, I pushed it aside along with the rest of his clothes.

The sun fell, providing just enough light to cast him in shades of gold and gray. I traced the shadows across his chest with my fingers, let my gaze trace others along his thighs. His penis twitched. I ran my thumb over the tip, liked the feel of it so much I did it again. I wondered how he would feel against my lips—both soft and hard, yet so alive. I went to my knees.

"Raye," he began, but when my lips closed over him, he stopped talking, started moving. In and out, slowly, deeply.

I wanted to try everything I'd ever read about, heard about, dreamed about, and I wanted to try it with him. He wasn't from here; he wouldn't stay. While that might make most women cautious, it made me throw every caution I'd ever had into the suddenly whistling wind.

Why was the wind whistling? Had the damn door opened again?

I drew back, opened my eyes, saw a shadow shimmer in the corner, then another near the door.

Ghosts.

The thought of being watched nearly made me put a stop to something I wanted more than I'd wanted anything, anyone, in . . . well . . . ever. Then I remembered the rosemary in my pocket.

Bobby's eyes were still closed, but they wouldn't remain that way if I didn't continue. I blew on the moistness left by my mouth, and he shivered. Apparently he hadn't felt the wind.

"Keep your eyes closed," I whispered.

"Mmm," he agreed.

"Don't move. I'm just going to lock the door." I removed the rosemary bottle.

In more ways than one.

I sprinkled the tiny leaves across the doorway. I tossed some of the herb into the air for good measure, then flicked the lock. I hoped that worked. I wasn't sure what I'd do if it didn't.

I glanced around the room, afraid of what I might see. But the shimmers had receded. The only shadows lay in Bobby's now open eyes. Either the rosemary had done the trick, or the ghosts didn't want to watch. Fine by me.

I went to him, and his thumb stroked my lip, pulled it free of my teeth. "We don't have to," he said.

"You're wrong." I lifted my mouth.

"About?" His lips hovered a breath from mine.

My fingers curled around his neck. "We have to."

I felt his smile when we kissed. But the humor soon fled, along with any gentleness. Laughter was for later, as were both slow and soft. Right now I wanted fast, hard, and serious.

His thumbs slid beneath the waistband of my jeans. He ran them along the hollow between hip and stomach. I went onto my toes, arching; my pelvis bumped his erection, and he hissed. I lost the jeans and the underwear. At least I'd remembered to put on a pair without holes. Not that it mattered now.

"Bedroom?" he asked.

I wrapped my legs around his hips, wiggled, desperate to feel him inside. "No time."

"Whoa." He pressed his forehead to mine. "Give me a sec."

He set me on the table. I came up on my elbows as

he leaned over and grabbed his jeans. Protection. At least one of us had a brain.

I was naked from the waist down, displayed like an offering to the gods and oddly enough . . . I liked it. I lay back and waited for the tear of the package, the snick of the condom. Instead, his shadow blocked the waning sun. Next thing I knew, he put his mouth to me.

Though my body shouted, *Shh!* my mouth said, "Wait."

"No."

"I can't."

"You will." He kissed the part of me that screamed for it. "Now."

He licked that part, tickled it with the tip of his tongue. Not only did that part scream, so did I.

"Then you'll come again when I'm here . . . " He put his tongue inside of me, then out. "I promise."

He continued until that promise was fulfilled, and I checked a few items off my to-do list.

He worked his way upward, shoving my shirt ahead of him, running his lips along my skin. My nipples were as hard as he was, and he spent a bit of time making them harder. By the time he lifted his head, I thought he was probably right about coming again.

"How about a shower?" he asked.

I blinked, my mind full of sensation, not sense. "Uh, sure. Go ahead."

That he could walk away for a shower—no matter how badly he wanted, and needed, one—kind of hurt. Was it only me who was crazy for this? For him? For us?

He stepped back, held out a hand, which, dazed, I took. Then he led me to my own bathroom, drew me inside, shut the door.

My gaze caught on my reflection in the mirror over the sink. Color bloomed in my cheeks, making my eyes shine very dark. My hair was tousled. I kind of liked it that way. My shirt had caught above one breast but hung over the other. I had beard burn on my neck, probably everywhere else too.

The water started. I turned away from the new me in the mirror.

One foot in the tub, one foot out, he offered his hand, curled the fingers inward. "Lose the shirt." His lips tilted. "You didn't think we were through."

I had. Silly me.

For an instant Bobby thought Raye would run. Then she lost the shirt, and her dark hair tumbled over one of those exquisite breasts. She'd been chewing on her lips and they were red, causing him to think again of Snow White. Did that make him the Huntsman?

She put her hand in his and stepped beneath the water, lifting her face to the stream, arching her long, slim, white neck like a doe worshipping the moon. He was so star-struck by the sight that he didn't shut the curtain until the sound of water peppering the tile made him snatch the end and drag it closed.

She resembled a nymph beneath a waterfall, a mermaid in the surf. And for tonight, at least, she was his.

He reached for the soap; she got there first, holding it out of reach.

"Let me," she said. Who was he to argue?

She lathered his chest, his arms and legs and what lay between. He had to still her hand before he lost what he'd saved just for her. He faced the water, to rinse and catch his breath. She soaped his shoulders, his spine, a bit lower, but when her fingertips ran over his hip, he flinched.

Her hands stilled. "What's wrong?"

He twisted, but the area that felt as if it had been scrubbed raw was too far around to see. "Something must have hit me in the explosion."

She brushed her hand over him again and this time he hissed. She lifted her eyes. There was something in them he didn't like. Did he have a chunk of the house stuck in him? He would have noticed that before now.

"What is it?"

"Just a scrape." Her mouth smiled; her eyes didn't. "I have something for it when we're done."

It didn't occur to him then to wonder how he'd gotten scraped so badly with his clothes on. He had better things to wonder about. For instance, how would her breasts taste beneath the water? How smooth would her skin be in rain? What would she sound like when he entered her? Could he last long enough to make her come again? How, precisely, did one have sex in a shower?

His answers came in a rush. She tasted like heat; she felt like cream. When he entered her, she whispered his name. The sound, the scent, the feel of her all around made him desperate. He had to still his body, move his hand along hers, and recite the Miranda warning lest he finish long before she did.

As for how? Several ways—her back against the wall, then his. Her cheek pressed to the tile as he slipped in from behind. Then atop a pile of towels on the floor, him watching her face bloom in wonder, that sight making him lose his last hold on control and empty himself, body and soul.

He lay with his head against her breasts as the damp

slowly cooled them. The shower still ran, the sound like rain, the steam a summer fog.

"We should get up."

"Mmm," she agreed. Her fingers stroking his back. Neither of them moved.

He wasn't sure how long they lay there but when he next opened his eyes, the steam was gone, though the mirror over the sink remained fogged. He'd slid to the side, resting his uninjured hip on the floor, his leg thrown over hers. The color that had been in her face had faded. She appeared as tired as he felt. All he wanted was to climb in bed and sleep for a day.

With her.

He withdrew his leg; she reached for him—lethargic, she missed. He sat up and turned off what must now be ice water. Her eyes opened, and she smiled. His heart went ka-boom.

He stood, grabbed a towel, and wiped the mirror. His reflection looked the same as always. Why was he so surprised?

"You okay?" Raye shoved her wild, dark hair out of her face. The way she sat there, naked, staring up at him made him want her all over again.

"Yeah."

"Want a drink?" she asked.

"Hell, yeah."

Her laughter made his gut clench. How could anyone want to remove laughter like that from this earth?

He offered a hand. His palm tingled when it met hers. He released her, and she rubbed hers along her hip as if it stung. When he did the same the slice of pain caused him to crane his neck so he could see his back in the mirror.

"That's not a scrape," he murmured. "That's a bruise."

"Does it matter?"

"A kindergarten teacher should know the difference."

"I was distracted."

Join the club.

She reached past him, opened the mirror, behind which lay a medicine cabinet. He caught a glimpse of aspirin and cough medicine, as well as a circular pill container marked with the days of the week. At least he wouldn't have to run out for condoms. He thought he'd just used his last one.

Raye withdrew a blue and white tube of ointment. "This will help."

"What is it?" he asked, but he offered his hip. If she planned to smooth it on with her fingers he didn't care if she used turpentine.

"Arnica. I use it for my bruises."

His gaze lowered to her arm, where she'd had some only a few days past. She didn't any more.

"Stuff must work pretty well."

"It does." She spread it on. He felt nothing beyond her touch. Apparently arnica also took away the pain. Or maybe she did.

She returned the cream to the cabinet, wiped her hand on a towel, and opened the door. "I've got wine and beer."

"Beer," he said, thankful when she shut the door behind her. He wanted to look at those marks again.

The bruises on Raye's arm had resembled fingers, and her explanation of a child grabbing her had made sense. It still did.

What didn't were the finger-shaped bruises on him.

Chapter 15

I retreated to my bedroom, dug around for a robe I never used, and put it on. Apparently my ease with naked only extended to the actual act and right after. I would have loved to be the kind of woman who could deliver a beer to a man unclothed. But I wasn't. If I had been I could have made a much better living doing it. Teaching didn't pay half as well as stripping. A fact that annoyed me daily.

In truth, I needed to get out of the bathroom before Bobby asked about that bruise. I had no idea what to tell him. I'd never seen another like it.

Except on me.

My hand on the refrigerator door, I glanced at my arm, but the bruises that had been there a few days ago—the ones made by the ghost of Anne McKenna—were gone. Arnica cream rocked, though usually not quite that well. However, I'd never had bruises caused by a ghost before. I hoped I never would again, though I figured that hope was doomed.

But now Bobby had them too. I had no idea what his meant either.

I thought back to the basement. Genevieve had been upset; her ghost-child hand had reached out in an attempt to snatch her father from danger. Her fingers had gone through his side—right where those marks were. He'd stopped and shuddered. Which meant he'd felt her, and that was . . .

Really odd.

According to Bobby, anyone who said they saw ghosts was a thief, a charlatan, or a liar—maybe all three. Considering his behavior today, I had to wonder if perhaps he'd been protesting too much.

I pulled a Miller Genuine Draft out of the refrigerator. I had a few Leinie's Summer Shandys left, but I doubted Bobby was a lemony-beer type of guy.

I popped the top, glanced at the bathroom door. Was he still staring at the bruises, trying to convince himself they'd come from four thin, short sticks of wood that had rained down from the exploding house, rather than the fingers of his dead child? Why wouldn't he? He had no idea his dead child, or anyone else, was following him.

And I really, *really,* didn't want to be the one to tell him.

I considered that ghost bruises weren't something reserved just for those who saw ghosts. People got bruises all the time that they didn't know the origin of. They passed them off as a bump they'd been too busy to register at the time, a thump in the night on the way to the toilet, forgotten by the light of day, even acute leukemia. In most cases, they were right—hopefully not about the leukemia. It helped that most mystery bruises were not shaped like fingers.

So why were his? Why were mine? Another question or two for Henry.

I poured some red wine, drank a healthy swallow, then took both it and the beer to the kitchen table, set them down, glanced at the door again, and picked up the clothes I'd promised to wash.

I removed Bobby's keys, his wallet, and his cell phone from the jeans, tossed them next to the beer and strode to the stacked washer and dryer in the corner of my rarely used kitchen. When I returned to my wine, I saw that his wallet had fallen open. I forgot all about the mystery of the ghostly bruises.

A photo of Genevieve occupied the space meant for a driver's license. Not a surprise. The surprise was the gorgeous redhead in the photo next to her.

Obviously Genevieve's mom—they had the same nose, a similar smile. But the woman's presence in the wallet brought up a question: Was Bobby married?

That would have been a good question to ask before now.

The bathroom door opened. So did my fingers. The wallet dropped onto the table. The leather folded closed on contact. Thank God.

Bobby wore nothing but a towel. *Num*. He picked up his beer, took a sip, smiled. He must not have seen me going through his wallet.

"I put your clothes in the wash."

"Thanks."

"I took the stuff out of your pockets."

"Thanks," he repeated.

"I . . . " I had no idea how to broach this subject. I'd never had to. The thing that annoyed me the most about dating in New Bergin, that everyone knew everyone else's business, meant I did too. No embarrassing surprises in the aftermath. All the embarrassing surprises were out in the open as soon as they embarrassingly happened.

"Remember that cold case?" Bobby sipped his beer. "We talked about it at Thore's Farm. Locked-room mystery. You suggested we check the floor in the locker."

"Okay." I remembered. How could I forget?

"Someone cut a hole in the floor through the ceiling of the room below, threw back the carpet and shot the guy."

Which explained why the ghost was gone from here. I hadn't seen that particular spook trailing in Bobby's wake since that night. Mystery solved. Case closed. The spirit had gone on to . . . wherever.

"How did you know that?" Bobby asked.

"I didn't." And because I hadn't—I'd only known that the dead man wanted him to look in the locker, not why—I even sounded convincing.

"You knew about the bomb in the basement too."

"Did not," I said quickly. Too quickly but it *was* the truth.

He drained the beer. I got him another. It gave me something to do other than panic.

"You walked right to it, Raye."

"It isn't as if the basement was huge, and you said that you'd searched everywhere else."

"I said that as you were walking over there, not before."

My mind scrambled for an excuse—anything other than that a seventeenth-century ghost-witch had been pointing to it. Amazingly, I found one.

"The other bodies were burned and Mrs. Noita wasn't. I figured there was a fire coming, and what better way than an explosion?"

"You jump to that conclusion rather than that I interrupted the guy before he struck a match?"

According to Mrs. Noita, it hadn't been a guy, but that was another bit of information I was going to have to keep to myself. At least until I figured out how to tell it without buying myself an express ticket to loony land.

"Don't you ever have hunches?"

From his frown, I figured he did, but he didn't like them any more than I liked some of mine.

"How did you get in?" he asked. "That cop-kid was supposed to keep everyone out."

I shrugged, not wanting to point fingers and tell tales. I didn't have to.

"He's gotta be the worst cop ever."

"Probably not the worst."

Bobby cast me a disgusted glance. I wouldn't want to be Brad the next time Bobby saw him.

"He just let you come in without trying to stop you?"

"He tried. I sicced Jenn on him and ran."

"Don't ever do that again." He opened the second beer. "You took ten years off my life when you walked down those stairs, and that was before I saw the bomb."

Silence descended. I wasn't sure how to bring the conversation around to the woman in the photograph.

"Are you married?" I blurted. Considering his face, that probably wasn't the best way.

"You think I'd . . . "—he waved at the table, causing me to blush—"if I were? Thanks." He sat on the couch.

"I said that wrong." I followed, perching on the arm. Near but yet so far. "I meant to ask if you'd ever been married."

"Why?"

"Isn't that what people ask . . . " My gaze drifted to the table. "After?"

"Usually it's before, Raye."

A point I'd already made to myself. "I'm not good at this."

"You're wrong. You're very good at this."

I blushed again, and he touched my knee. I felt that touch everywhere.

"I've never been married," he said.

Was that good news or bad? Truth or another lie?

"Do you have kids?" My voice was too bright. He snatched his hand back as if I'd let off an electric shock.

"No." His voice was hoarse. He slugged more beer.

"I'm sorry."

"Why? Do I seem like the kind of guy who should have kids?"

As a kindergarten teacher I'd learned that, for most people, "should" had very little to do with having them.

Luckily he didn't require an answer. He stood, and for a second I feared he'd leave. Instead, he took my hand. "How long until my clothes are done?"

"An hour."

"That might just be enough time." He drew me toward the bedroom.

I glanced at the wallet, now closed over the photo. If I hadn't met Genevieve, I could brush off the picture as a niece and a sister.

But I had met her, and I was pretty sure I would again.

Really, Genevieve wasn't the issue, and wasn't that a surprise? The ghost wasn't the problem. The problem was her mother. Where was she? Who was she? *Was* she?

Bobby had denied the mother and the child. I didn't blame him. At least one of them, maybe both, was the source of great pain.

He closed the bedroom door and took me into his arms.

How did one bring up dead children?

One didn't. Especially if one had been talking to them.

Henry stood on the landing outside Raye's apartment. He couldn't get in. Every time he tried, he wound up right here. Raye had warded the door. He wondered who had told her how.

"Daddy!"

Henry jumped. A child stood next to him. Her shirt identified her as a princess. Strange. He'd thought there was no royalty in America. Perhaps she wasn't from here. However, it was best to be safe and not sorry.

"Your Royal Highness." Henry bowed.

The child wrinkled her nose. "Who are you?"

"Henry Taggart at your service, ma'am."

"You talk funny."

"No doubt." He had a Scottish accent. He hadn't heard too many in this area.

The child had an accent too. Definitely not Scottish. "Where are you from, ma'am?"

"Ma'am." She giggled. "I'm not a ma'am."

"You are a princess." He indicated her shirt. "Yes?"

Her giggle faded. She glanced at the door again. "My daddy says I am."

"Then you are royal and must be addressed as 'ma'am.' " After he'd first addressed her as "your royal highness." Henry might be a Scottish witch, but he knew what was right.

"Okay," she said, still more interested in the door than him. "Why can't I get in?"

"The door has been warded against ghosts."

"What's *warded*?"

"A way to keep us out."

She turned wide blue eyes in Henry's direction. "How?"

"Herbs. Perhaps a spell."

"Like A-B-C?"

"Not that kind of spell, child." He cleared his throat. "Ma'am."

She nodded, as regal as any Stuart, and flicked her hand. "Make it stop."

"If I could, I would."

"But you can't, so you won't," she recited.

She really was adorable. He wished, not for the first time, that he'd been able to see all his daughters grow up.

"What's your name?" he asked.

"Genevieve." She lifted her chin. "Princess Genevieve."

"Why do you want to get inside?"

"My daddy's in there." She stomped her foot. "Daddy, come out!"

Henry blinked. He'd been startled, then distracted, then charmed by the girl, which was his only excuse for being so slow. The child and the detective from out of town shared not only an accent but similar blue eyes. Best, still, to be sure.

"And who is your daddy?" he asked.

"Bobby Doucet."

Henry suddenly understood the reason for the ward. He didn't much like it. Certainly, his daughter was old enough to do what he strongly suspected she was doing with the detective—though they weren't married and he should probably take umbrage with that. However, he had learned that in this time many did not marry before having knowledge of one another. He didn't like that either, but no one had asked him, and he doubted they would.

Presently he had more pressing concerns than his daughter's honor. Whatever Raye had used would keep him out, but it would allow those with a pulse in. And those with a pulse, and a weapon, were the ones that needed to be kept out. He just wasn't sure how.

A car drove past slowly on the street below. For an instant Henry thought the driver was looking at him. No matter how many centuries passed, he couldn't get used to being invisible to the majority of the world.

Considering that he was invisible, the woman wasn't staring at him but at Raye's apartment. The place appeared deserted. The car sped up and disappeared around the corner.

The woman might have been an acquaintance of Raye's, but Henry doubted it. He'd been at his daughter's side since birth, and he'd never seen that face before in his life.

Bobby's phone rang. He reached for his nightstand, where he usually kept the thing, and instead encountered a woman.

He opened his eyes; his fingers were tangled in Raye's hair. He wanted to tangle other parts of himself with other parts of her all over again.

Except the damn phone was still ringing. Where was it?

He sat up. The bedside clock read midnight. They hadn't been asleep that long, though it felt like it. Sexual satisfaction and exhaustion will do that to a man.

Apparently it did the same to a woman. Raye muttered, "Shhh," and turned over.

Bobby followed the distant sound of his phone, which lay on the kitchen table next to his keys and wallet. He picked it up. "Yeah?"

"We got a problem."

"Johnson?" Bobby asked. He hadn't bothered to glance at his caller ID. His eyes were still fuzzy.

The chief grunted. "Someone broke into Larsen's Bed-and-Breakfast."

A jolt of adrenaline rushed through Bobby, and his eyes focused just fine. "Who?"

"All John saw was a woman running out the door. Very tall, brown hair that reached past her butt. She jumped in her car and drove away. She had a weird knife."

"Weird how?"

"Long, two sided. He said the blade was ripply."

"No idea what that means."

"Squiggly?"

"Not helping."

"How about this . . . the description of the knife matches the description Christiansen gave of the weapon probably used on Mrs. Noita."

"Fantastic." It appeared that the killer, this time, was a woman.

"It gets better."

"How can it get better than that?"

"Sarcasm. Thank you." The chief's voice was dry.

Bobby couldn't blame him. He needed to zip his lip. The guy was doing his best, and in truth the man's best wasn't half bad. Bobby wouldn't mind working with him again. But he'd prefer it if he didn't have to.

"The woman had been in Raye's room. The pillow and the mattress were hacked to pieces."

"At least Raye wasn't."

"True. But John doesn't know where Raye is."

Bobby's gaze flicked to the bedroom doorway. She lay in the middle of her bed, hair tousled from his hands, mouth swollen from his lips, her body lethargic from his—

"She's at her apartment."

The chief cursed. "I'll get someone over there."

"No," Bobby said.

"Doucet, the first guy tried to kill her. Now this woman did too. She needs to be protected."

"She is."

"Oh." Silence settled over the line.

Bobby drew his hand over his jaw, the rasp of his beard so loud the chief had to have heard it. Bobby hadn't wanted to announce his business. Then again, in a town of this size, his car parked on the street out front already had. He was surprised the chief hadn't heard about it before now.

"I won't let her out of my sight," Bobby promised.

Johnson sighed. "I suppose I have to be the one to tell her father."

Bobby remembered the Magnum. He wished he hadn't given it back.

"Maybe you could just say she's safe at home."

"Not a chance, hotshot." Johnson hung up.

"Dammit." While he wouldn't wish away the hours he'd just spent, he did find himself wishing away this town and everyone in it but them. Perhaps when this was over he'd take Raye . . . where? New Orleans?

Why not?

She lay crosswise on the bed, one bare, smooth, pale shoulder gleaming in the faint silver light of the moon.

The thought of her anywhere, looking like that, was nearly impossible to resist. Considering the danger here he should take her anywhere. Immediately.

He spotted her laptop on the table. The "sleep" light pulsed, and he opened the top, clicked a key, waited while the machine sprang to life. It wouldn't hurt to check airline reservations, just for the fun of it.

He never got that far. When the screen went live, so did the last thing Raye had been searching for.

"Venatores Mali," he murmured.

How in hell did she know about that?

Chapter 16

I awoke confused.

Where was I? Who was I? What day was it?

I didn't care for the feeling. I couldn't recall ever having it, except for the never-voiced concern over the second question—would I ever truly know who I was?—I was always in New Bergin and every day was similar enough to the last so as not to matter. Unless it was a weekend.

I opened my eyes. My apartment. Nine A.M. I certainly hoped it was the weekend. Had to be. If I weren't in class by now, the phone would have rung. Someone would probably have pounded on the door too.

I sat up, realized I was naked at the same time I saw Bobby Doucet sipping coffee in my living room. Everything came back—the good along with the bad. But the best realization . . .

It was Sunday.

My robe lay on the floor. The sight of it there explained my confusion upon waking and the—for me—late hour of doing so. Every synapse in my body and my mind had been fried by a plurality of orgasms. I retrieved the robe and put it on.

Bobby wore jeans and nothing else. My lips curved. Perhaps one more wouldn't kill me.

He must have sensed my stare, or heard me move, because he looked up. "Morning."

Something was wrong. Had there been another murder? Was my father all right? Had Bobby seen or sensed Genevieve or one of the others?

My eyes cut to the door, but the rosemary still lay across the floor at the base, undisturbed. I should probably disturb it. Lately, the ghosts had been all that stood between me and death. I shouldn't bar them for long.

Bobby sipped his coffee, staring at me over the rim with a strange expression in his eyes. As if he didn't know me, or, maybe, he just didn't trust me.

After last night, I thought he knew me pretty well. But trust? That was a different ball game.

"Morning," I returned, my voice cooler than it should be, considering, but so was his. Was that normal? I had no idea. I'd never had a morning-after experience. My single time sleeping with someone had not involved sleeping, or the morning. Still, I'd thought it would be better. Cuddling, coffee, reading the paper in bed.

The paper! I crossed to the door, opened it. The day was cool and clear, a glorious autumn morning. One of the reasons—perhaps the only reason—to live in Wisconsin at all was autumn. Summers were short and often shitty. Winters were long and always so. Spring? Never saw one. But autumn in the Badger State was as close to bliss as it got.

A crisp breeze blew the rosemary away as I snatched the paper off the landing.

New Bergin still published a newspaper, which was delivered to everyone's doorstep. It only came out on Sundays, but that was enough most of the time. I glanced at the headline, which blared *MURDER!* What had I expected? The usual rehash of the town council meeting and the high school football score?

As I set the paper on the kitchen table I noticed my laptop. Open, running, and revealing the last thing I had Googled.

Venatores Mali.

I glanced at Bobby. He lifted a brow. He'd seen it. He'd have to be blind not to.

While I had left my computer out, I hadn't left it open. Though considering that I'd shared my body, why wouldn't he think I'd be happy to share my search engine?

I waited for the questions, the accusations. Instead, he sipped more coffee, which looked like a good idea. At the least I'd have something to do with my hands. At best maybe my head would clear enough to figure out how to explain myself.

I drank half of a cup before I faced him and tried another smile. He wasn't buying this one any easier than he'd bought the last.

We continued to drink coffee as the silence stretched. I'd watched enough *Law and Order* to know what he was doing. Silence begged to be filled. If he waited long enough maybe I'd confess.

Not a chance. He wouldn't believe me anyway.

My landline rang, so shrill I gasped. No one ever called me on it anymore. I wasn't even sure why I kept it.

"Raye?" My father's voice sounded rushed and breathless. "Thank God you didn't come home."

I wasn't sure what to say to that. *Gee, thanks?*

"I should have called." Would have if Bobby hadn't arrived, and then— "Why didn't you call me?"

"Your phone's dead."

"Oh." I guess calling my father wasn't the only thing I'd forgotten to do last night. "You could have called this phone if you needed me."

"I would have. Then Chief Johnson told me."

I stilled. "Told you what?"

"That Detective Doucet was keeping an eye on you."

"An eye on me?" I echoed as my gaze lifted to Bobby's. Was that what they called it now? "Why?"

"He didn't tell you?"

My gaze narrowed. Bobby's eyebrows lifted as he sipped more coffee. "Tell me what?"

"A woman broke in here last night. Stabbed your mattress and pillow."

"What would anyone have against my mattress and pillow?"

"I think she meant to stab you, Raye."

I'd figured that out for myself. Hence the attempt at tension-diffusing humor.

"She didn't hurt you, did she?" I asked.

"She was already running out the door when I saw her."

"Lock up from now on."

"As I told the detective when he suggested it, I don't have a key."

"You don't need a key to lock the place from the inside."

He gave a short sharp laugh. "It's been so long since I locked anything, I forgot."

"Don't forget any more." I rubbed my forehead.

"I hope they catch this woman quickly, then everything can go back to the way that it was."

I had my doubts that everything was ever going back to the way that it was, but I kept them to myself. Who knew? Miracles happened. Though usually not to me and mine.

"Why would anyone want to hurt you?" my father asked.

"I don't know," I lied. "Why does anyone want to hurt anyone?"

"The world is full of crazy people," he said. "I never thought any of them would come here."

The curse of a small town—no one ever did. Which made them woefully unprepared when crazy arrived.

I offered the most comfort I had at the moment. "I'll charge my cell. We'll keep in touch."

"You'll be back at school tomorrow. It's safe there."

"It is." Another lie, but why stop now?

Maybe I shouldn't go to school. I hadn't wanted danger spilling onto my father, and it had anyway. I certainly didn't need to bring more of the same to my kids and the school.

I said good-bye and glanced at Bobby. "When were you going to tell me about the break-in?"

"Right after you told me why you were researching *Venatores Mali*."

He had me there. What should I say?

"Mrs. Noita was a witch."

Huh, hadn't planned to lead with that.

"She was not."

"You didn't even know her." Neither had I but that was beside the point. "Jenn lived next door as a kid. She and her brothers called Mrs. Noita a witch. To be fair, that was because they weren't allowed to call her a bitch."

Bobby's lips twitched. "I still don't see how you knew about the *Venatores Mali*."

"What do you mean by know?"

"It's a stretch to jump from *mean old lady* to *secret witch-hunting society* unless you knew."

I spread my hands, refusing to be drawn into admitting I'd known anything.

"Tell me how you made that jump."

I didn't like his tone, but I figured I could answer him here or in front of the chief.

"When we heard the fire was at Mrs. Noita's, Jenn said that they called her a witch. She even got a potion from the woman once."

"Seriously?"

I shrugged. "The whole thing made me curious. I looked up *witch,* which led to *witch hunters* and"—I waved my hand at the computer—"that's what I got."

"Did you find anything on that ring?"

"The leader of the hunters branded those he burned with his ring. But I couldn't find any pictures or descriptions of it."

"Me either."

Which was just plain strange. How had that been kept a secret? And why?

"What else do you know about Mrs. Noita?"

"Nothing but what Jenn told me. The woman kept to herself. There's one in every town. She probably didn't like people." After parent-teacher conferences, I didn't like people much myself, so I could relate. "I didn't live near her, so I didn't think much about her."

Until she spoke to me from the great beyond.

"You and everyone else," he muttered. "You'd think the chief had never met the woman either for all that he could tell me."

That was bizarre. Though if Mrs. Noita stayed out of trouble, why would the police know anything? Still . . .

"Did you Google her?" I asked. When Bobby shook his head, I tapped the keyboard, typed in the name. "You should probably see this."

"Just tell me."

"*Noita* means witch."

"It does not."

I was getting tired of him arguing with everything I said. I turned the computer in his direction. "See for yourself." I went into the bathroom and closed the door then stared into the mirror and considered what I'd read.

Noita was the Finnish word for witch. Originally applied to those who fell into a trance, it was believed that while in such a trance their spirit traveled through a hole between heaven and the underworld. There they met the souls of the dead, who offered knowledge that was otherwise lost.

Maybe I was Finnish, because the similarities between a *noita* and myself were pretty damning.

I showered, giving Bobby time to dress and leave. But when I opened the door, he was still there.

"I'm sorry," he said. "I don't know why I jumped to conclusions."

"What kind of conclusions?" I'd be interested to know what he'd thought when he'd opened my computer. He certainly couldn't suspect that I saw dead people.

"I have no idea," he admitted. "I was surprised to find the words *Venatores Mali* since I was alone when Mrs. Noita told me . . ." He paused. "Do you think Noita was her real name?"

"That's more your department than mine."

"I'll check. Anyway . . . " He rubbed a hand through his hair, which was already messy from my hands doing the same. Just the sight of it made me want to do it again. "She said the *Venatores Mali* killed her."

I blinked, and gave a short bark of laughter.

"I know. How could a seventeenth-century Scottish witch-hunting society kill someone in America in the twenty-first century?"

"There are still Nazis," I said.

"Why?"

"I don't know. Who'd want to be a Nazi?"

"I meant, why would you bring up Nazis?"

"Any society can be revived. For that matter, anyone can start a society and slap any name on it that they want. It's America."

Land of the free, home of anyone—including Nazis and witches.

"But a witch-hunting society?" Bobby persisted. "That's crazy."

"They're definitely crazy."

"There's no such thing as witches."

"There are, Bobby."

His expression went mulish.

"Just because they don't fly on broomsticks doesn't mean they aren't witches. Or at least that they believe they are or say they are. All it would take is for someone who hates them . . . "

I paused as a thought trickled through my head but thankfully not out of my mouth: *Someone like you.*

I pushed it away and continued. "For someone who hates them to get it into their head to eliminate witches. Add a few more crazies, and you've got yourself a tribe. There isn't anything much stronger than insane people with a cause."

"Just look at the Nazis," Bobby murmured. "You think Mrs. Noita's niece was a witch too?"

"Only one way to find out. Bowl of blood, call forth a demon; he should be able tell us."

Bobby's mouth opened and shut, like a goldfish that had done a triple reverse Moses and landed on the floor.

"Kidding." I really needed to stop messing with people when I was uncomfortable. It didn't make me feel any less so and usually made the recipient more so. Lose-lose.

"You could go to her house, her work, ask questions." I lowered my voice to a conspiratorial level. "Like a detective."

What had I just thought about messing with people? It was pretty hard not to.

"Good idea," he said.

"Let me know how it goes."

"Won't have to. You're coming with me."

Although I would like nothing better than to spend a day with Bobby Doucet, witch hunting wasn't what I had in mind. Pretty soon it was going to occur to him to ask why the witch hunters were after me.

"I have papers to correct. Lessons to plan." At least there wasn't a Packer game—bye, week—or my day would really be rushed.

"Bring it along. I promised Chief Johnson I wouldn't let you out of my sight."

"But—"

"Get dressed, Raye. We're going to Madison."

Bobby had flown into the Dane County Regional Airport. He'd been told it was five miles northeast of the business district. He hadn't cared since he wasn't staying.

"Anne McKenna lives on State Street," he said. They were headed southeast on Interstate 94. Late Sunday morning traffic was moderate. "Is that the business district?"

"Depends what kind of business you're talking. The university is huge—over forty thousand students, add professors and support staff, that's a lotta business. The capitol is right smack in the center of town—even more business."

"Are the university and the capitol far apart?"

"They're connected by State Street."

That hadn't really answered his question. State Street could be ten miles long.

"I'll direct you," she said. "We'll have to park a few blocks away, if we're lucky. State Street is pedestrian traffic only." She laughed at his expression. "Don't look so sad. It's nice not to have to look for cars while you stroll."

It sounded like she knew the area well. "Did you go to college there?"

"I went to Eau Claire. Closer. Cheaper. Easier to get into. But I knew people who went to Madison. I visited. It's *the* place to be for college students all over the state."

"They don't like their own colleges?"

"Sure. But Halloween in Madison is a two-day party. There's also a spring street festival called Mifflin."

"What's a Mifflin?"

"The name of the street."

"Clever." He passed a slow-moving semi.

"Mifflin's pretty wild; the city has clamped down on it. But they couldn't do much about Halloween on State

Street. People dress up. They go from bar to bar. Sometimes they climb the sidewalk like it's a mountain." She held up a hand. "Don't ask. They did start charging admission, figuring that would cut down on the attendees. It didn't."

"I take it you've been there for the Halloween party?"

"Once. When Jenn insisted. It was insane. So many people. So close. There was one point where I got picked up by the crowd and carried along. My feet didn't touch the sidewalk. Freaked me out."

"I've seen that happen at Mardi Gras. It can be scary."

"I pushed my way to a store stoop. Everyone was drunk and not very accommodating." She rubbed her arms as if she were cold. He wanted to hold her, to warm her. "I haven't been back since."

She stared out the window, her fingers curled so tightly around her own arms they'd gone white.

"What did you wear?" he asked.

Her breath rushed out. She'd been holding it. He didn't like the idea of her in a crowd, panicked, alone. He should probably have changed the subject completely, but he'd also been intrigued by the idea of her in costume. What would Raye Larsen wear to the Halloween party of the year?

"I was a witch," she said, as if it were a new and interesting revelation.

He made a soft sound of amusement, and she smiled, letting her arms fall back to her sides. Mission accomplished.

"I had the choice of being a black cat or a witch. As the cat costume consisted of a black bodysuit with a studded collar and leash, very Jenn, I picked the witch outfit."

"Pointy hat?"

"Check."

"What else?"

She slid a glance in his direction. At least she'd stopped holding her breath and rubbing herself as if she'd been dumped out of the car in the middle of a snowstorm.

"The last time someone asked 'what are you wearing?' I hung up on them."

"I promise not to breathe too heavily."

"You won't want to. My costume consisted of a puffy black dress that reached to my knees, purple and white striped wool socks, ruby slippers, a broom, and green makeup."

"Wart?"

She touched the tip of her nose. "Yep."

"Very 'I'll get you, my pretty.' With that getup, Jenn should have dressed like Toto and not a cat."

"Jenn would never consent to being a dog."

"Good point."

They continued in silence for several miles. The sign for the next exit proclaimed a variety of fast food choices. "You want something to eat?"

They'd dressed and left without bothering to down anything more than coffee. He was fine; he'd done the same a thousand times before, but she looked pale.

"McDonald's," she read. "Taco Bell. Dunkin Donuts is tempting. But if I'm going to blow the diet I'd rather go to State Street Brats."

He eyed her. "Diet?"

"Not so much for weight loss as for health."

"You're twenty-seven. Don't you have a few years before you need to watch your food choices?"

"I have no idea of my health history. For all I know my parents had diabetes, high cholesterol, and the fat gene."

He'd never considered all the issues that an adopted child would have to face. In this day and age, most knew their parents, or they could if they wanted to. They definitely had access to their medical records. What would it be like not to know anything about where you came from?

"I watch the salt, the fat, the junk," she continued. "But I'm a sucker for State Street Brats. That's my splurge."

Bobby had heard of bratwurst, never had one, wasn't sure he wanted to. His thoughts must have shown on his face because Raye patted his knee. "The place is legend. Brats in nearly every menu item. They even have a red bratwurst."

"Why?"

"Badger spirit. Red brat, white bun. Go Big Red." She pumped her fist into the air.

People *were* crazy. But he'd known that as soon as he understood the meaning of the word. If people weren't, he'd be out of a job. Some days he didn't think that would be such a bad thing.

Raye indicated the next exit. "This one."

He followed her directions. The big white capitol dome loomed above streets that were a maze. He could have plugged the address into his GPS but why bother when he had her?

Memories of last night surfaced—the way that she'd tasted, the sound of her cries, the brush of her breath, the clasp of her thighs.

"Take the next parking place you see."

He snapped out of the past. He was on a case. Now was not the time for pornographic daydreams and bad poetry.

Bobby saw a space half a block up. He had to parallel park, but he was good at it, even with a car that wasn't his.

"Nice," she said as they climbed out. "You didn't even tap the curb."

"As if."

She smiled, and for an instant he thought she'd take his hand. For an instant he almost took hers, until he remembered.

Case. Victim. Murderer. He swooped out his arm in a "be my guest" gesture, and she led the way.

They took one turn and State Street spread out before them like a Midwestern French Quarter. Shops, taverns, restaurants. People milled about, walking dogs, sipping coffee.

"Is this it?" Raye peered at the numbers above the nearest doorway—a used bookstore.

"That one." He lifted his chin to indicate another farther down.

Raye stopped in front of it and frowned.

"Is it closed?" he asked.

She didn't answer, just pointed to the sign above the doorway, which read: *PRACTICAL MAGIC.*

Chapter 17

"Just because she lives above a magic shop doesn't make her a witch," Bobby said.

"It's not a magic shop." Raye tapped the star surrounded by a circle. "A pentagram is a Wiccan symbol."

"How do you know this stuff?"

"Don't you? You live in New Orleans."

He rubbed his forehead. "I try to avoid the weird shit."

Or at least he had after he'd met Audrey. She'd brought enough weird shit into his life to last the rest of it. He'd never been sure if she believed in all the kooky crap she and her friends spouted, or if she'd only pretended she had in order to dupe the pathetic, unsuspecting, and desperate.

"I'd think that in New Orleans there'd be tons of 'weird shit,' especially in homicide."

"You'd be surprised."

There was Sullivan's loup-garou incident, of course, but Bobby hadn't been involved and most thought that Sullivan had had a breakdown. It made more sense than a werewolf running loose in the Crescent City.

"Homicide is pretty cut-and-dried. It's almost always the husband, sometimes the wife. On occasion, a sibling. People kill the ones they love. They don't off the passersby."

"I still can't believe you haven't run into a witch or two. Maybe a voodoo priestess?"

"Despite the press, voodoo is a fairly peaceful religion."

"So is Wicca. I'm pretty sure that's one of their tenets . . . "

She pointed at the painted sign in the window, which read: HARM NONE.

"Probably why I haven't met any."

Homicide began and ended with harm.

"Just because she lived over a Wiccan shop doesn't mean she was a witch either," he said.

"Sooner or later, Bobby, one and one is going to have to equal two." Raye opened the door.

Inside a young man stood behind the counter. His nametag read TODD. He was dressed in jeans, Nikes, a red T-shirt sporting that big-headed badger. Bobby had lost track of how many of those he'd seen in the few yards they had traveled to arrive here. The guy's strawberry-blond hair was short, his lightly freckled face clean-shaven. He was the least likely Wiccan shop worker Bobby could have imagined.

"Blessed be," Todd said.

Bobby flashed his badge. If he was lucky, the clerk wouldn't look closely enough to read NOPD. He didn't.

"Do you have a key for the apartment upstairs?" Bobby asked.

"Annie's place?"

"Is there more than one apartment?"

"Got me there." Todd opened the register, removed a key, held it out. "You know who's gonna be taking over?"

"Taking over what?"

"The shop. Man, I sure hope it doesn't get sold. I like this job."

"Anne owned the shop?" Raye asked. She was quicker on the uptake than he was.

"Of course."

"Why 'of course'?" Bobby wondered.

"She was a high priestess."

Bobby glanced at Raye. She shrugged.

"The leader of the local coven," Todd continued.

"It's like a witch club," Raye said.

"That's right, dude."

Bobby had never gotten used to women being referred to as *dude*. From Raye's bemused expression she hadn't either.

"I thought Ms. McKenna was a hospice worker."

"She is." The young man's bright, eager expression fell. "Was." He shook his head. "Why would anyone hurt her? She was a saint."

"Can a witch be a saint?" Bobby asked.

"Joan of Arc," Raye murmured.

"Good one." Todd nodded approvingly. "Annie's gift was to relieve suffering. She helped ease people from this world."

That smelled like euthanasia. Which was still a crime as far as Bobby knew. "How?"

"Once people are in hospice, there's not much to do but manage their pain, which usually means boatloads of narcotics. Some don't want to spend the time they have left drugged out of their mind. Annie used herbals and massage instead of pills."

"Herbals." Bobby knew what that meant.

Todd rolled his eyes—part disgust, part amusement. "Dying people, dude."

He had a point.

"Annie was gifted," the kid continued.

"I'm not following."

"She was an air witch."

He still wasn't.

Todd grabbed a piece of paper, drew a five-pointed star. "Four elements." He tapped the eraser side of his pencil on each of the four nonascendant triangles. "Fire, air, water, earth." He moved the eraser to the single ascendant point. "Spirit. Point up, shows spirit is more important than earthly concerns."

"What about point down?" Bobby asked. He'd seen that too.

The kid made a face. "The earthly over the spirit. Satanism. Crazies."

"Because witches are so sane," Bobby muttered, ignoring Raye's annoyed glance.

"Those who follow this path . . . "—Todd tapped the center of the pentagram—"are some of the sanest people I've ever known."

Bobby was getting too much information out of this guy to argue and risk his clamming up so he swallowed further comments. "Anything else?" he asked.

Todd stared at him for a few seconds as if gauging how much he should say, then shrugged and went on. "The continuous line used to draw the star symbolizes the interconnection between the divine and the earthly." Flipping the pencil point down, he drew a ring connecting the points of the star. "All is unified. Life is a circle—birth, death, rebirth."

Bobby nearly said *blah, blah, blah,* but managed to stop himself. From the glance Raye shot his way, his expression had said it for him. At least Todd didn't notice.

"Witches are elemental," Todd continued. "An earth witch is good with herbs, a water witch with healing and cleansing."

"But Anne was an air witch?" Raye asked.

"Right. If her talent had been medicine or healing, she would have been a nurse. Hospice isn't about that. An air witch alleviates pain, and air rules the crossover."

"Lost me," Bobby said.

"The gates of death. An air witch is a necromancer. They can communicate with the dead."

Raye started so violently, Bobby took her hand. It was freakishly cold for the warmth of the autumn day. He glanced at her. She wasn't looking at him but at the kid.

"Communicate how?" she whispered.

"Hear them mostly. Clairaudience. But really powerful air witches can bring the dead across."

"I refuse to believe in zombies," Bobby said.

"We're talking ghosts, dude."

"Of course we are," Raye said.

"Annie not only helped the dead cross over, she helped the living communicate with those they've lost."

"Séances?" Bobby's lip curled.

"Sometimes."

"And I suppose she charged a hefty fee for them."

"That wouldn't be ethical. Besides, how can you charge the dead?"

"That wasn't . . . " Bobby began, but Raye set a hand on his arm. "Shh."

"Annie was training me," Todd continued. "Now what am I going to do?"

"You seem to be doing just fine here," Bobby said.

"She wasn't training me in the store; she was training me to be a witch."

"Isn't that a warlock?"

"It's the twenty-first century. No one uses that word anymore."

"Except on *Bewitched*," Raye said, and Todd snickered. "I thought witches were born not made."

Bobby cast her a quick glance. How much research had she done before he arrived last night?

"To be an elemental, like Annie," Todd said, "you have to inherit the craft. If you don't you can still learn the way, assist the others, but real magic is beyond us."

"Real magic," Bobby repeated, managing, barely, not to sneer. "Isn't that a simile?"

"I think you mean oxymoron," Raye said.

"Moron is right."

"What is your problem?" Todd asked.

"He's a cop," Raye said. "They don't believe anything."

"Or anyone," Bobby agreed. Especially about this. It was all such BS. But as Raye had pointed out, it didn't matter if he believed it, what mattered was if the killers believed and acted on it.

"Did you know Anne's aunt?" Raye asked.

"Mrs. Noita?" Todd nodded. "Earth witch."

Bobby groaned.

Todd's eyes narrowed. "Does she have a great garden?"

"Didn't notice," Bobby said. He'd been a little busy with her dying on him, then there'd been the running for his life.

"I think so," Raye said slowly. "I remember my father saying something once about buying her tomatoes instead of going to the store."

"Lots of trees with stuff hanging in them," Todd continued. "Symbols drawn on the leaves." As Todd wasn't asking, Bobby didn't answer. "For protection."

"Didn't help."

Todd straightened. "What happened?"

Raye's breath caught, and she cast Bobby a horrified, helpless glance. The kid didn't know. Now Bobby would have to tell him. He hated informing next of kin. Not that Todd was *next*, but he still had to be told.

"Her too?" Todd asked, their discomfort and silence telling the tale without them having to. "Damn."

"Sorry," Bobby said.

Raye reached over and patted the boy's hand. Todd didn't seem to notice.

"How?"

"Murdered."

"The same guy?" His eyebrows drew together. "No. Some cop killed him."

Bobby must have made a movement because Todd's gaze widened. "You?"

Bobby shrugged.

"Thanks, man."

"What about 'harm none'?"

"He started it," Todd said.

Bobby would have had a hard time accepting thanks for killing someone, even if that someone had been a murderer about to kill again, but thankfully Todd moved on without waiting for any acceptance or acknowledgment on Bobby's part.

"Did Annie go to New Bergin because her aunt died?"

"Mrs. Noita died yesterday," Bobby said. "You have no idea why Ms. McKenna went to New Bergin?"

Todd shook his head. "She called me in to work, said her aunt needed her and she'd be gone a few days."

"Did she visit a lot?"

"She'd go see her around the sabbats—before or after. Annie had duties here on the actual days. Just like Mrs. Noita had duties there. She was the high priestess in that area."

"How many witches are there in New Bergin?" Raye asked.

"Hard to say. Mrs. Noita's coven was made up of the people from all the little towns between here and Eau Claire. There's a fairly large coven in Eau Claire."

"There's a sentence I never thought I'd hear in this lifetime," Raye muttered.

Bobby rubbed his forehead. He wasn't sure what to make of the fact that the two victims had not only been witches, but the leaders of groups of a whole lot more. It might explain how Mrs. Noita had survived as long as she had, considering the nature of her injury. Then again, maybe not, since the explanation was magic.

"What's a sabbat?" he asked. He'd heard the word, but he wasn't sure what it meant, and apparently he needed to know.

"You should take Wiccan 101, dude."

"Just catch me up," Bobby ordered, then added, "Please."

"There are eight sabbats—celebrations, feast days, gatherings. They're seasonal and solar. There are four major sabbats." Todd held up a finger. "Imboic." He added an additional finger for each one. "Beltane, Lughnasadh, Samhain. Four minor." He continued on the other hand with four more fingers. "Yule, Ostara, Midsummer Eve, Mabon."

"And what happens during these celebrations?"

"Not what most people think."

Bobby lifted an eyebrow. "What do they think?"

"Naked dancing. Orgies. Human sacrifice. At the least we must kill a chicken, maybe a lamb."

"You don't?"

"Harm *none,*" Todd said. "We sing, dance, eat, chant. It's like church in the forest. You should come."

"In the forest?" Bobby fought a shudder. He liked his church in a nice cathedral, with lots of candles and Latin. Although, remove the cathedral, and the dancing, add a ton of trees and the two were probably very similar. Too bad he had a thing about trees.

"What happens if the high priestess dies?" Raye asked.

Sadness flickered over Todd's face before he answered. "There's a ceremony in the place they felt most at peace. Probably the clearing where we hold our sabbats. In days gone by, the body was wrapped in a shroud and consigned to the earth. No casket. The sooner we return to the mother the better."

"Is that even legal?" Bobby asked.

In most cemeteries, a grave liner, or vault, was required to keep the ground from settling and creating a very unappealing pockmarked appearance. Cemeteries preferred to look like the front lawn of heaven's golf club.

And wouldn't bodies buried in the soil without protection contaminate not only the ground but the groundwater? There was a reason folks died young back in the day, and that might be one of them.

"Cremation is common now," Todd said. "We'll spread Annie's ashes in the clearing instead, though—" Todd frowned. "Usually the high priestess presides."

"Who'll take over?" Bobby asked. Power and prestige were always on the hit parade of motives.

"We'll elect someone. Usually it's the person with the most experience. But not always."

"Person?" Raye repeated. "Not woman?"

"Most leaders are women. Wicca is a very feminine religion. The goddess, right? But some covens elect high priests. Many of the larger ones have both a high priest and a high priestess."

"Who do you think will take Anne's place in your coven?" Bobby needed to have a talk with whoever that was.

"I haven't been involved long enough to guess."

Bobby handed one of his cards to the kid. "Let me know about the funeral arrangements."

"You wanna come?"

He didn't want to, but it was standard procedure in a murder case. Sometimes the murderer showed up at the funeral of his victims. Anne's wouldn't. But as there was more than one killer, there was probably someone pulling the strings. Maybe that person would show. Stranger things had happened.

What he really needed to do was attend the maniac's funeral. However, the way things were going, he doubted he'd be able to make a quick trip to Ohio. He should get in touch with local law enforcement, ask someone to take photos. Although the FBI was probably all over that already, or they'd better be.

"Why would anyone want to kill such great ladies?" Todd wondered. "They were healers, helpers. Everyone loved them."

"Not everyone." Raye's eyes widened as if she hadn't realized she'd said it out loud. "Mrs. Noita was kind of cranky. Some of the kids called her a witch."

"She was a witch. You think kids killed her?"

"No." Bobby cast Raye a quelling glance. The information about the *Venatores Mali* was not information he wanted to get out.

"How'd Mrs. Noita die?"

Bobby hesitated, but as the generalities had already been reported in the Sunday paper, he went on. "Throat cut."

"Bloody."

"Very."

"Was there anything odd about her death?"

"I like to think, or at least hope, that every murder is odd," Bobby said. But the kid was right. "It was pointed out that she should have died more quickly than she did."

Todd nodded. "Blood magic is the most powerful kind of magic there is."

"What's blood magic?" Raye asked.

"Using blood in a spell makes that spell not only personal but permanent. Blood magic binds through life and death and eternity. It isn't used unless there's no other choice."

Though Bobby didn't believe a word of this, he still got a shiver. From the way Raye hugged herself she had too.

"The results of a blood spell are stronger. They can't be undone."

"Why not?" Raye's voice was just above a whisper.

"A fire witch would burn the blood, an earth witch would drop it onto the dirt, a water witch would disperse it into the water, and an air witch would release it to the wind. You can't unburn something. Once liquid sinks into the earth, it can't be drawn out. Blood becomes one with the water and once the wind blows past it's irretrievable."

"You think Mrs. Noita used blood magic?"

"To delay death from a wound like that, she would have had to use something. Did you find a magical instrument near the body? Maybe an athame?"

"Which is?"

"Double-edged knife." Todd moved to the glass case, opened the back, reached in. "Like this."

The weapon appeared normal enough—for a weapon. Silver blade, honed on both sides. It was the two sides that drew Bobby's interest.

"Are there any athames that are squiggly?"

Todd's lips twitched. "That is not a word I'd have thought would come from your mouth, dude."

"Me either." And it wouldn't have if he hadn't heard it from Johnson. "Are there?"

"Not so much anymore. But I have seen one."

"Where?"

"Here."

Bobby peered through the glass top of the case. He didn't see any squiggly knives.

"Dude," he said, and Raye coughed.

"I didn't say it was here." Todd indicated the display with the tip of the knife he still held then lifted it toward the ceiling. "Annie had it at her place."

"Why?" Bobby asked.

"To cut herbs, draw a sacred circle." Todd shrugged. "Whatever."

"Ms. McKenna used an athame in her spells?"

Todd shook his head as he returned the knife to the case. "Fire witches use athames. Annie was an air witch. She would use a wand." He moved to another case, where a selection of amazingly different and intricate wands was displayed. They had carved wooden handles, onyx, amethyst, crystal. In the corner of the case equally elaborate cups had been grouped.

Todd tapped the glass above them. "Chalices for a water witch." He frowned. "Come to think of it, Mrs. Noita wouldn't have used an athame. She was an earth witch. Her instrument was the pentacle." He pointed at the wall where several necklaces were displayed, each with an amulet bearing the five-pointed star. "Used to call spirits."

Raye, who'd been leaning close, peering at the designs on the amulets, stepped away.

"Also to invoke the goddess," Todd continued, then shrugged. "But mostly for protection."

"Protection again," Bobby said. "Did they hang them over the door, in the trees?"

The kid's gaze sharpened. "You should have found one hanging around Mrs. Noita's neck."

Mrs. Noita's neck, chest, pretty much everything had been covered in blood. But not so much that Bobby couldn't see a marked lack of a pentacle.

"It wasn't."

"Might be why it didn't help." Todd chewed his bottom lip for a second. "She wouldn't take it off. Maybe it was torn off in the struggle. It has to be there somewhere."

Bobby decided not to mention that Mrs. Noita's "there" wasn't there anymore, along with most of Mrs. Noita. The guy was having a hard enough time as it was.

"What are these?" Raye asked, lifting a ring from a box atop one of the cases.

"Also pentacles. Men aren't big on necklaces."

"Ever see a ring with a snarling wolf?" Bobby asked.

"Wasn't a ring."

Bobby and Raye exchanged a glance.

"The athame with the curving blade has a snarling wolf carved into the handle."

"Is that common?" Bobby asked.

"Carvings, yes. But they're usually runes and such."

Bobby almost asked what a rune was, then decided to keep his eye on the ball. "No wolves?"

"That was the only one I ever saw. Witches are associated with cats. Wolves?" He lifted one shoulder. "Not really. But after Annie showed me that athame, I did a little research. There was one group that used a snarling wolf as their symbol."

Raye's breath caught. Bobby set a hand on her arm to keep her from speaking.

"A particular coven?" he asked.

"No. A bunch of witch-burning bastards from the seventeenth century."

Bobby's fingers tightened as Raye leaned forward. "What were they called?"

"*Venatores Mali,* hunters of evil. They hunted witches with the blessing of some Scottish king. Their symbol was a snarling wolf, which was seen as a great hunter in many cultures. The Norse often wore wolf skulls on their heads when they went a-viking. A lot of the Plains Indians did the same."

"The Scots?" Bobby asked.

"Apparently they carved the wolf into their implements of torture."

"They did?" Bobby couldn't remember any of that from *Braveheart.*

"Maybe it was just the *Venatores Mali.*"

"Why would the symbol of a witch-hunting society be carved into the hilt of a witch's ritual knife?"

"Christians liked to appropriate everything pagan. There's a reason our sabbats fall near Christian holidays. They put the holidays next to the sabbats."

Bobby must have looked skeptical because Todd continued, "You think Jesus was born on December twenty-fifth?"

"Yes?"

"No, or at the least, no one knows for sure. The Bible is vague about his birth, oddly specific about his death. Part of that is because they weren't really birthday-party people back then. One of the few references to the time of year among the apostles' writings was 'shepherds watching their flocks.' Flocks would have been corralled in December. If you take the Bible literally, that means Jesus wasn't born in December."

"Pretty slim," Bobby murmured.

"My middle name, dude. A lot of experts think the early Christians needed to offset the sabbat of Yule and decided December was a nice place to plop Christ's birthday. Get the common people to confuse the two and pretty soon you've got a congregation instead of a coven."

Bobby felt vaguely sacrilegious, and he wasn't even the one plopping Christ's birthday in any old place.

"What does this have to do with the wolf on the ritual knife?"

"Why stop at appropriating pagan holy days? What if a witch hunter took the athame off one of his victims and carved his crest into it, thus changing a peaceful pagan ritual knife into a Christian tool of torture?"

"Interesting theory."

"It's a little more than that," Todd said. "I found mention of a squiggly knife in a seventeenth-century text."

"They actually used the word *squiggly*?" Raye asked.

"Even better. There was a drawing, which matched Annie's athame."

Bobby got a chill. "What did Anne have to say about that?"

"She didn't seem surprised."

"I bet not," Bobby said. He was starting to think Anne had hunted down that athame with the same intensity that the *Venatores Mali* had hunted her.

But why?

Chapter 18

"Why would Anne want an athame when she wasn't a fire witch?" I asked. From Bobby's glance, he'd been about to ask the same thing.

"Who wouldn't want it? It was probably worth fifty thousand dollars."

"Fifty thousand for a knife?" Bobby blurted.

"Not just any knife. If it was the same one, that athame belonged to Roland McHugh. The founder of the *Venatores Mali*."

My breath caught. *Uh-oh.*

"How do you know all this?" I asked.

"You notice no one's come in since you did?" Todd indicated the books lining the walls of the shop. "I got nothin' but time to read them."

Bobby rubbed his eyes. "What else do you know about the *Venatores Mali*?"

"I never heard of 'em before I saw that carving on the athame. They were a *secret* society."

"They were burning people on the orders of King James. You'd think someone would have kept records."

"If they did, they hid them well. The only information I found was in diaries. McHugh scared everyone, including his followers. He was obsessed with witches, and once on the trail of one, he didn't stop until they were ashes."

I got a shiver, which was silly. McHugh had been dead for centuries.

"All of the witch hunters and black-robed inquisitors were fanatics," Bobby said. "It was kind of their thing."

"For McHugh the hunt was personal. Sure, he fried anyone he could along the way, but he was obsessed with one witch in particular for the rest of his life."

"The one that got away?" Bobby asked.

"Unfortunately, no. He burned both her and her husband."

"End of story," Bobby said.

"Not quite. The woman was a midwife who attended McHugh's wife in childbirth. His wife and the child died."

"That happened a lot back then." Bobby took a breath, let it out. "Although I can see how the man became unhinged."

He tried to keep his voice neutral, but I heard what lay beneath. I took his hand, and, though he cast me a curious glance, he let me.

"The problem was that the midwife gave birth to three healthy girls shortly after. Back then, more than twins were rare and kind of witchy, their surviving even more so. McHugh got it in his head that the woman had sacrificed his wife and child so that hers would live. He vowed to find those devil-spawned children, no matter what it took."

"How'd he lose them?"

Both men glanced at me, and I continued. "He murdered the parents. Did they sense the end was near and hide the babies?"

Todd actually rubbed his palms together. Considering all the blood and fire and death, he was enjoying the tale a little too much. "Here's where it gets interesting. The *Venatores Mali* surprised the couple in a cottage in the deepest, darkest forest. They built a pyre."

"Huge mistake in a forest," I observed.

"They'd made enough of them to know what they were doing," Todd said. "McHugh believed both mother and father were witches. Strapped them back-to-back on the stake and lit them up."

I must have flinched because Bobby's fingers tightened around mine. "The children?" I asked.

"Held in the arms of three hunters."

"They made them watch?"

"They were a few days old. Doubt they could focus on much, or remember anything at all."

For an instant I felt the fire hot against my face, the smoke, the smell, the shouts, and the terror. My imagination working overtime again.

"If the triplets were there, then why would McHugh spend his life searching for them?" Bobby asked.

"They disappeared." Todd flipped his fingers toward the ceiling. "Like magic."

Bobby snorted. "The men holding them ran off. Protected them. Hid them."

"Those dudes? Not a chance. Even if they'd suddenly sprouted a conscience, they were scared of McHugh. Those who crossed him were labeled devotees of Satan, and they fried too."

"There has to be a better explanation than magic," Bobby insisted.

"According to the diary I read, the parents chanted as they died. The flames burned so high and hot, they were incinerated in an instant. Nothing left but ashes, and if you know anything about burning bodies, that ain't easy. The children vanished, and they were never seen again."

"That's impossible," Bobby said.

Todd lifted one shoulder. "Blood magic is the most powerful kind. Their disappearance made McHugh nuttier than before. He vowed vengeance on his deathbed."

"He could vow whatever he liked," Bobby said. "Death is the end."

Not always.

The words whispered through my head. I glanced around, but I didn't see any ghosts.

"He swore death wouldn't bind him. That he would come back and obliterate the line of the witches that had obliterated his."

"He could have had more children," I said. "His line didn't have to end."

"Because a kook like him was such a great prize," Todd muttered. "I bet he had a damn hard time getting dates when he smelled like dead people."

"How did he die?" I asked.

"Plague of 1636 in England. He should have used fire for more than killing. A little sterilization would have worked wonders."

"Not a word of him since?" I continued.

Bobby cast me a glance. "Really?"

I shrugged and spread my hands.

"Not that I've heard, though if the *Venatores Mali* are trying to raise him—"

"Raise him?" Bobby interrupted. "Dude."

"The *Venatores Mali* are killing witches," Todd began.

"I didn't say that."

"I can add. Witches are dying. The snarling wolf symbol is involved. If McHugh isn't back—"

"He's dust," Bobby said tightly.

"If there are people calling themselves *Venatores Mali,* following McHugh's rules, hunting, killing, burning, then McHugh isn't really dead. He never will be."

"Why now?" I asked. "Why here?" I left out *why me*. But from the glance Bobby gave me, he heard it anyway.

"If we find that out, we might find them," Bobby said. "I should take a look at that athame."

"You've got the key to her apartment." Todd indicated the stairs to his left. "Knock yourself out."

"You know where she kept the knife?"

"Last I saw the thing it was on her bedside table."

Bobby went up the stairs with me close behind. He inserted the key into the lock and pushed open the door.

Expecting the apartment to be dark and musty, I was pleasantly surprised by a room full of sunshine, which smelled of mint. The reason for both was immediately apparent. The shades on Anne's eastern windows were up, the sill lined with tiny pots of herbs. Even without the scent I would have recognized mint leaves.

I crossed the room, set my fingers on the soil. "I should water these."

Bobby didn't answer; he'd already stepped into her bedroom. I followed, curious to see the athame. He stood next to her bed. The only thing on the table was a lamp. He opened the drawer; stuff rattled; he cursed.

"Not there?"

"No." He went onto his knees and peered beneath the bed, then straightened. "We're going to have to toss the place."

The apartment was smaller than mine, and that wasn't easy. "It shouldn't be hard to find."

Bobby headed for her dresser. I found the watering can next to the kitchen sink and sprinkled the pots before I forgot. Besides mint, she had basil, thyme, and rosemary. I plucked a few leaves of the latter and tucked them into my pocket. Just in case.

A loud smack had me spinning, sloshing water onto my foot. A Siamese cat sat on the coffee table, peering at me with the bluest eyes I'd ever seen on an animal. The face was such a dark brown it was nearly black, which might have contributed to the intense shade of those eyes. The ears were huge, also deep brown, matching the paws and the tail. Everything else was the shade of sand.

The cat let out a long, loud, very human yowl, and the tail twitched once as it stared pointedly at the book on the floor before lifting those freaky eyes to mine. He, she, it must have knocked the volume off the table.

"Raye?" Bobby appeared in the bedroom doorway. "You o—" He saw the cat. "Where did that come from?"

"Must be Anne's. It knocked something on the ground." The cat jumped down and sat on the book, claws flexing against the binding and making a sound that caused my skin to prickle.

"I'm fine." I kept my gaze on the cat. "You can go back to what you were doing." When he did, I moved closer. "What's your name?"

The cat didn't blink. I wasn't sure what to do. I'd never had a cat, or a dog either. I'd once had a goldfish from the goldfish game, but it hadn't lasted long enough for us to bond.

I knelt and the cat scooted behind the sofa so fast, I

barely saw it move. I considered following and trying to coax the animal out, then I saw the title on the palm-sized volume that lay on the floor.

Book of Shadows.

Compelled, I opened the cover and forgot all about the cat.

This Book of Shadows belongs to Anne McKenna, an air witch. Should any harm befall her, the book is gifted to the next witch of that element who beholds it. Use the information wisely and well. Harm none.

The pages ruffled forward, as if blown by a breeze, but the windows were closed. I turned back to the first page. Though I knew it was impossible, there was more writing there now than there'd been before.

The new words seem to be inscribed by the same hand as all the rest, which made me think at first that I'd just missed the final line. Anne was dead. Even if a ghost could write, I hadn't seen her here, and seeing ghosts was what I did. The new entry read: "Raye Larsen's Book of Shadows," followed by today's date.

I dropped the book. It made less of a smack this time since I was on the ground. Good thing too. I might have fallen if I wasn't already there.

"Raye?"

I shoved the tome into the pocket of my jeans. How was I going to explain why my name was in it?

"The cat," I said, then peered behind the couch.

No cat.

Bobby appeared next to me. He held out a hand, and I took it. He frowned. "You're like ice."

He folded me into his embrace. I spent the time worrying that he'd feel the book in my pocket, rather than enjoying the hug.

"There isn't a knife in her bedroom. Did you find anything out here?"

I hadn't had much of a chance to look. "Not yet."

Together we made our way around the room, rifling drawers, peeking under cushions and furniture. Bobby went into the teeny bathroom and from the increase in volume of the slams and thunks, he wasn't having any luck finding it there either.

He stepped out. "No athame."

"No," I agreed.

"Shit."

"You think someone stole it?"

"Yeah."

"She could have taken it with her when she left."

"I read the reports. It wasn't on her body, or in her car."

"So if it wasn't stolen here . . ."

"It was stolen somewhere." He let out a breath. "I figured the chances of there being two squiggly knives was pretty damn slim."

A crash from below was followed with cries of "Help!" and "Go away!" and, oddly, "Shoo!"

We hurried down the stairs. At the bottom, Bobby drew his gun, glancing over his shoulder with a stern "Stay" before he went around the corner.

"Don't shoot!"

Todd's voice. No others. Curious, I took a look.

The cat sat on the counter, staring at the kid, who cowered in the corner. The only movement from the animal was a twitch of the tail, back and forth, back and forth.

"Get it out of here!" Todd sneezed—once, twice, again.

Bobby reached for the cat and it hissed, arching like a Halloween decoration. He dropped his hand.

Todd coughed. His eyes were already red. "You gotta get her out of here. I swear she comes by me on purpose."

"You're allergic," Bobby said.

"Y-y-ya . . . think!" The last was emitted with a sneeze.

"What's her name?" I asked, stepping into the room.

"Samhain."

The cat leaped into my arms. I waited for the spike of her claws. Instead, she rubbed her head under my chin and began to purr.

Todd straightened from his cowering pose. "I've never seen her act like that with anyone but Annie."

"Has she been locked upstairs by herself?"

"Natasha, the other employee, fed and watered her."

"She seems lonely," Bobby said.

"Dude," Todd murmured, "aren't we all?"

Bobby snorted. Todd kept a wary gaze on Samhain. "I think she loves you."

Personally, I thought she hated Todd, or maybe she just liked messing with him. I stood with my arms full of cat, my pocket full of *The Book of Shadows* as the kid sneezed and coughed and dribbled. If I didn't know better I'd think Samhain was sending waves of dander his way on purpose. Todd was so pathetically pathetic, I felt bad. Then he said it.

"I'll have Natasha drive her to the shelter as soon as she comes in."

I swear Samhain's purr lowered to a growl. But how could she know what he'd said?

"She can't stay here," the kid continued. "I was going to have Mrs. Noita take her. But now . . . "

"Can't you leave her upstairs where she's comfortable?"

"She sneaks down here whenever she can. Scares the crap out of me sometimes."

"It's a cat," Bobby said.

"Sure it is," Todd muttered.

"What about Natasha?"

"No pets at her place."

"Give her this place."

"It isn't mine to give."

"I can't." I tried to put Samhain on the counter. She clung to me like a baby monkey—with claws.

"I don't think you're going to be able to get rid of her," Bobby said.

"I have a job. What will she do all day?"

"Same thing she did here. Sleep on the back of the couch, maybe on your pillow." Todd's lip curled, and he sneezed just thinking about it. "You find the athame?"

"No," Bobby said. "Did Anne carry it with her?"

"I doubt it. Like I said, an athame wasn't her ritual instrument."

"Do you have security cameras?" Bobby asked.

Todd's eyes widened. "You think someone stole it?"

"Yeah," Bobby said, and we exchanged glances.

We had a pretty good idea who'd stolen it too—the tall brown-haired woman who'd murdered my pillow and mattress. But we'd never seen her. A video would be very helpful.

"Sorry, dude. No need for cameras. The people who come here are peaceful. Harm none."

"Yet you sell knives."

"Athames."

"Which are sharp enough to kill."

The thought seemed to upset Todd so much he went into another sneezing fit.

Bobby lifted his chin in my direction. "Maybe you should . . . "

I went upstairs to gather cat things—food, bowls, litter box, toys. I had to set Samhain down to do it, but in the apartment she let me.

I came down the stairs, hands full; the cat hovered at my heels as if she were herding me. I reached the last two steps, and Bobby spoke.

"Did the couple with the triplets have a name?"

I paused. Samhain bumped her head against my ankles. I couldn't move. My ears strained; what was coming next was important.

"Taggart," Todd said.

Or not. Never heard that name in my life.

I lifted my foot, planning to take the final steps and rejoin them.

"Henry and Prudence Taggart."

My heel caught. I pitched forward, everything in my hands flew upward, and I fell downward. It was only two steps. I shouldn't bruise too badly. Then Samhain appeared right in my path. I was going to fall on her if I didn't—

She flew across the floor as if the wood had been greased like a bowling alley. Her claws scrambled for purchase. There wasn't any. She clumped against the counter at the same time all of her necessities rained around me.

The return to New Bergin was uneventful. They'd had enough eventful already.

"You sure you're okay?" Bobby asked.

"As okay as I was the last three times you asked."

"Bruises and strains don't hurt right away."

"I caught my foot. Scared the cat, dropped the stuff. Not a mark on me. I swear."

But there was something wrong. Bobby could feel it. Or maybe it was just the cat, which had decided her favorite place in the world was lying across the back of his seat.

If he got too close, she batted at his head. Claws sheathed, lucky him, it was still distracting. Raye had tried to get the animal to rest in her lap, on the seat, the floor, the dash. Samhain preferred staring at the back of Bobby's neck.

"I should buy a carrier," Raye said, and Samhain growled. "You can't just sit wherever you want."

"Are you talking to the cat?"

"Someone has to."

He glanced in the rearview mirror. Samhain stared out the back window. "She isn't listening."

"Oh, she's listening. She's just pretending not to."

"You're not going to become one of those cat ladies, are you?"

"Spinster schoolteacher with a cat? I think I already am."

"Twenty-seven does not make you a spinster, and one cat doesn't qualify you for cat lady. Relax."

She was so tense her fingers were white from being wrung in her lap, and he could almost feel her vibrating. No wonder the cat wouldn't sit by her.

"You should eat," he said.

They'd skipped State Street Brats, not wanting to leave Samhain in the car alone. But that meant neither one of them had imbibed anything but coffee. If Bobby hadn't been doing just that for most of his adult life he'd be jittery. Raye had to be.

"Not hungry," she said.

"What's wrong with you?"

The question came out too loud and too sharp as evidenced by Raye's widened eyes and Samhain's smack on the back of his head.

"I just . . . " She glanced out the window. "Have so much to do before tomorrow."

"What's tomorrow?"

"We call it Monday. First day of the workweek."

"You're not going to work."

"Am too."

"Someone's trying to kill you."

"Thanks to a world full of crazies, the school has more security than Area Fifty-one."

He cast her a glance. "Area Fifty-one?"

"All I'm saying is that I'm safer at school than at home."

"I'm with you at home."

"Twenty-four/seven?"

"Don't you want me to be?"

She hesitated, and he experienced a moment of uncertainty. He shouldn't have touched her, but all he wanted was to touch her again. However, if she didn't want him to— "If you'd rather I stay somewhere else, I can talk to Johnson and—"

"I don't want you to go." She set her hand on his leg, her fingers stroked, but absently, a movement meant to soothe not arouse. "It's just . . . you will go."

He would. He had a job, a life, a history in New Orleans. "Maybe you could come with me."

Her hand froze. "I don't think so."

He was more disappointed by her words than he'd thought he could be. "You might like it in New Orleans. You won't know until you try."

"It isn't the place for me. I'm sorry. And the more we . . . " She shrugged. "The harder it'll be when you leave."

It was pretty hard right now. Just her hand on his knee and he was having a difficult time focusing on the road.

The cat batted him in the head—twice. There was something about that cat.

"We don't have to," he began.

"I know. But . . . " She let out a breath. "Even though we shouldn't, don't you want to?"

"Raye, if you take your gaze off the . . . " He frowned at the fields, which appeared recently planted. What could they plant in the fall? Did he care? "Look at me, and you'll see how foolish that question is."

She turned her head. He lowered his eyes, indicating her hand, which had crept upward as she stroked. Her fingertips were centimeters away from his erection.

She stilled; he could swear his penis stretched ever nearer. Seconds later her thumb brushed the tip and he cursed, his palms clenching the wheel.

"Sorry," she said, but she didn't sound sorry, and she didn't move her hand.

The next hour was one of the most excruciating of his life, and he'd had some pretty excruciating hours. He didn't think an erection could last that long without chemical aid. Then again, he'd never had occasion to find out.

Outside Raye's apartment, they gathered the cat's things, as well as the cat, and hurried up the steps.

"Detective!"

Bobby ran through a litany of curses in his head before he turned. "Chief."

Johnson contemplated Bobby's hands, full of litter box

and *Meow Mix,* which he'd lowered so they hid his arousal, before moving on to Raye, who had her hands full of Samhain and kitty toys. "You spend the day getting a pet?"

"Long story. We're kind of in the middle of it."

"I've been waitin' on you."

Bobby's teeth ground together. "Problem?" He hoped with all the hope he had that there hadn't been another murder.

"We need to talk."

"I'll come by the station in a bit."

"Now would be good."

Bobby's penis thought now would be good too, but not for what the chief had in mind.

"We—uh—haven't eaten. I've got a pretty bad headache."

Raye choked. Bobby kept his gaze on Johnson. If he glanced at her, he wasn't sure what he'd say or do.

"All righty. I'll just see you at the station in . . . an hour?"

"Um . . . yeah. We'll be there."

"We?" Raye repeated.

"You can't stay here alone."

"I don't—" she began.

"I'll send a man over." Johnson backed away. "In an hour."

"Okay," Bobby said, but the chief was already headed toward the station.

"You think he bought the headache excuse?" Raye asked.

"Not a chance."

Chapter 19

Though Bobby wanted to throw open the door, toss everything, including the cat, on the couch, then toss Raye on her back on the bed, he couldn't. There was still a murderer on the loose. He made Raye stand just inside the door with Samhain while he checked the apartment.

"It's all good," he said as he came out of the bedroom.

Raye, crouched next to the closed door, straightened and a bell jangled. She must have been picking up a toy she'd dropped. But . . . hadn't he told her to leave the door open? He couldn't remember.

What if there'd been someone here? What if she'd had to run? Every second counted. However, the sight of her, even with an armful of cat toys and cat, made every thought but one disappear.

She must have seen the intent in his eyes because she shook her head. "Let me get her settled."

And though his body howled, so did Samhain, at least until her vittles and water were set down and her restroom facilities established.

"All right," Raye said. "What—"

His mouth came down on hers. For an instant Bobby thought the cat was yowling again, but it was merely need screaming through his blood. He'd spent the last hour with an untamed erection, the soft stroke of Raye's hand on his thigh, the murmur of her voice, the scent of her skin—

He couldn't take it any more. He lifted her into his arms and did what he'd been imagining.

She bounced when he tossed her on the bed. He shut the door, flicked the lock. He knew the cat couldn't open it, but he wasn't taking any chances. Not with this. Not with her.

Raye's face flushed with laughter. Her lips, damp and a little red from his, parted. He licked his own and tasted her. The beast that had been mumbling just below the surface of his blood roared. He pulled his shirt over his head, kicked off his shoes, laid his gun on the bedside table, and shucked his pants. His skin heated beneath her gaze.

"You're so beautiful," she said.

"I'm a guy." He flexed his biceps like Arnold. "I'm manly, not beautiful."

"Can't you be both?"

His arm lowered. "I'll be anything you like."

Something flickered across her face, and his playful mood died. "What's wrong?"

"Nothing."

He didn't believe her, but when she held out her arms he went into them and forgot everything but the desire to surround himself with her.

He should have slowed down; he should have taken his time, but his body kept shouting that there'd been foreplay enough in the car. She seemed to agree because when he began to unbutton her shirt, she shoved away his hands and did it herself, so fast he was afraid she lost a few buttons.

She pressed the front clasp on her bra, and her breasts

sprang free. He reached for them, and his fingers closed on nothing as she sprang off the bed, removed her shoes, then tossed every last stitch away.

He would have enjoyed the view—creamy smooth skin he wanted to lap like a cat, raspberry nipples that begged him to discover if they were as sweet as they looked—but she pressed his shoulders onto the bed and straddled him.

His gasp was a curse when she took him inside. Her mouth captured his. Her hips rocked, back and forth, lift and lower—the speed blinding. He placed his palms on her waist, tried to set a rhythm, but she had her own, and he was helpless to fight it. He could barely think beyond, *yes, now, more.*

"Raye," he managed—a warning, a promise. She arched, taking him even more deeply, and as she tightened around him, her breath caught, her breasts jiggled, enticing him to taste.

Not raspberries. Better. Heat and life. Sweetness and light. Raye.

Together they gasped, moaned, came.

She collapsed on top of him, as boneless as he felt. He wanted to lift his arms and hold her, but he couldn't quite manage it. He buried his face in the curve of her neck and inhaled the scent that both matched and enhanced her taste—sweet and spicy, cool and warm.

She was everything.

He must have dozed because when the bedroom door rattled, he came awake with such a start she slid off his chest, mumbling words he couldn't understand.

He turned his head, hand reaching for the gun on the table, then falling away when he saw the paw that shot through the gap between door and floor, curving upward, yanking on the portal and making it clatter.

"Stop that," he ordered. Samhain only did it again.

He laid his arm over his eyes. As annoying as it was to be woken like that when all he wanted to do was stay here and sleep all tangled up in her, he was due at the police station. He peeked at the clock.

Five minutes ago.

I was in the middle of a lovely dream of a future without maniacs. No knives, witches, or ghosts. Just me and Bobby, maybe a baby or two. A boy with his hair and my eyes, a girl just the opposite.

Foolish dream. I knew that even while I was having it. The ghosts had been with me always. Why would they suddenly go away? And how would I explain them to a husband who didn't believe and to children who wouldn't understand?

Ghosts. There was something about ghosts that needed my attention.

I opened my eyes. Twilight and I was alone. If the pillow hadn't smelled like Bobby I might have thought I'd imagined everything. Then Samhain landed on the mattress, and I knew that I hadn't.

"Is he gone?" I asked.

The cat blinked.

"One for no, two for yes."

Samhain blinked twice.

I stared at her. "That was just a coincidence."

Her freaky blue eyes closed, then opened.

Great. I was halfway to being a cat lady just by talking to her. If she started answering . . .

I got out of bed, padded into the living room naked. When I heard a creek on the landing, I dived into the bedroom, scaring the cat so badly she jumped straight up in the air, hissed, and scooted under the mattress. I nearly followed. Managed not to only by remembering that the chief had promised to send a guard to stand outside my apartment while Bobby was at the station.

I got dressed before I peeked out the window. In New Bergin the choice of officers other than Johnson was limited. I was glad to find Larry Abel leaning against the railing, his gaze on the quiet town. The last time I'd seen Brad I'd duped him. I'd prefer not to see him again for a very long time. Knowing Brad, he would pout.

I poured a glass of wine. The bottle was almost gone. If I wasn't careful I'd have to buy more sooner than usual—something a kindergarten teacher shouldn't do in a town like this. Everyone would notice. They would talk. I should be more worried about that than I was.

"Henry?" I said, not too loudly. I didn't want Larry to hear, think there was someone inside and burst through the door.

Henry didn't materialize. Had he ever when I called? Then I remembered the rosemary I'd scattered over the threshold upon our return and hurried to the door.

But the line of the herb had been disturbed when Bobby left. I found only a few leaves in place, the rest scattered by his feet and the wind.

"Henry!" I said again—more urgently but no louder. I received the same results.

I needed to speak with him before Bobby returned. Perhaps Anne's *Book of Shadows* would light the way.

The volume was still in my pants, one of the reasons

I'd tossed off my own clothes rather than letting Bobby do it. The second reason being my impatience to have him inside me.

My cheeks heated. I'd never wanted a man that badly, never felt for anyone what I felt with him. I'd wanted to whisper in his ear, against his skin and mouth, things I'd never thought, heard, dreamed of in my life. I'd managed not to by making the encounter all about speed, about need. Only in that way could I keep my thoughts and feelings to myself. Now was not the time to fall in love, and Bobby Doucet was not the man to fall in love with. He was as haunted as I was.

I pushed aside such thoughts. I had things to do and very little time to do them in.

I found my pants, removed the book. The handwriting throughout matched that on the first page, which claimed the book as Anne's. The same writing that had then made the book mine. Those words were still there. Had I thought they wouldn't be?

Only if I'd imagined them, and I knew better.

"All right," I said. "I don't suppose you have a spell for calling reluctant spirits."

The pages fluttered in an invisible breeze. I lifted my hands as if they burned. They kind of did. The pages stopped fluttering, several stood on end. It was almost as if the book itself were thinking, searching, maybe listening. Then they slowly fell away, yawning open near the end of the pages that held writing. Many more remained in the volume that didn't.

I took a healthy gulp of cabernet, set the glass down, swallowed. The page twitched as if saying, *Look at me!*

So I did.

* * *

Bobby walked into the police station only ten minutes late. An officer named Larry had stood on the landing outside Raye's apartment. Bobby was glad it wasn't Pretty Boy Brad. He wouldn't have been able to refrain from ripping into him about the previous day's fuckup and then he would have been even later.

Chief Johnson and Dr. Christiansen sat alone in the single office, a half-empty bottle of Jameson on the desk, coffee cups that didn't hold coffee between their hands. Bobby found a cup, filled it, took a sip, then a seat.

"Where you been?" Johnson asked.

"Madison."

The man's brows shot up. Before he could ask why, Bobby told him.

The two older men lifted their cups and together they drank. The clicks when they set them back down were indistinguishable from each other.

"Some of the kids called Mrs. Noita a witch," Johnson said. "I never considered she was one."

"You believe that?" Bobby asked.

"Doesn't matter if I do, only matters if the killer does."

"Do you know if Noita was her real name?"

"Why wouldn't it be?"

"*Noita* means witch in Finnish."

"Huh," both Johnson and Christiansen said at the same time.

Bobby wasn't sure her name even mattered any more. "You know anything about a coven near here?"

"A coven," Johnson repeated, then shoved his hands through what was left of his hair. "I can't believe I'm having this conversation."

That was more like it. Sure, there were people who

practiced Wicca. That was probably less weird than some of the things others practiced. But covens and witches and spells—oh my—those Bobby had a hard time getting his mind around. And he was glad Johnson felt the same. He was tried of being the only skeptic.

"What about that call you had last month?" Christiansen asked.

"You're gonna have to be more specific, Doc."

"Full moon, bonfire in the woods. Naked people fleeing when the cops showed up."

Bobby lifted his eyebrows. "Seems like that might have been something you would have shared."

The chief snorted. "Stuff like that happens all the time."

"How often?"

"'Bout once a month." Johnson frowned. "It's just kids. Drinkin' beer, makin' out."

"Is it always around the full moon?"

Johnson thought a minute then muttered, "Hell." His gaze flicked to Bobby's. "Any of your vics involved in witchcraft?"

Bobby shook his head. That he'd remember. Then again, in New Orleans something like that might not even be worth mentioning. He pulled out his phone. "I'm gonna call Franklin."

He'd asked the FBI agent to check on other brandings and burnings. He hadn't heard back, which made Bobby think maybe there weren't any except . . .

He wasn't that lucky.

The man answered on the third ring. Bobby identified himself.

"I've been meaning to call," Franklin said. "It's been a little nuts here."

Despite the agent's words, wherever he was didn't sound busy. Bobby couldn't hear anything from the other end at all—no doors slamming, no phones ringing, no FBI agents murmuring. If he were in the field, wouldn't there be sounds of traffic, music, dishes rattling in a restaurant? Now that Bobby thought about it, he'd never heard anything on the other end of the phone but Franklin. However, the man's next words made him forget his suspicions. Whatever they were.

"There have been other bodies burned in other locations."

"How many?"

The agent paused a beat. "Dozens."

"Dozens?" Bobby repeated, and the chief and the doc sat up straighter, both reaching for, then finishing their whiskey.

"So far," Franklin allowed.

"And you didn't connect them?"

"Burned bodies? No. They were in different places, different methods of death, different means of burning."

"What about the brand?"

"Once I started asking, the brand turned up. Some thought it was a tattoo. Or some new fad. I've seen similar marks on a lot of professional athletes lately. Not the wolf brand, but brands. I don't get why kids would mark themselves that way, which my wife says makes me old."

The guy must be beyond tired to ramble like that. Bobby could relate.

"Anyway, the brand was in the reports—at least for those bodies where there was enough left of a body to find one."

"Did you get anything off Wellsprung's ring?" Bobby asked.

"No."

Figured.

"Was he obsessed with witches?"

Silence loomed. "How'd you know that?"

"Wild guess. What about the victims? Any of them practice Wicca, belong to a coven?"

Papers rustled. Franklin cursed, and Bobby knew.

The *Venatores Mali* had been busy.

" 'The Raising of Spirits-Both Good and Evil,' " I read. "Why would anyone want to raise an evil spirit?"

Samhain, who had just crept out from beneath the bed and into the living room, made a gurgling-purring sound and scooted back where she'd been.

One spell required the breath of a witch, the other the blood of one. I'll let you guess which was which. Witch.

"Black candles. Sage." I moved into the kitchen holding the book, opened the corner cabinet. Bizarrely, I had both.

I had gone shopping with Jenn on State Street, right after Halloween last year. I'd bought a deeply discounted bag of votive candles in black and orange. I snatched up the bag, started extracting the black. "Is four enough for a circle?"

Samhain yowled once from the bedroom.

"Five?"

She yowled twice, and I pulled another candle free.

The spell called for a sage stick, but I only had flakes in a jar, which I pulled from my spice rack. It would have to do.

I used chalk to draw a pentagram on the table. I erased and redid it twice before I got the thing right. My hands were a little unsteady. Then I set the candles at each of the five points, which formed a circle.

After dropping the sage into a glass bowl, I went over the spell one more time, then lit everything and chanted the words written there. As instructed, I allowed my breath to cast over the flames so that they flickered but didn't go out.

"I call the spirit Henry. Come in peace or not at all. As I will so mote it be."

My gaze flitted around the room. Nothing. The book said this was a spell to call good spirits, burning the sage would ensure no evil ones slipped through. But what if I really needed a sage stick instead of just sage? Would that difference keep Henry from coming? Would it allow evil to arrive instead? What if Henry was evil?

Was there a spell to determine evil?

I closed my eyes and recited the spell again. Chanting *did* indicate more than once. Probably more than twice. I continued to say the words, the scent of the sage and the candles, the sound of my own voice, the lethargy left by the long day, several long nights, and—I admit it—the great sex made me trancelike. For an instant, I saw Henry—I saw Pru—in another town, with another woman who looked a lot like me, except for her hair, which was as red as flame.

"Henry," I said, and he glanced over his shoulder, right into my eyes. His mouth formed my name, then, *No!* and then . . .

He flickered.

Pru howled so loudly the sound trilled along my skin like an ill wind. Outside my door, Larry cursed. Had he heard it too? That was impossible. However, so many things I'd once thought impossible no longer were.

The air stirred. My eyes opened. I held my breath.

And the candles went out.

Chapter 20

"Raye?" Larry knocked on the door. "You okay in there?"

"Fine." I kept my gaze on the man-shaped shadow in the corner. "Thanks."

"You hear that wolf?"

Henry stepped forward, and I held up my hand. "You'd better check that out, Larry."

"I'm not as dumb as Brad. Your new boyfriend would kick my ass if I moved an inch away from this door."

Henry's eyebrows shot toward his eternally black hair.

"All right. I'm headed to bed."

"It's seven-thirty."

"Good night." I went into my room. I didn't bother to wait for Henry before I shut the door. He walked right through.

"Why did you summon me like that?" he demanded.

"That's the way the book told me to."

"I didn't mean—" He frowned. "What book?"

I held up Anne's *Book of Shadows*, and his frown deepened. "Where did you get that?"

"Does it matter?"

"Yes."

I sighed and told him.

"All right," he said. "That could be helpful."

"It brought you here so I'd say it was very helpful."

"You can't just summon me like that, Raye."

"Apparently, I can."

"You shouldn't. I didn't come when you called because I was in the middle of something very important. I need to—" He flickered.

"Don't you dare!"

My voice was too loud. I listened for the sound of Larry crashing through the door, but silence reigned.

"I'll just call you back," I warned.

He let out a breath. "It's too late now anyway. I'm sure your . . . " His lips tightened. "I'm sure Pru was able to handle things."

"Who was that woman who looked like me?"

"You saw her?" he asked, and I nodded. "It's a long story."

"Then you'd better get started. You can begin with what happened to your daughters."

"How do you know about them?"

"Three people can't disappear into thin air without someone talking about it. Even though McHugh's followers were terrified of him, some of them still wrote things down." I lifted the *Book of Shadows*. "Books last longer than memories."

He hung his head. "Your mother wanted to tell you."

My heart took a hard, fast leap. "You know who she is?"

He coughed and, from beneath the bed, Samhain growled. "Since when do you have a cat?"

"She came with the book," I said absently. "Is my mother alive?"

"Yes."

"Where is she?"

His gaze met mine. "With your sister."

"I have a sister?"

"Mo leanabh." That dark gaze gentled. "You have two."

Bobby ended his call with Agent Franklin. "He's on his way."

Johnson grunted. Though he might have called the feds for help, no local really wanted them in their town, even when they needed them. Christiansen poured the chief another drink.

"He's bringing some sort of witch expert," Bobby said.

A few seconds with his computer, clicking away while Bobby waited on the line, and Franklin had connected the burnings and brandings, and the *Venatores Mali.* He'd also used whatever resources he had, wherever he was, to check the backgrounds of Bobby's victims. Several of them were involved in the occult—voodoo, hoodoo. Who knew? In truth, he wasn't surprised.

"It might take them a few days to get here," he continued. The witch expert was in high demand.

"What is a witch expert, and why do we need one?" Johnson asked.

"The *Venatores Mali* were witch hunters. They branded victims with their symbol—the snarling wolf. They also burned them. Mrs. Noita and her niece were witches who were branded and burned."

The chief rubbed his forehead. "Is everyone crazy?"

Bobby figured that was rhetorical.

"Is there anyone in town who doesn't belong?" he asked.

"You," the chief answered.

"Thanks."

"Sorry." Johnson appeared contrite. "People drive through on their way north. They stop and gas up. None of them belong."

"Whoever killed Mrs. Noita broke into Larsen's house and killed Raye's pillow. Wouldn't crazy like that stand out?"

"You'd be surprised," Christiansen murmured.

"Probably not. I stayed at Raye's dad's because there wasn't a hotel."

"What's your point?" The chief drained his coffee cup.

"This killer, and the maniac too, were in town more than a day. Where did they stay?"

Johnson spread his hands and shrugged. So did Christiansen.

"There's one question that's been keeping me up at night," Johnson said.

"Only one?" Bobby asked. Lucky man.

"Why are they trying to kill Raye?"

"A less likely witch was never born," Christiansen agreed.

Bobby frowned. Both men sat up and asked, "What?"

"She's adopted."

"Point?" the chief repeated.

This time the doctor answered. "We don't know *what* she was born."

"Two?" I asked.

I understood the implication, but I didn't want to believe it. I couldn't believe it. Because the implication was insane.

"The young woman you saw is named Becca. She's a veterinarian in Three Harbors."

"That's about a hundred and fifty miles from here."

"Miles don't matter to me."

"Do miles matter to Pru?"

"Are you asking if she's a supernatural wolf?"

Was I? Why not? I nodded.

"She can share her thoughts with those who have the ability to hear them. Does that mean she's supernatural or that they are?"

"You're making my head hurt," I said.

"Wolves can run up to forty miles an hour. They can cover one hundred and twenty-five miles in a day, though forty is average. They've been known to follow their prey at a run for five or six miles and then accelerate."

"What are you trying to say?"

"Wolves that are merely wolves can travel much faster than humans."

"You still haven't answered the question."

"It will take her longer to get here than it took me, but less time than it would take you."

I gave up. "How do you know so much about them?"

"Even before my wife became one, her affinity for animals was so powerful that wolves flocked to her. They adored her, worshipped her. They would follow her anywhere, do anything for her."

And the weird continued.

"The triplets in the legend," I began, then chickened out. "They were witches too?"

His gaze held mine. "They are."

Again, one and one was adding up to two. Despite my occupation, I was starting to hate when that happened.

"What does *mo leanabh* mean?"

He gave me that look again—the one that made me

feel as though he'd put his arm around me. The one that made me want him to.

"My child," he answered.

I let out a breath, drew in another, did it again. There were so many things I wanted to ask, and then again I didn't.

"You left me on the side of the road." I was still upset about that.

"I left you nowhere, *mo leanabh,* I sent you through time. I wish I could have landed you in a feather bed, but some things are beyond our control."

My throat ached from suppressing inappropriate laughter. This was ridiculous. And yet . . . I believed him.

"How did you send me?"

"Blood magic."

"The pyre," I said. "You wanted McHugh to kill you."

"I never wanted that. But to save my family I gladly gave my mortality."

"If you were powerful enough to send three children through time, why weren't you powerful enough to save yourself?"

"I did."

I waved my hand right through him. He shimmered, broke apart, faded. "You don't seem saved to me."

Henry returned, scowling. "Was that necessary?"

My fingers tingled with cold. I shook them and shrugged.

"I'm still here," he said. "So is Pru; so are you and your sisters. McHugh is not. I win."

"You're dead, Henry."

"Not really."

His definition of dead and mine weren't the same.

"I'm immortal now. As a witch, I wasn't."

I suppose that was true or he wouldn't be a ghost.

"Witches have powers that protect—others as well as ourselves. Some of us, like your mother, can heal. There is a reason most images of witches depict ancient crones. With healing powers, witches live longer than most. It caused suspicion."

"I bet." I imagined a woman in seventeenth-century Scotland talking to animals. That would have gotten her burned, even without the supernatural ability to heal.

"Why didn't Pru heal herself and you?"

"Blood magic requires sacrifice."

Henry and Pru had given up everything for me. I wasn't sure what to say, what to do. For so long I'd despised my unknown parents for what I thought they had done. But none of what I'd believed was true, and it would take me longer than an instant to get my mind around it.

"I would do anything to protect you," Henry continued.

"You did."

His lips curved, and I wished I could touch him.

"I should say thank you, but that sounds so . . . lame."

"Lame?" He lowered his gaze to my leg. "You seem to walk quite well."

Not only was it going to take a while to get used to the fact that I had parents, sisters, a family—as well as the bizarre nature of that family—but it was going to take some time to learn to communicate with the ones who'd come here from the seventeenth century, even without factoring in that one wasn't human at all and the other wasn't any more.

"I meant *thank you* is inadequate."

"You're my child. You always will be. I will protect you no matter the cost."

Something in my chest shifted, warmth spread, my eyes burned, and I swiped at them. I could hear the love in his voice, see it in his eyes. Love like that was what I'd always dreamed of.

"Your mother and I cast a spell to send our girls to a place where witches would be safe," he said.

"Whoops."

"You were safe. The persecution of witches is no longer."

"Tell it to Mrs. Noita and her niece."

"The *Venatores Mali* have been reborn."

"Like you."

Henry tilted his head, considering. "The spell was cast to save our children. Blood and death fueled its power. But we never asked for this." He swept his hand down his black-clad form. "It merely happened."

"No place is safe forever," I said. "No one can predict what people will do. How things might change. Maybe you became a safeguard, a watchdog. Without you in my life to warn me of danger, I'd be dead now. I'm still safe."

"But for how long?"

That I didn't know. And there were others to worry about besides myself.

"Have they found Becca?"

"Not yet."

Relief flooded me for the safety of someone I didn't know. If there was such a thing as twin telepathy, what did triplets have? Something stronger? If so, why hadn't I ever felt either one of them? Unless that emptiness inside of me had been born of their lack. Would that change once I met them? I wanted, desperately, to find out.

"Where's the third?"

A shadow passed over his face. "We don't know."

"How can that be?"

"You and I have an affinity for ghosts, hence my attachment to you. Becca has an affinity for animals."

"Which brought Pru to her. What other powers do the two of you have?"

"Pru can talk to animals and heal. I can talk to ghosts, affect the weather, and—" He flicked his hand and Samhain skidded out from beneath the bed. She hissed at him and scurried back.

"If you can toss things, why didn't you toss McHugh?" Into a tree.

"He brought minions—a lot of them. Using our powers takes energy. Your mother was still weak from your births. I needed to have enough strength to send three souls though time. We could fight, or we could save our children."

"Why didn't you run? Hide?"

"Even if we triumphed that day, over those hunters, there would always be more. Once we drew the attention of the *Venatores Mali,* we were marked for as long as we lived. It wasn't as if we could move quickly or easily with three infants. We definitely couldn't move silently and avoid notice for long."

"So you stood your ground, and you died for us."

"I didn't mind."

I felt the urge to thank him again, but words would never be enough. I considered his seemingly solid form and thought of how my fingers had ached with cold after swiping right through him.

Hugs weren't going to work either.

"Protecting you and your sisters was my purpose in life. It is also my purpose in death. I loved all of you from the moment I saw you. I love you still. I will *always* love you. I will never let anything hurt you if I can stop it."

I swallowed, nodded, lowered my gaze until I was able once more to speak. "I want to love you, but I don't know you. You're a stranger." And an odd one at that. "I'm sorry."

"My love isn't based on your loving me back. True love never is."

I didn't know much about love, though I wanted to learn. I hoped I'd have time.

"We have other things to worry about," Henry said.

He was right. It would take me time to come to terms with who he was, who I was. But, in the meantime, I had so many questions.

"I had bruises on my arm where Anne McKenna grabbed me. I never had bruises from a ghost before." I stared at my fingers, wiggled them. They tingled but they weren't black and blue. "What gives?"

"You're sensitive," he said. "I'll assume she was agitated?"

"Getting an arm hacked off can do that to a person."

"Indeed."

"Bobby had bruises too. Why?"

"Same reasons."

Genevieve had been understandably agitated, but—

"He can see ghosts?" That might be the reason he was so snarly about the supernatural.

"No. But he feels them. He refuses to acknowledge anything that hints at the mystical, but he has magic in his blood."

I wasn't sure what to do with that. Right now I had more important questions.

"Someone suggested that the *Venatores Mali* might be trying to raise McHugh." From the expression on Henry's face, he'd already gotten there before me. "Is that possible?"

"It isn't easy, but it's possible."

"How?"

"Raising the dead is dark magic. I'm not familiar with the particulars."

"You're dead."

"Is there a reason you keep pointing that out?"

"You're here. You've been raised."

"I'm a ghost not the risen dead. There's a difference."

I lifted my eyebrows and waited.

"I'm spirit not form. Here for a purpose and then I'll be gone."

"And the risen dead?"

"Once raised they remain until they are vanquished. They are form and not spirit. Solid without a soul."

"McHugh will come back without a soul?" That sounded worse than his coming back at all.

"He never really had one in the first place," Henry said.

"How do you vanquish a risen spirit?"

"I have no more idea about that than I have about how they're raised."

I let out a breath. "Now what?"

"You're going to have to familiarize yourself with dark magic. Only by understanding it can you thwart it."

A shiver traced my spine. "Isn't that dangerous?"

"Very." His gaze looked beyond me and into the past. The high collar of his coat shifted, revealing the brand of a snarling wolf that matched the one on Anne McKenna's ghost. "But so is McHugh."

Henry made me promise not to summon him again unless it was life or death.

"If you call me, I'll come if I can. If I don't come—"

"You can't. Got it."

Henry began to fade. "Get rid of the sage and the candles, brush away the pentagram. Those are always so difficult to explain."

Not exactly fatherly advice, but good advice just the same, because not long after I dumped the sage, hid the candles, and wiped the table, the door opened. Bobby sniffed a few times, but I gave him a hug before he could ask any questions. He seemed like he needed one.

He kept his arms around me, and I didn't mind. I laid my head on his chest and listened to the steady beat of his heart.

"Did I wake you when I left?" he asked.

"No. I just . . . woke."

He kissed the top of my head and released me, which was good because if I'd still been pressed against him he would have felt the jolt his next words caused. "The officer said you'd been talking to yourself."

"That's only a problem if I answer."

"Ba-dump-bump," he said, making a motion like a drummer in a vaudeville act. Then he tilted his head and waited for me to go on.

This was the problem with cops. They couldn't be distracted by hokey humor like any garden-variety kindergartner.

"Maybe I was on the phone."

"Were you?"

I discovered I could only lie so much. Especially when all he had to do was glance at my cell phone, or use his powers of cop-hood to check my landline, and discover the truth. Though why he would, why he'd care . . .

"No."

He lifted his eyebrows, still waiting.

"I was practicing my lesson for tomorrow."

And the lies returned with ease. Though I *should* have been practicing, or at least preparing, rather than messing with magic. Maybe I could use what I'd learned so far as a Halloween lesson for my class.

How was that for a horrible, no-good, very bad idea?

"There is no tomorrow."

My gaze cut back to Bobby. I must have looked as panicked as his words had made me feel because he muttered, "Sorry. I meant that you're not going to work."

"We've had this argument. I am."

"We didn't finish it. You're not."

He seemed more upset about that than he should have been.

"Did you hear something at the police station?"

He glanced toward the door. "Not really."

"Liar." I ignored the voice in my head that taunted: *Takes one to know one*!

I did spend most of my time with five-year-olds.

He let out a long breath. "There've been other deaths, in other places. All of the victims were associated with witchcraft in some way."

"We suspected that."

He inclined his head. "The maniac was obsessed with witches. Had altercations with several. There was a restraining order against him from one."

"Probably the reason he came here. No one knew him well enough to hide."

"How did he know you?"

"I . . . what?"

"He killed a witch, then he tried to kill you. Twice."

"I was there. I remember."

"Why you?" I spread my hands and he continued. "*Witches* are dying. Why you?"

"Not dead."

"Not for their lack of trying."

"I'm not sure what to tell you."

Actually, I just didn't want to tell him. I hadn't gotten my own mind around my heritage, how was I going to get his around it? Especially since he'd made his opinion on the subject quite clear. Those who said they had supernatural abilities were liars, cheats, and charlatans.

"They could have made a mistake," I continued.

"Or they know something about your parents that you don't."

He was right. Again, I couldn't tell him. Unless I figured out how to explain that my real parents were a four-hundred-year-old witch and his wolf-wife.

"Unfortunately, no one's owned up to dumping me on the side of the road in the last twenty-seven years; I doubt they're going to come forward now. Especially if they're a witch and witches are dying."

He made a sound of aggravation. "This is so nuts."

"I know."

"Thank you." He collapsed on the couch. "I'm glad someone can see reason."

"Meaning?"

"Witches. Psychics. Auras. Supernatural powers. Magic. Ghosts. It's all bullshit."

If I'd had any question about his views—and I didn't—they'd have been thoroughly answered now.

I joined him on the couch and took his hand. "You seem pretty adamant."

"Shouldn't I be?"

"Usually there's a reason behind such strong opinions."

"Sanity?"

"Sanity's more of an excuse than a reason."

He gave a short sharp laugh. "I've never heard sanity used as an excuse. Crazy is another story. Not guilty by reason of nutso."

"That's the legal term?"

"Should be."

I tightened my fingers. "In my experience those who have the deepest feelings against something are the ones who have the greatest fear of it. And that comes from some experience with it."

He pulled away. "I don't know what you mean."

My eyes met those of Genevieve as she materialized in the corner. A tear slid down her cheek.

"Don't you?" I asked.

Chapter 21

Bobby's stomach churned. He was so cold, he wanted to take Raye into his arms and hold her until the ache went away.

Except the ache never went away. Not since Genevieve had.

He couldn't talk about her. He just couldn't. So why did he want to?

"You can tell me."

Sometimes he felt as if Raye could read his mind. Which was as crazy as all the rest of it.

"Tell you what?"

"Why the idea of psychics and ghosts makes you so angry."

"When people die, Raye, they don't come back."

No matter how much we might want them to.

"They don't come back, no, but some of them might hang around."

"And go bump in the night?"

"Has anything gone bump in your night?"

"Just you."

"That's not what I meant."

"What do you mean?"

Her eyes flicked to his, then to the far corner of the room. Though her lips curved a little, she seemed sad. "You're haunted, Bobby."

The chill that had been pressing on his chest jolted through his blood. "What?"

Her gaze returned to his. "You've lost someone."

"Everyone's lost someone."

"Not like you have. It hurts." She set her hand on his cold, cold heart. "Here."

He couldn't help it. He tangled their fingers together. Hers were so warm and alive. "You're psychic now?" He put all the scorn he felt for the "profession" into the word.

"I'm not." Silence fell between them. She drew their joined hands to rest on his knee. "Tell me," she said, and though he'd sworn never to speak of it again, he did.

"Everything started with Audrey."

A crease appeared between Raye's eyebrows.

"We weren't married," he said quickly, and the crease deepened. "You asked if I was married, if I'd ever been married. I wasn't. We weren't."

"Okay."

"I arrested her."

"For?"

"What I arrested her for in the first place isn't the issue. The issue is what I should have arrested her for later and didn't. Then she died. End of story."

"That isn't the end of her story."

"It was for me."

Raye's lips tightened, released. "How did she die?"

"Overdose."

"Accidental?"

He shook his head, swallowed.

"All right," Raye said slowly. "You feel guilty that you didn't know what she was doing? You didn't stop her? You weren't there? What is it?"

"I wasn't there *because* I knew. I couldn't stop her from using. I did try."

Raye peered into his face. "There's more."

Bobby tried to pull away, but this time she wouldn't let him. "I . . . " he began, meaning to tell her that he hadn't just left Audrey, but also— "I can't. I—" To his horror, his voice broke. He had to swallow or choke, and then he had to keep swallowing or sob.

"It's all right," she said.

"It isn't," he managed, his voice both dry and damp—hoarse and brimming with tears.

"I know."

She pressed a kiss to his temple, lifted her palms, and cupped his face. He stared into her eyes, and that cold weight on his chest shifted. It didn't go away, but it lightened. He didn't understand why. He hadn't shared his burden, but still she seemed to understand.

He couldn't help himself. He kissed her.

And then he couldn't stop.

I should have pulled away, backed away, run away. I'd been so close to getting Bobby to tell me everything. If he stopped now, would he ever share? And if he didn't admit everything, everyone, that haunted him, how could I admit everything and everyone that haunted me? How could we have a future if we didn't?

We couldn't and we wouldn't, which meant I should stop this. But at the first brush of his mouth I was lost. I wrapped my fingers in his shirt and held on.

I tasted tears, though he'd shed none. Perhaps if he had, he wouldn't taste of desperation too. He needed me, needed this, needed us. Whether to forget or to avoid, I didn't know. Right now that distinction didn't matter.

Later, I promised myself. *Later.*

He licked my lips, lifted his own. I opened my eyes to his frown. My fingers tightened. "Don't."

I wasn't sure what I was protesting, then he lifted a hand, traced my cheek, turned his finger upward and I understood the taste of tears had been my own.

"Why?" he asked.

I shook my head. How could I tell him his daughter followed his footsteps every day, sat next to him in the night, worshipped him, ached for him, and would not leave until he let her go?

"Raye," he whispered, and the sound of my name in his broken voice only caused more tears to flow. He kissed them away as if I were a child, making me think he'd done the same before.

Though it wasn't the same; it couldn't be.

"He's always so sad."

I jerked at Genevieve's voice, closer than she'd been before.

"Hush." Bobby pressed his lips to my hair.

I rested my cheek on his chest and met Genevieve's gaze. She was still crying. Poor kid.

"Tell him it wasn't his fault. Mommy fell asleep and I ate her candy."

I shuddered in sudden understanding, and his arms tightened. "Are you cold?"

I was so cold I'd probably never get warm, but I shook my head.

"He likes you," Genevieve continued. "He's never liked anyone before the way he likes you. Can't you make him happy?"

I could, but not while she was watching.

As if in answer to the thought, maybe it was, Henry appeared. He held out his hand. "Come along, child."

She went with him as if she knew him; she definitely trusted him. Her tiny, pale fingers tangled with his much larger ones. For an instant I mourned the thousand and one times I'd never been able to hold his hand like that, as well as the thousand and one times I never would. I'd never be able to hold my mother's hand either. She no longer had one.

Together they walked through the eastern wall of my home. I remained where I was, enjoying the steady beat of Bobby's heart beneath my ear. He ran his palm over my hair. My eyelids grew heavy, and I straightened.

"What's wrong?" He tried to tug me back.

"I'm supposed to be soothing you."

His head tilted. "Who said?"

I nearly blurted, *Genevieve*. I was more tired than I'd thought.

"You're upset," I began.

"I wasn't crying."

"Sure you were."

In places no one could see, which was the very worst kind.

"Let's go to bed," he said.

He undressed me like an overtired toddler, and I did the same for him. We crawled beneath the covers, and I laid my head on his shoulder, pressing my hip, my leg, my foot against his.

"I don't want you to go to work tomorrow."

"I have to. It's a small town. There aren't very many subs." And the ones there were didn't sign on for a return engagement to my room. Freaky things happened in Miss Larsen's kindergarten class all the time, but when there was a substitute, they happened worse. For some reason, Stafford took my absence as a personal affront.

"Everyone deserves a day off."

"I just had two." Though they hadn't been very restful.

"Raye."

I kissed him. It was the best way to stop an argument. With Bobby, sometimes it was the only way.

I worshipped his mouth—kissing, nipping, suckling, licking. I hadn't made out like this in . . . ever. Because I'd never done so naked, in my own bed, with a man who knew what he was doing.

He took possession of the embrace, slowing me down, revving me up. By the time he touched my breasts, I was so aroused just by the play of our mouths, the brush of his toe along my instep, the tickle of the hair on his legs against mine, I cried out and arched into his hand. One tweak of my nipple between his thumb and forefinger and I came, gasping.

He slid into me while I shuddered. His mouth played over my eyelids, my cheeks as he thrust—over and over—deeper, harder, and somehow my orgasm continued, or perhaps the first just ran into the second. Who knew? Who cared?

I opened my eyes as his breath caught, our gazes met, and he shuddered too. Eventually he lowered his forehead to mine.

"I can't lose you."

"You won't."

"That's right." He rolled to the side, stared at the ceiling. "Because I'm not going to let you out of my sight."

* * *

"Are you a grown-up?" Genevieve asked.

She and Henry stood outside Raye's apartment. Sunday night in New Bergin and they were the only souls on the street.

"I'm a ghost," Henry said. He wasn't sure if that made him a grown-up or not.

The child studied him, lower lip caught between her tiny, slightly crooked teeth. "I don't think he meant you."

"Who?"

"Stafford."

That beastly ghost child who had been tormenting his daughter for years. Henry had tried to get rid of the fiend, but Stafford wasn't a fool. He knew if he told Henry why he was still here, Henry would make certain he soon wasn't. The child had avoided him of late, and Henry had been too overburdened with the *Venatores Mali* to notice. Or perhaps he'd just been so glad not to see the imp he hadn't wanted to.

"What did he say?" Henry asked. If the urchin had upset her he would—

"He told me something that no grown-up is supposed to know." She worried her teeth harder. If she'd had blood, she might have bloodied them. "But I think someone should." Her eyes filled with tears again. "It's bad."

Henry sighed. When wasn't it?

Morning came and with it the usual rush, made even more so because I wasn't used to sharing my space. Everywhere I turned, there Bobby was. At the sink, in the shower, on my way to the coffeepot. But we managed.

Bobby insisted on driving me to school rather than walking, which helped me to be more on time than when I had to wait for—

"Jenn!" I shouted as we rolled down Main Street.

"Where?" He glanced around, frowning when he saw no sign of her.

"I'm sure she's still putting on her ankle breakers or searching for her most expensive, inappropriately tight shirt."

His frown deepened. "She works at an elementary school."

"Preaching to the choir." I pointed in the direction of her cottage. "Pull over and I'll—" I had my finger poised above her number on my cell when the front door opened, and Brad Hunstadt stepped out.

"Oh, that's not good." It got worse when Jenn followed, and they proceeded to play tonsil hockey on the front porch. I winced. "No one wants to see that."

"I think you're wrong." Bobby indicated several passersby that had stopped to watch.

"They'll be married by sundown."

"Really?"

"If they aren't she may as well buy her scarlet letter today."

"She's a big girl." He eyed Jenn once more. "Figuratively speaking."

"He spent the night. She's toast."

"I spent the night."

My eyes met his, and my heart skittered. Hell.

I was toast too.

Chapter 22

When had he fallen in love with her?

First kiss? First touch? More likely first sight.

Since Bobby had driven into town and almost driven over her, he'd been tumbling head over heels in this direction.

What was he going to do about it? He couldn't stay here forever. Or could he?

She muttered something that sounded like a curse as Jenn followed blond beauty around the corner of the house. Seconds later a boxy blue Ford four-door with Brad at the wheel and Jenn in the passenger seat turned onto First Street.

"She didn't even text," Raye murmured.

"Must be love."

Her cheeks flushed. "Must be."

They were both in big trouble, even without the crazies that were trying to kill her.

Bobby followed Brad's car to the school, pulled into the lot just behind but lost sight of it in the traffic. Seemingly every teacher in the place had arrived at precisely the same time. As they climbed out, Bobby leveled his cop stare at several gawkers.

"What are you doing?" she asked.

"Trying to keep you from earning a scarlet letter."

"That ship has sailed."

He came around the car and took her arm, planning to escort her through the front doors and to her classroom, but she held back. "You don't have to stand right next to me all day."

"I'm protecting you."

"Is that what you call it?" She lowered her voice and wiggled her eyebrows. "Protect me again."

Now he was the one whose cheeks warmed.

"We have top-of-the-line security," she said. "I'll be fine."

"I—" He swallowed and straightened. "So will I."

"Why wouldn't you be?"

That was a conversation he didn't plan on having.

"I—uh—I meant I wouldn't interfere with your day. Do you have a computer in your room? There are things I can work on."

"Uh-huh." Her gaze went to his holster. "You're going to have to lose the gun."

"No, thank you."

"You aren't getting that through the metal detector."

"I'm one of the good guys."

"A metal detector can't tell good from bad. It only knows metal."

"What if the *Venatores Mali* come? They have guns."

"So far, they don't." She held up her hand before he could protest. "They won't get a knife through security either." She set her fingertips on his arm. "Put it away, please. It makes me nervous to have a gun in a kindergarten class." Her lips tightened. "In any class."

"I could be a guest speaker. Cop for a day. The kids will love it. I'll answer questions."

A bead of sweat ran down his cheek. He felt a little ill. The idea of going inside was bad enough. But talking to them, listening to them, learning their names, seeing their faces—

"What's wrong?"

He swallowed or tried to. His throat was so tight he coughed instead. Her expression told him that this was a fight he wasn't going to win. In truth, he was afraid he'd be so distracted by the kids, he might not keep as sharp an eye as he needed to on his weapon.

Bobby withdrew his gun, popped the trunk, and stowed it.

"Thank you." She began to reach for his hand, glanced about, thought better of it and led the way inside.

By the time they reached her classroom, Bobby had broken out in a cold sweat all over, and the tightness in his throat had spread to his chest. If he hadn't felt this way before—every time he saw kids the age of his daughter when she died—he'd think he was having a heart attack.

"Miss Larsen!"

Several of the children ran to her, all talking at once. Bobby backed up, bumping into the doorjamb, then sidestepping quickly to avoid the brush of the bodies still flowing into the room.

Raye cast him a concerned glance before she was enveloped. A redheaded boy grabbed her hand; a girl with huge, brown eyes wrapped her fingers in Raye's belt loop. One chattered about what his dog had done; the other shared how she had finally learned to ride her bike without the little wheels. Raye miraculously carried on a conversation with both of them.

He could tell by the way they touched her that they adored her. Her smile blossomed as she spoke to them. She looked so right, standing there in the sun with all the little children around her, that Bobby's chest hurt even worse at a sudden realization.

They could never have a future together.

A woman like Raye, with a gift like that, should have a passel of kids. Not only did she deserve them, but the as-yet-to-be-born children deserved her. What they didn't deserve, what she didn't, was to be saddled with a man who'd squandered the gift of his own child and was so weakened by the sight of any others that he could barely function.

Right now the joyous sound of their voices, the scent of peanut butter and juice, the whirl of their little bodies made Bobby want to run as fast and as far away as he could. Instead he remained pressed against the wall just inside the door until one little girl saw him and stopped.

Her face lit up. "Hi!"

Bobby's mouth opened, but nothing came out. The kid didn't mind.

"Whose daddy are you?" she asked.

He ran like the coward he was.

In the hall the cacophony became louder and his ears rang. Several kids bumped into him as he made his way toward the nearest exit and burst outside. He had the sense to check the door, make sure it locked behind him. Then he walked around the entire school and did the same with every single door that he found. He had to say the security was excellent, which made him feel better about wandering to the empty playground and taking a seat on a bench that faced the school.

Bobby was breathing faster than if he'd sprinted five miles. He tried to calm himself, but he didn't have much luck. He could still see the tops of little heads through the windows. He wanted to close his eyes, turn away, but he had promised to keep Raye safe.

He already had the death of one person he loved on his conscience; he didn't need two. So he forced his gaze forward, even though his stomach continued to roil and his eyes began to ache. He should probably blink a few times—maybe throw up.

He did the first, managed to avoid the second. The wind kicked up and tumbled leaves over his shoes. Strangely it smelled like rain despite the lack of a single cloud in the sky. He sniffed again, and his skin prickled.

Who was making cinnamon toast?

For an instant the world shimmered behind a veil of tears. Then, oddly, the chill that had washed over him fled. He could still smell rain and cinnamon and sunshine, but his stomach settled, his breathing evened out, and as his gaze touched Raye, who stood at the window of her class, an odd sense of peace came over him.

As always, after a weekend apart, the children surrounded me and began to share what they had done. I listened, commented, let them ramble until I heard Carrie's voice.

Whose daddy are you?

By the time I turned, Bobby was gone.

I went back to what I'd been doing. I didn't have much choice. I knew better than to leave the kids alone. Even without Stafford—though where he was this morning, I had no idea—there'd be trouble if I went in search of Bobby.

I should have known he wouldn't go far. Something might be wrong—and I had a pretty good idea what—but nothing could be wrong enough for him to break his promise to keep me safe. Within minutes I saw him sitting alone on the playground. He appeared so wan and sad I wanted to ply him with ginger ale and kisses.

Then he lifted his head. The breeze stirred his hair, and Genevieve appeared on the bench at his side. He drew in a deep breath; his forehead crinkled. For an instant I thought he might cry. Then she leaned her head on his shoulder; his breath rushed out and some of his color returned.

He might say he didn't believe in ghosts, but he felt them. Or at least he felt her.

"You're going to have to tell him."

Both my own and Henry's reflection appeared in the glass.

Out of the corner of my eye, I checked on the kids. Everyone was doing as I'd asked—writing and/or drawing the story of their weekend to share with one another. I had a few minutes, maybe less.

"Tell him what?" There was so much Bobby didn't know.

"Her presence has soothed him, and he doesn't know she's there. If he did, it might help."

"Him or her?"

"Both. Maybe if he knew she was all right, he'd be all right too."

"Then she could move on."

Henry's black-clad shoulder lifted and lowered. "She doesn't belong here."

"Neither do you."

"We aren't talking about me."

"We will."

"You aren't gonna take her away from me."

Stafford stood on my other side. From his expression

he'd heard the whole exchange—or at least enough of it to worry.

I jabbed my finger in his direction. "You will not pull the fire alarm, young man."

His expression went canny. "You promise not to send Genevieve away?"

I hesitated, but in the end I couldn't lie to the child, though I probably should have. "I can't do that."

Stafford disappeared. I waited for the alarm to shrill. Instead, one of the windows shattered.

The kids started screaming.

Bobby shouted, "Get down, Raye!" and sprinted for the front door.

I'm sure he thought someone was shooting at me. I'd have thought the same thing if the glass hadn't shattered outward—and I didn't know about Stafford.

"Stop that," I said.

The children listened. Stafford did not. A second window went *sploosh*.

"That's it," Henry snapped.

Spink. A third window cracked, tiny tributaries spreading outward from the center, the sound similar to ice during the spring thaw. Pieces fell away like the parts of a puzzle. *Tink, tink, tink*. They bounced onto the blacktop outside.

"Everyone in the coat room," I ordered.

Just because Stafford was sending the glass outward at the moment, didn't mean he couldn't change directions.

"You need to go to the apple tree."

"Not now, Henry." I was busy herding the stragglers.

"I don't care when, though the way he's behaving, it should be now."

"He?"

"The horrid little imp. His bones are buried beneath the apple tree."

People started appearing in the doorway—Mr. Jorgensen, the janitor, the principal, Mrs. Hansen, and Jenn.

"What the hell?" my friend asked as Mrs. Hansen went straight to the children and began to usher them out the door. Mr. Jorgensen stood over the broken glass shaking his head.

I ignored them, my attention on Henry. "You're sure?"

"Genevieve told me what happened to the child." He glanced through the hole where a window should have been and then back. The concern in his eyes made my heart tumble toward my feet. "Perhaps once it is known, he will be on his way."

I nodded, not wanting to continue my conversation with air now that there were more adults in the room than myself.

Bobby burst in. "Why didn't you get down? You could have been shot."

"No one's shooting." I lifted my chin in the direction of the windows. At least Stafford had stopped at three. "Look for yourself. The glass shattered outward."

His scowl deepened. "How?"

"That's your department." And I couldn't exactly explain about the ghost child having a temper tantrum any more now than the two dozen times it had happened before.

I spent the rest of the day trying to calm my now wired class enough to teach them something, as well as ignore Mr. J as he taped cardboard to the window holes.

"Had to order the glass," he said. "Won't be in for a week."

The glance he gave me made me want to apologize.

The man spent more time in my room than almost all the others combined.

Then there was Bobby, who tried very hard to discover why my windows had exploded at all, never mind in which direction.

"Kindergarten classes always seem to have a lot of stuff go bad," Mr. Jorgensen said.

He'd been the janitor at this school since I'd attended kindergarten.

"Though I ain't never seen three windows crack like that without somethin' hittin' 'em first."

Something had hit them—though I wasn't sure if it were Stafford's fists, feet, or the power of his ghostly mind. Did it matter?

Bobby spent a few hours after lunch surfing the office computer. I'd offered him the one in my classroom, but he'd studiously avoided looking at the children, shaken his head, and fled.

I was going to have to tell him about Genevieve. Not telling him certainly wasn't helping.

First I had to deal with Stafford. And to do that, I needed to be alone.

After story time, I texted Jenn: *Is Bobby still at the computer?*

No. He's in with Mrs. Hansen.

Excellent. Mrs. Hansen would talk his ear off for at least a half hour. It was what she did.

Can you come and sit with my class for a few?

Her answer was quick and brief. *No.*

They're asleep.

You told me that last time. Then they woke up.

It hadn't been pretty. I'd have to make sure I was back before that happened again.

Ten minutes, I promised. If I hadn't found Stafford's bones by then they were buried too deeply to be found with a shovel anyway.

Jenn arrived, scowling. She probably would have bitched at me some, but she was afraid to wake "them" up. If I hadn't been the same, and in a big hurry, I would have bitched about her evening with Brad.

I'd been around to pick up the pieces when the two of them had self-destructed the first time. What had she been thinking to allow him into her house, let alone allow him to stay the night? Then again, she'd told me he was ridiculous in bed.

Another reason I zipped my lip and left the room without a word. My ears still burned from her telling me all about it years ago. Jenn had always had a tendency to overshare.

I snuck into Mr. J's office. He was rarely in it, unless he had to retrieve a tool or a cleaning solution. A school of this size kept him hopping. He could probably use part-time help, but I think they'd spent all that money on the metal detector. People had panicked big-time after the last school shooting, and, really, who could blame them?

I snatched a shovel—Mr. J did all the gardening too—and hurried to the apple tree that swayed at the very edge of the property. Lucky for me it was on the gymnasium side of the school. No windows. Not that I couldn't have explained away my behavior as a treasure hunt or some other kindergartenesque project. But I'd rather not.

I contemplated the circle of earth around the tree. Under the apple tree could mean anywhere, and I didn't have the time.

"West side." Henry materialized. He had to duck or

get a branch through his brain. I wondered if that would hurt.

"Here." He pointed to the foot of the tree.

I started to dig. "How do you know that?"

"The property line is . . . " He sliced his hand across the tree.

I didn't bother to ask how he knew where the property line ran. All that mattered was the digging.

"The boy was buried on school grounds, which is why he's attached to the place."

The first few shovelfuls weren't easy to remove. The grass was thick and the ground was dry. But after that, things got easier. If you call tiny pieces of bone tumbling from the earth easier.

"You should probably use your hands now," Henry said. I glanced up. "You don't want to break the skull."

I dropped the shovel.

The idea of using my hands, of touching a skull, made me a bit woozy, but I did it. I had to. I couldn't just leave him there.

My fingertips met something solid, and I yanked them back.

"Go on," Henry urged.

I brushed away the dirt from the slightly rounded protuberance. If I'd just been digging, for whatever reason I might do such a thing, I'd have thought I'd found a rock. In seconds the skull of a child emerged in the bottom of a hollow; bone fragments littered the overturned dirt. I sat on my heels, rubbed a thumb gently over the crack in the skull.

"Oh, Stafford," I whispered.

"Is that a skull?"

Chapter 23

Raye snatched her hand out of the hole. She glanced to the right of the apple tree before lifting her gaze to Bobby's. "Yes."

"Why?"

"Someone died."

"I figured that out for myself." He went onto his knees at her side, careful not to disturb anything. "That's a kid-sized skull."

It also had a kid-sized fracture. He'd seen enough of them to know.

"Why did you dig it up?" he asked.

"Someone had to."

"And it was you because . . . ?"

She didn't answer.

"How did you know to dig here?" He remembered what she'd said as he walked up. "Is that Stafford?"

"Yes."

She seemed pretty certain, which made Bobby nervous. How would she know who it was and where it was unless . . .

His mind shied away from the rest of that sentence. There had to be another explanation.

"Did someone confess to you where he was?"

"Confess?" she repeated.

"The kid has a skull fracture. Whether it was an accident or on purpose, the fact remains that someone buried him where he shouldn't be buried."

"We have to put him to rest." She reached for the bones. He grabbed her hands.

"You shouldn't touch anything more than you have already."

"Right." She set her hands on her knees, but she remained where she was.

"I have to call the chief."

Raye nodded.

"Is there anything you want to tell me before I do?"

She shook her head.

"Raye, he's gonna ask how you knew that kid was buried here."

"I just—"

"You didn't just know. The only person who 'just knew' would be the one who put him there."

Her forehead furrowed. "You think I did?"

He scrubbed his fingers through his hair, tempted to yank it out. "I don't. No." Anyone who'd seen her with children couldn't think that. Then again, he'd been hoodwinked before. "But others will."

"I was going to bury a prize for a treasure hunt, and I found him."

He bit the inside of his lip. "You're going to have to do better than that, Raye." He pulled out his cell, dialed Chief Johnson. "Not only do you have no prize to bury, but it doesn't explain why you think you know who that is."

After informing Johnson of what was going on, Bobby did the same with Mrs. Hansen. She handled the news with fewer hysterics than expected. Or at least fewer hysterics than Jenn had showed when she was told she'd have to stay with Raye's class for the rest of the day.

"It's only an hour until school's out," Mrs. Hansen said.

"But they're *awake*!" The emphasis Jenn put on the final word carried all the horror of an ingénue in a zombie flick.

They're alive!

Raye sat on the bench where he'd put her, staring into the distance. A few times Bobby could have sworn he heard her speaking, but when he glanced in that direction, she was alone.

Johnson arrived shortly thereafter with Christiansen in tow. It wasn't every day they found the bones of a child buried on a playground. Or at least Bobby hoped they didn't. The two stood at the edge of the hole, staring at what lay on the bottom.

"Any missing kids in the area?" Bobby asked.

Johnson didn't even look up. "No."

Bobby eyed the forest. "You've gotta lose a few in there."

"We might lose 'em, but eventually we find 'em again."

"Ever hear the name Stafford?"

The chief's head lifted. "My granddaughter used to talk about Stafford."

"Yet you don't have a missing persons report on him?"

"You think that's Stafford?" Johnson pointed at the skull. "Not possible."

"Why not?"

"Because Stafford is an invisible friend."

Bobby laughed.

The chief didn't. "Who told you about him?"

Bobby didn't answer. Had finding the bones of a child caused Raye's mind to go slightly awry so she'd applied the name of the classroom's imaginary playmate to the skeleton? Sadly, he liked that explanation better than any of the alternatives.

"My niece talked about him too," Christiansen said. "A lot of the kindergarten kids see Stafford." At Bobby's quick glance the doctor shrugged. "I figured it was a harmless delusion. Or maybe . . . " He frowned into the hole again.

"Maybe what?"

"A ghost." Bobby snorted, and the doctor lifted his eyebrows. " 'There are more things in heaven and earth, Horatio.' "

"Huh?"

"Shakespeare. *Hamlet.* Which, considering the skull, is apropos."

"Raye found this?" Johnson asked.

"She was burying something for a treasure hunt."

Johnson grunted. He didn't sound any more convinced than Bobby was.

"She thinks this was Stafford?" The chief pointed at the bones, and Bobby nodded. "Maybe you should call the FBI guy and see if they have any missing Staffords on their list."

"Really?"

"There've been more times than not when Raye knew things she shouldn't. And she was right."

"What's that supposed to mean?" Bobby asked.

"It means you should call the FBI guy," Chief Johnson said, and walked away.

* * *

"Why'd you do that?" Stafford materialized next to me on the bench.

"It's time."

"I'll be good." A tear ran down his cheek. I felt like a wicked witch.

"You can't stay forever."

Although . . . I had found his bones, and the kid was still talking to me. Maybe there was more that needed to be discovered.

"What happened to you, Stafford?"

Bobby was on the phone. Suddenly his gaze met mine, and I folded my lips together lest he see me talking to myself. Again.

"You'll see."

Stafford's voice was faint and, now, so was he. As Bobby kept talking, the little boy sitting next to me disappeared. The breeze ruffled my hair. I swore it whispered good-bye.

Bobby ended his call and strode toward me. Before he could question me again, I questioned him. "Who was he?"

That phone call had revealed the truth or Stafford wouldn't be gone. Unless the kid was screwing with me.

Wouldn't be the first time.

Bobby sat down. "James Stafford junior. J.J. to his friends."

"Where was he from?"

"Chicago."

"What else?"

"The mother thought the father had taken him. But the guy turned up in St. Paul without the boy. They could never prove he'd run off with the kid, let alone that he'd . . . " Bobby waved in the direction of the grave.

"They will now."

"They will," he agreed.

Silence fell between us. I didn't know what to say.

"You didn't just find him by accident," Bobby said.

"No."

"You want to tell me how?"

"No," I repeated. "But I will."

He waited. I couldn't find the words to start.

"Raye . . . " he began.

"I see dead people," I blurted.

That probably wasn't the best way.

"Did you see the father bury him? Did one of the children find a bone?"

"You're not listening to me. Stafford's been a thorn in my side since the day I started teaching."

"Stafford's dead."

"But not gone. He broke the windows today."

"You expect me to believe the child in that hole, who's been dead for five years, who's in pieces in a grave, broke the windows."

"You wanted to know how I knew, that's how."

"The chief said his granddaughter talked about Stafford."

"Some of the kids can see him too."

"Kids are suggestible. If their teacher tells them they have an invisible friend who causes mischief, they believe her."

"Ask them."

"This is crazy."

"You mean I'm crazy." I'd thought that often enough.

I knew others thought it too. Why it hurt that Bobby did, I wasn't sure. He'd told me he didn't believe in ghosts.

"I didn't say that."

"You didn't have to. How do you think I knew about the locker at that hotel?"

He blinked. "What?"

"Your cold case."

He glanced away. "We discussed it."

"Not that much."

"If not that then what?"

"Your victim told me."

"That's—" His lips tightened; he still refused to look at me.

"Crazy. I know. But he did."

"Why would he tell you?"

"Because he could. I saw him. Heard him."

At last he met my gaze, his both curious and wary. "Here?"

I nodded.

"Why would he be here?"

"He is—was—attached to you." At his obvious confusion, I continued. "Some ghosts attach to a person. Some to a place—like Stafford."

"Why?"

"Unfinished business. Either the ghost's or the person they follow."

"I don't understand."

"Excessive grief or guilt over a death by the living can keep the spirit from moving on."

He rubbed the back of his neck. "You know an awful lot about ghosts."

"Been seeing them all my life." I still didn't know as

much about them as I should, but I did know more than most.

His expression closed. The air around him seemed to chill. I could tell he wanted to say *Bullshit*, but he didn't.

"You said *was*."

I lifted my brows.

"The hotel victim *was* attached to me."

"Once you discovered how he was killed, he went on."

"Where?"

"Wherever ghosts go."

"You don't know?"

"Once they go, they don't come back and share."

"Why would some guy I didn't know follow me around?"

"Maybe the same reason they are." I indicated the man and woman who materialized near Bobby every once in a while. I hadn't seen them often since that first time at my father's house, but I had seen them.

"There are more?"

"An older woman. African American. Graying Afro."

"Hey!" the woman in question exclaimed.

"Sorry," I said. It was gray. Always would be. "Beautiful hands. Very tall."

"My name is—" the woman began.

"Geraldine Hervieux," Bobby murmured.

"Oui." Geraldine's face softened. She set her hand on his shoulder. "He has never given up on finding me."

"She disappeared," he continued. "It was one of my last cases in missing persons before I transferred to homicide. Her daughter still comes in every month to make sure I keep searching."

"You would anyway."

"Yeah, I would."

"I'm in the Honey Island Swamp," Geraldine said.

"She's in the Honey Island Swamp."

Bobby closed his eyes. "That's seventy thousand acres of land and a million alligators. Literally. I'll never find her."

The woman stroked his hair. "He doesn't need to find me; he needs to let me go."

"She wants you to let her go."

His eyes opened. "I can't let go what I don't have."

"He continually thinks about my case, reads the file, dreams about it. I could be at peace if he would be."

I told him what she had said.

"If I just knew who killed her . . . "

"No one killed me. I went to gather wild iris for my daughter's birthday. She loves them. A gator got me."

"You didn't tell anyone you were going there?" I asked.

She shook her head. "More fool me."

"What?" Bobby asked.

"A gator got her while she was gathering wild iris for her daughter."

"I'm supposed to tell her daughter that? I can't prove it. And the poor woman would—" Bobby made an aggravated sound and stood, paced a few steps away, then came back. "This is ridiculous. You aren't talking to Geraldine."

"How would I know what she looks like if I wasn't talking to her?"

"People like you have your ways. It's easy enough to search the *Times Picayune* for my cases."

He was right. I'd even done so.

"People like me," I echoed. "Those liars, thieves, and charlatans? Why do you hate them so?"

He gave me a wary glance, then his shoulders dropped on a sigh. "Audrey sold jewelry and drugs. Some of her pals sold lies."

"How can someone sell lies?"

"Fortune-tellers. Psychics. They have all sorts of methods to find out information about people. Once a fool believes they have a connection to the great beyond, he'd give anything, everything, for that connection. For one more second of a loved one's presence. A single word. For anything that might make the pain—" His voice broke.

"Oh, Bobby," I whispered. He shot me a glance that very clearly said *drop it*. I wasn't sure I could.

He might have been duped and lied to by another, but I was who I was. While I'd spent my life trying not to be, I knew now I had little choice. I was a witch born, and a witch I would stay.

"Leave him be, *cher,*" Geraldine said. "You can't make him see. He has to want to."

Geraldine took the hand of the man who'd been hovering a few feet back. His eyes were as sad as hers. If Bobby didn't believe me about Geraldine, he wasn't going to believe me about that guy either. The two of them would be stuck haunting him until he did. No wonder they appeared so sad.

Geraldine and the mystery man strolled west, walking right through one of the gawkers—Mrs. Knudson, who must have either closed her yarn shop or just walked away and left it open. She wrapped her arms around herself as if a winter wind had blown past, then Geraldine and her friend disappeared.

"Ask her—" Bobby began.

"She's gone."

"Convenient."

I tightened my lips so I wouldn't say *fuck you*.

"How did you know about those bones, Raye?"

"I told you. I see ghosts."

"If the kid's been a thorn in your side for years, why didn't you . . . " He waved his hand. "Exorcise him before now?"

"I didn't know where he'd been buried. And he was having too much fun to tell me. He didn't want to leave."

"Then why did he?"

"My—" I bit my lip. Telling him my father was a centuries-old, time-traveling witch-ghost, who'd heard it from Bobby's dead child, was probably not the way to go. "One of the other spirits shared what Stafford had told her."

"Why would a ghost do that? Don't they have some kind of code?"

He was never going to believe me. Of course the alternative was letting him think I'd killed a five-year-old and buried him under a tree. Was it better to have the man I loved believe I was a murderer or a kook? I voted for kook.

My eyes burned. I wasn't sure if I was crying for Stafford, Bobby, myself, or all of us.

"Don't," he snapped.

I didn't bother to bite back another burst of: "Fuck you."

"You have."

My fingers curled inward. The spike of my nails only fueled my desire to punch him.

"You're going to have to come up with a better explanation than one ghost told another ghost who told you—the ghost whisperer."

Ghost whisperer. Wasn't he clever?

"I don't have one."

"Well, at least tell me who the rat-fink ghost is." His hand wrapped around my arm. I could tell he wanted to shake me, just a little, but he didn't. "Don't stop to think. I don't want a made-up ghost. I want the real thing. What's her name?"

"Genevieve," I snapped.

Then I wished that I hadn't.

Chapter 24

"I—" Bobby managed through the screeching in his ears.

"You—" he tried again between great gulps of air.

"We—she—" His heart thundered so loudly he was dizzy, and his stomach rolled.

Raye went as pale as he felt. "I'm sorry. I shouldn't have said that."

"I never told you about her." He couldn't remember once saying his daughter's name since he'd found her, still and cold, on the floor next to a passed-out Audrey.

"You didn't," Raye agreed.

"Then how—" He pursed his lips before the stupid question could escape. If she could look up his cases, she could certainly discover the name of his dead child.

"Why?" he whispered, horrified when his voice broke. He swallowed the tears—once, twice, again.

"She's—"

"No!" He leaped to his feet. Several of the bystanders frowned in his direction. He lowered his voice. "You will not tell me she's here."

A memory of himself at her father's place surfaced. He'd caught the scent of his daughter—sunshine, cinnamon, and rain. Had she been there too?

He shook his head—hard. What was wrong with him? His daughter wasn't here. She hadn't been there. She was gone. Forever.

Because of him.

He didn't remember moving, but the next thing he knew he was climbing into his rental car and driving off very fast. He didn't plan to stop until he reached the airport. Except . . .

Someone was trying to kill Raye. Was it because she'd done the same thing to them that she'd done to him? Had she said she could see departed loved ones, talk with them, impart a message from beyond? He supposed it wasn't easy to live on a teacher's salary, even here. Though . . .

If she'd been taking money for ghost whispering, wouldn't he have heard about it by now? That was the kind of thing small towns talked about.

Bobby smacked himself in the forehead. It didn't help. He still wanted to believe anything but what he'd heard.

However, Raye's claim might explain the question he hadn't before been able to figure out an answer to. Why did the *Venatores Mali* want Raye dead? Perhaps someone thought that seeing ghosts was a little witchy. He certainly did.

Just that morning Bobby had decided he loved her. He'd been thinking about staying here—with her, for her—just so he wouldn't have to leave and never see her again.

Now all he wanted was to leave and never see her again.

Bobby pulled to the side of the road. He couldn't go.

Raye might be bad, sad, evil, crazy—even all four—but he'd promised to protect her, and if he didn't what did that make him?

At least three out of that same four.

He had to make sure someone was watching over her if he wasn't. No matter what she'd said, done, he didn't want her dead. He dialed Chief Johnson.

"I have to leave," he said in lieu of hello.

"Doucet?" Johnson asked. Bobby heard him shifting, moving, probably looking around. "Where are you?"

"On my way to the airport."

"What happened?"

He wasn't touching that question. "Make sure Raye is protected. I'll call you." He hung up before the chief could ask anything else.

He made it another mile or two before he stopped again. He rested his forehead on the steering wheel and tried to calm his heart, his breathing, his mind. It wasn't easy.

No one spoke to him about Genevieve. No one. As a result he hadn't heard her name in so long the first mention of it nearly broke him.

Her death had driven him insane with grief. To be fair, it had had the same effect on Audrey. He didn't know if her overdose was accidental—the result of her overmedicating her pain—or on purpose for the same reason. When her supposedly psychic pal Marlene had offered to use her "gift" to contact his child—for a price—he'd agreed. Certainly he'd been self-medicated at the time—whiskey not coke—but that didn't excuse the second or third time. And definitely not the fourth.

When Marlene had disappeared with most of his savings, he had no one to blame but himself. But he didn't have to like it. And he didn't have to let anyone ever make a fool of him again.

Nevertheless, he'd traveled to New Bergin because what he'd thought was a serial killer had come to the small Wisconsin town. Now he knew that the killer was, in fact, killers, and they weren't going to stop. No matter how much he might want to leave, he couldn't. He wasn't that guy.

His phone vibrated. As it was most likely Johnson calling him back, and Bobby would rather speak to the man in person, he nearly ignored it. Could be Raye, though he doubted it. His reaction had shocked her. Though what she'd expected, he wasn't sure. Nevertheless, old habits died hard, and he couldn't keep himself from glancing at the caller ID.

Franklin.

"Where are you?" the FBI agent asked.

"Where are you?"

"I was at the crime scene."

"Which crime scene?"

"J.J. Stafford's. Why'd you leave?"

Bobby resisted the urge to bang his head against the steering wheel. "I'll be right back."

"I'm not there anymore. I need you to meet me in the woods, about half a mile off Route Seventy-three. Walk in from the mile eight marker sign."

"It's getting dark."

"Don't ever let anyone tell you you're not a trained observer," Franklin said. "Just get here. Cassandra heard of a place that's perfect for the kind of things that have been going on."

"Who's Cassandra?"

"Voodoo priestess."

Bobby was tempted to laugh, but he had a feeling the FBI agent wasn't joking. Did they ever?

Franklin let out an exasperated huff. "I said I was bringing a witch expert, who better than a voodoo priestess?"

What was Bobby supposed to say to that? Luckily Franklin didn't wait for an answer.

"I'm surprised you don't know her. She runs a voodoo shop in New Orleans."

"I don't go to voodoo shops." Ever. Despite his many greats-removed grandmother—or maybe because of her—voodoo gave him the heebie-jeebies.

"She knows your partner."

"Sullivan?"

"You got more than one?"

"No." Bobby found it odd that Franklin's witch expert was from his own hometown. Then again, voodoo capital of the world. But was a priestess a witch? Did one have to be a witch to be an expert on them?

Bobby groaned. His mind hurt.

"You okay?" Franklin asked.

"Not really."

"Finding a kid is always tough. I'm sorry about that."

"Me too." Bobby pulled onto the road and headed for mile marker 8. He was already on Route 73. There weren't exactly a lot of roads into or out of New Bergin. "What's so special about this place anyway?"

"According to what Cassandra heard through the spooky grapevine, there's a natural sacrificial altar."

Bobby leaned forward, his eyes straining to distinguish the numbers on the markers. The sun had fallen beyond the tree line, casting wavering shadows everywhere. He hated it.

"What in hell is a natural sacrificial altar?"

"A rock, a burial mound, something raised in a clearing that's used for sacrifices."

"You think it's where the coven meets?"

Silence settled over the line for a minute. "There's a coven?"

"Apparently, though I've never met any witches here that aren't dead. Why do you want to look at this altar?"

"You said your first victim wasn't killed where you found her."

"You think she was killed there?"

"Considering we've got witches and witch hunters, as well as an increasing number of dead people, I think we should look."

Unfortunately . . . so did Bobby.

A woman spoke, her voice muffled, then Franklin cursed and his voice lowered. "Someone's coming. A lot of someones. Get here, but quietly." The line went dead.

Bobby reached the marker. A black sedan sat right next to it. The FBI had never been very invisible. He didn't think they tried to be. Although if they did they were really bad at it.

Dusk was nearly gone and true night was falling. The trees whispered. Bobby wanted to bring his flashlight—and several very large friends—but he'd been told to come quietly. He didn't want to come at all.

Before he'd traveled the prescribed half mile, Bobby heard voices, saw the flicker of flames. He walked more slowly, more carefully, afraid he'd step on a stick and alert everyone to his approach.

As if his mind had conjured it—nice choice of

words—a stick cracked. He froze, waiting for figures to fly from the darkness like the monkeys from the witch's castle.

He shuddered. Oz had always freaked him out.

Someone clapped a hand over his mouth, and his hand went to his gun. It was gone.

"Calm down." Even at a whisper, he recognized the voice as Franklin's.

The man released him, and Bobby spun. There was just enough light left for him to see that the agent was older than Bobby had imagined. Or maybe it was just the sheen of silver that glinted in his dark hair, or the lines around his eyes, which could be the result of too much sun, or too much death. Either one aged a man.

Franklin handed Bobby his gun. "I counted about ten or so."

"You want me to help you arrest them?"

"They haven't done anything yet."

"They will." A woman swam out of the gloom.

"Cassandra?" he asked.

Despite talking just above a whisper, his voice must have revealed his skepticism. She smiled. "I know. I'm the least likely candidate for a voodoo priestess in the world."

She was tiny, with a pixie haircut and big blue eyes. If it hadn't been for the white streak at her temple, she wouldn't have appeared a day over twenty.

"She consults with the FBI on certain paranormal occurrences," Franklin said.

"Like when people think they're witches?"

Cassandra cast Franklin a glance. He shrugged. "Skeptic."

"Don't tell me you believe this crap?" Bobby asked.

"Once you've seen enough crap, you start to believe." Bobby opened his mouth, but Franklin shook his head. "Later." He beckoned Bobby to follow as Cassandra led them closer to the leaping flames.

In the center of a clearing a bonfire blazed in front of a tall, flat stone. Nearly a dozen people—men, women, young, old—milled about chatting as if it were a social gathering. If they weren't all naked, it might have been.

"Skyclad," Cassandra whispered. "Some covens prefer it when they do rituals."

Bobby wondered where they'd left their clothes, then caught a glimpse of a decrepit cabin at the edge of the trees, which answered that question as well as where the maniac, and any other strangers in town, had most likely been staying.

"Not a coven." Franklin lowered the smallest set of binoculars that Bobby had ever seen and handed them over. "Check out their fingers."

Bobby wasn't sure what fingers had to do with anything until he peered through the spyglass. Every person in the clearing wore the snarling-wolf ring of the *Venatores Mali.*

"They aren't witches," Franklin said. "They hate witches."

"Doesn't mean they aren't about to perform a ritual," Cassandra observed.

"Hypocritical much?"

"When dealing with dark magic and crazy people, you'd be surprised."

"I doubt it."

Bobby used the binoculars—which had the best night vision adjustment he'd ever seen—to get a better look at the rock altar. Streaks of brownish-red marred the top and the sides. If it hadn't been stained by blood, it was doing a pretty good imitation.

"I think you found your crime scene," Franklin said.

"Or *a* crime scene." If that wasn't Anne McKenna's blood it belonged to someone else.

Everyone in the clearing turned to face the path on the far side. Bobby lifted the binoculars again, making sure to keep the eyepieces high enough to avoid another unappealing view of several backsides that should not be skyclad. A new arrival appeared at the edge of the clearing, and Bobby nearly dropped the spyglass.

What was Pretty Boy Brad doing here?

The kid had seemed so innocent—he'd thrown up at the sight of Mrs. Noita—that Bobby hadn't suspected him of much beyond overeagerness and stupidity. But his appearance wherever the action was, as well as his sudden reconnection with Raye's best friend, had become worrisome.

Bobby must have made a forward movement because Franklin set a hand on his arm just as a woman appeared. She wore a brilliant scarlet robe that she dropped from her shoulders and became skyclad too. Tall as Brad—maybe six feet—her dark hair brushed the tops of her thighs. Bobby doubted there were two women of that height, with hair that long, running around a town of this size. She had to be the same culprit who'd broken into Larsen's Bed-and-Breakfast, and most likely the one who had killed Mrs. Noita.

Everyone went to their knees and bowed their heads. "Mistress." The word swirled around the clearing in a dozen different voices.

The woman walked to the altar. "Those of you here

tonight have done what was necessary. You have killed the witches. Spilling their blood, marking them as evil."

She lifted her hands toward the sky. One sported the snarling-wolf ring; the other clasped a squiggly knife. Even before he caught sight of the pentacle around her neck, he knew it was the knife they'd been looking for. If the woman hadn't killed Mrs. Noita, as well as her niece, then taken their ritual instruments, someone here had.

"You have burned them as they should be burned," she continued. "Each death is an offering to the one we adore. The more you burn, the higher you rise."

The others came to their feet, faces upturned to the night. Bobby got a Nazi Germany vibe. Switch out the wolf for a swastika, a tall woman for a psycho little man, and it could be 1939. He wiped a shaking hand over his sweaty face.

"If one day you kill more than I have, you could take my place as our leader. Remember that. Strive for it."

"Freaks," Cassandra muttered.

"Tonight we will meet our maker."

"Works for me." Bobby set his hand on his gun.

"We will raise Roland McHugh to life everlasting, and he will show us the way."

His fingers stilled. "They think they're raising a dead guy?"

Cassandra and Franklin exchanged glances.

"Wait," Bobby murmured. "Do *you* think they're raising a dead guy?"

"Stranger things have happened," Cassandra said.

"Where?"

"Never mind that," Franklin whispered. "Our orders

are to find out what they're up to and how. So, for right now, let's just watch and learn."

"The FBI wants to know how a group of serial killers are planning to raise a dead serial killer?"

Franklin shrugged. "I do what I'm told."

Bobby was tempted to ask who was telling him such insane things but now wasn't the time for that either. Especially when the athame wielder motioned to Brad and said, "Bring the sacrifice."

Brad disappeared from view, returning almost immediately with a struggling figure wrapped in a blanket.

"Shit," Cassandra snapped. "Goat without horns."

Bobby cast her a confused glance.

"Human sacrifice. Only a life buys a life. In light magic, sacrifice is given. But in dark, it's taken."

A chill trickled over Bobby that only increased in depth as Brad carried the "goat" to the stone, set it on top, and drew off the covering.

"Raye," Bobby whispered.

Chapter 25

When Brad said he'd take me home, I didn't think anything of it. Why should I? Someone had to. Bobby'd brought me to work that morning, then driven away without a backward glance.

I couldn't get past the expression on Bobby's face when I'd said his daughter's name. I'd broken him, and I wanted nothing more than the chance to put him back together again.

But what would I tell him? I couldn't continue to deny what I saw, who I was. I'd tried to all my life and denying it hadn't changed anything. It had only made me ill prepared to handle the truth.

I was a descendant of witches. I saw ghosts. I had powers. And parents. Sisters.

I was so preoccupied with my weird life I didn't notice that Brad had turned away from town instead of toward it until he pulled onto a rutted service road.

"Brad? Why are we—"

I didn't see the left cross until it connected with my jaw. The next thing I knew I was on the ground, tied to the bumper, mouth gagged. All my muffled questions were ignored as he sat on the hood of the car and stared back the way we'd come.

I tried to toss his ass, and while he did frown in my direction, he didn't fly through the air. I should have practiced that more—or at least asked Henry the rules. Did I need my hands? I'd only moved three things so far—a cell phone, a knife, and a cat—and I'd had no idea I was doing any of them until they were done.

Moments later another car pulled in; a woman I'd never seen before climbed out. That was odd in itself, considering this was New Bergin, even without her long, scarlet robe and the squiggly knife.

Squiggly knife. Hell. It was the woman who wanted to kill me. Lately, who didn't?

"Mistress June." Brad bowed.

If the robe and the knife and the bowing hadn't made me nervous, Brad's reaching into his glove compartment and pulling out a *Venatores Mali* ring, which fit him just right, would have done it for sure.

"Cloak the witch. Carry her," June ordered, and strode into the woods.

How did these people know I was a witch when I'd just found out myself?

Henry! I need you. Now!

I thought the words very hard. No Henry. Did I have to say them out loud? Perform the spell? Perform the spell out loud? I wish I'd known that before Brad had gagged me. I wish I'd known he was going to gag me before I'd gotten in his car. Unfortunately premonition was not one of my superpowers.

Too bad. I would really have loved to avoid the clearing full of naked people, even before they began to chant. I think it was Latin, though it was hard to be sure. Brad hoisted me onto a tall, flat rock. I had no idea why, but I got the gist when Mistress June lifted her athame high above me, point down.

I tried to roll out of the way, but several chanting underlings held me in place. I tried to fling Mistress June with the power of my mind. She took a single step back and cast me a considering look. She tightened her grip on the athame, so when I tried to toss it, nothing happened. I should have paid better attention in tossing class.

If only there'd been one.

The voices rose in pitch and volume and then, suddenly, stopped. The silence was chilling. So was Mistress June's smile.

"Welcome, master!" she shouted, and plunged the knife toward my chest.

A shot rang out. Her shoulder jerked back. The knife stuck in my arm and not my heart. It still burned like a bitch.

"Let her go."

Bobby stood at the edge of the tree line on the opposite side of the clearing. How had he found me?

Suddenly the knife was pulled from my arm—*ouch!*—and pressed to my neck. "Back off or I'll slit her throat."

Bobby froze. I wanted to shout *bullets beat knives!* but I was still gagged.

My arm was bleeding pretty badly. My entire left side felt both damp and on fire.

The naked followers began to chant again, and the world kind of shimmied. My head went light, my eyesight dark. I must have lost even more blood than I'd thought.

"What the fuck?" Bobby muttered as the sky above the altar rippled.

Raye had gone limp. He hoped she was playing possum, but from the amount of blood dribbling over the sides of the rock, he didn't think so. He needed to end this, but he wasn't sure how.

Though Franklin had no doubt called for backup, Bobby didn't think help would arrive in time. It was just the three of them. However, if Franklin and Cassandra walked out of the woods with guns, it would only cause the crazy lady to panic. With that knife at Raye's jugular, panic would be a bad thing.

"He's coming," the woman said. "The sacrifice of a witch by a *Venatores Mali* with the most kills. Add the chants of the worthy believers and our master will rise."

"You think you're raising a dead witch hunter?" Bobby knew she did, but if she was talking to him she wasn't speaking Latin, even though all the rest of them were.

The air crinkled again. Though he shouldn't take his eyes off the woman, Bobby couldn't help but stare as the sky seemed to stretch outward, as if something—someone—were, indeed, coming.

"Group delusion," he said.

The followers chanted louder, faster, and the woman laughed. "You should have killed me right away. Now it's too late." She lifted the knife above her head, her knuckles nearly touching the shifting, shimmering air that looked so much like the face of a man that—

Bobby pulled the trigger. Everyone stopped chanting.

The woman stood for another instant, poised above Raye, knife just about to swoop down. Then blood bloomed across her chest, and she fell.

The face in the sky stared right at Bobby. The eyes blazed like stars; the mouth curled. He thought he actually heard a snarl, right before the thing disappeared.

"You bastard!"

Bobby was so freaked by the face that couldn't have been there but somehow was that he wasn't thinking, or moving, as fast as he should have been. Brad had his gun pointed in Bobby's direction before he remembered the kid was there.

He was going to get shot, and there wasn't a damn thing he could do to stop it.

Then Brad's gun flew through the air and landed fifty feet behind him in the trees. The officer stared at his empty hand, then his fingers curled into fists. He lifted his gaze and started across the clearing in Bobby's direction.

Bobby could take Pretty Boy, no problem. Even without the gun.

Then someone jumped Bobby from behind, and he went down in a flurry of fists and feet and fury.

I wasn't out long. I heard June, Bobby, the *Venatores Mali*. But everything sounded so far away.

Until the gunshot. That was very close.

My eyes snapped open as Mistress June fell backward. Above me the sky rippled. I blinked, but the face was still there. In the sky. Behind the sky. Trying very hard to get out.

The thought made me so dizzy I shut my eyes for a minute, but that only made everything swirl faster.

Something snarled, and my eyes snapped open again. The face was gone. The sky was just sky. So what had snarled? I'd only heard a sound like that once before.

From my mother.

I tried to call out, *Pru?* but my mouth was still full of cloth.

I sat up, glanced around for my wolf mother, and saw Brad lifting his gun, pointing it at Bobby. Panic flared so bright my chest hurt. Then the gun flew out of Brad's hands.

Just like a ghost's agitation increased its ability to connect with the living, my agitation appeared to increase my ability to toss things.

Brad started toward Bobby, who also had a gun and seemed about to use it. Then one of the naked people jumped on Bobby's back, and all the rest followed. He fell beneath them, amid the dull thuds of flesh on flesh.

A dark-haired man in an equally dark federalish suit and tie appeared at the edge of the clearing. He slid a bit on the damp grass and fallen leaves. Bright, shiny shoes were not the best idea in the forest. He pointed his gun first at the pile, then at Brad who appeared ready to join in. "Stay," the man said.

Brad smirked. "You can't shoot all of them with him in the middle. And you can't make them stop unless you do. They'll tear him apart."

My heart jittered again, and one of the followers flew across the clearing. Both Brad and the fed glanced in my direction. I kept tossing. The more I did it, the easier it became. Embrace the panic, let it expand, send that energy outward, and voilà. Flying people.

The instant Bobby was alone, Brad took a step forward, so I tossed him too. He hit a tree, slid down, and went still. Considering that he'd kidnapped, punched, and gagged me, I didn't feel bad about it.

The rope at my ankles had loosened. Had I done that or was luck coming my way at last? Didn't matter.

I jumped off the rock and ran to Bobby. I didn't even consider that he'd left me behind, disbelieving and furious, at what I'd told him. I had to make sure he was all right.

I fell to my knees; at first thinking the ground was wet, then realizing my clothes were covered in blood. My arm should hurt worse than it did. Adrenaline was a wonderful thing.

Bruises had begun to darken Bobby's face. Several livid scratches marred his neck. His lip was swollen and bloody. Anger bubbled, and I glanced at the nearest *venator,* who had started to get shakily to his feet. He flew another three feet and lay still.

"Whoa." Bobby touched my leg. "Calm down."

I tried to talk, chewed on cloth instead. He pulled away the gag. His fingers traced my jaw, which must have a matching bruise from Brad's left cross, and his gaze was gentle, the way it had been before I'd mentioned Genevieve's name. Hope blossomed.

A movement at the edge of the forest had my head jerking up, my eyes narrowing. A dark-haired woman with a white streak in her hair stepped into the clearing, her hands lifted in surrender. She was so tiny I wondered for a minute if she was a fairy.

"Still a skeptic?" she asked Bobby.

Another of the *Venatores Mali* moved, and I gathered my energy to make her stop. But the new arrival said, "I've got it," then began to chant in a language I'd never heard before. It sounded French and then again it didn't.

Whatever she was doing, saying, worked because the faces of the groggy *Venatores Mali* took on an even more dazed expression, as if they'd all been conked on the head with a brick.

"Voodoo priestess," Bobby said, and sat up.

I tried to get my mind around that, then gave up.

"Blood loss," I murmured. "Cheapest high in the world."

Bobby pulled the knots free and released my wrists. "We need an ambulance."

Concern flooded me. "Are you hurt that badly?"

"Not me, Raye. You and the crazy woman."

"Crazy?" I repeated, then followed his gaze. "Oh, Mistress June."

The fairy girl walked behind the stone. "No ambulance for her. She's gone."

"Morgue then."

"Not gone dead. Gone gone."

"But I killed her." Bobby got to his feet, and I followed.

" 'Fraid not," the woman said. She peered into the trees. "Should I go after her?"

"No." That was the federal agent. "I called for backup. I need you here, Cassandra."

Cassandra crossed the clearing toward us. "I should probably do something to stop the bleeding."

"Okay."

"You'll need to sit so I can reach."

"Okay," I repeated, and sat abruptly in the grass. I probably shouldn't have gotten up in the first place.

"Raye?" Bobby sounded panicked.

"Shh," I said. My head swam.

Cassandra shoved it between my knees. "Breathe."

"Okay."

"I need your shirt."

I lifted my head as Bobby shrugged out of his. I wanted to enjoy the view, but the bruises on his torso and my still swimming head prevented it.

"Lie down before you fall," Cassandra ordered, and

because she was right, I did. She tore Bobby's shirt into strips, made a pad out of the largest one and pressed it to my wound. The pain that had been numbed by adrenaline came screaming back.

"Sorry." She set her hand on my forehead, chanted a few words in that pretty language, and when she lifted her hand, the pain withdrew. "Better?"

"Mmm." The pain was still there, but removed, as if I'd been stabbed weeks, not minutes, ago. "What are you speaking?"

"Haitian."

The idea of this itty-bitty white woman speaking Haitian made me smile.

"I know," she said. "I feel the same way every time."

I wondered momentarily if she could read minds, but the idea made *my* mind hurt, so I let it go. There was enough for me to think about right now to make me need extra strength Tylenol for the next several years. I wasn't going to worry about a voodoo priestess too.

"Just lie still and stay calm," Cassandra said. "Help's on the way."

Almost immediately sirens shrilled, and they sounded close, but out here in the middle of a great big nothing, everything did.

Cassandra moved off to speak quietly at the edge of the clearing with the suited guy. Bobby sat next to me and took my hand. "You're cold."

"I'll live."

"No thanks to me."

"You saved my life."

"After I put it at risk by leaving you."

"You couldn't have known Brad was a lying, witch-hunting bastard." I hadn't and I'd known him all my life.

"True." Bobby took a breath, then continued very softly. "But it would have been nice to know that you were a witch."

My gaze met his. I should have told him, except—

"You didn't believe me about the ghosts. I certainly wasn't going to tell you about . . . " I waved at the clearing. "This."

"I'm sorry I behaved the way I did."

I tilted my head. "You believe me now?"

"You tossed a dozen people while your hands were tied. Either I'm seeing things or you're special."

"Everyone's special in their own way," I said in my best Miss Larsen voice.

"Got that right." He rubbed his thumb along mine. "How did you manage to hide what you were for so long?"

"I didn't do a very good job." I lifted my chin to indicate the still dopey *Venatores Mali*. "They knew."

"But no one in New Bergin did."

"That's not true." I kept my gaze on Brad. Perhaps knowing him all my life meant that he, in turn, had known me. He'd seen something, told someone.

"I always saw ghosts," I continued. "But I learned not to talk about it. Freaked out my parents."

"Can't imagine why," he said, and I tightened my fingers around his. We'd need to talk about Genevieve, but not yet.

"That I'm a witch too is new information."

"I don't understand."

"I was adopted."

"I thought you were abandoned and had no idea who your natural parents were."

"I was, or I thought I was but—" My mind whirled

at all I needed to tell him. By the time I was done, those sirens were closer. At this point, they had to be.

"Your dad's a ghost and your mom's a wolf," he repeated. "From seventeenth-century Scotland."

"Yes."

"And as they died at the stake, they cast a time-traveling spell to send you and your sisters, whom you've never met, forward."

"Technically, they sent us to a place where no one believes in witches anymore."

He grunted and his gaze wandered around the clearing. "I'm not so sure they sent you to the right place."

"Who would have thought an ancient witch-hunting society would be revived in this day and age?"

"Not me."

"Franklin," Cassandra said. "You got silver in that gun?"

Something in her voice, if not her odd question, made my skin prickle. I lifted my head as Pru stepped into the clearing.

"Always," Franklin answered and pointed his weapon at my mother.

I tried to toss his gun, but the man had already seen my show and held on tight. I leaped up, nearly fell back down.

"No!" I cried. I couldn't lose her when I'd only just found her. She wasn't the usual mother, but she was the only mother I had.

Cassandra glanced in my direction. "You know this wolf?"

"It's—uh—" My gaze met Bobby's, and he shrugged. "My mother."

Chapter 26

"When was she bitten?" Franklin asked.

"Could be cursed," Cassandra put in.

"Bitten?" Bobby repeated. "By what? Cursed? By whom?"

Cassandra spread her hands.

"Look at her eyes," the FBI agent said. "Human eyes in the face of a wolf."

Now that he mentioned it, the wolf's eyes were strange. "What does that mean?"

"He thinks she's a werewolf," Raye said.

Bobby laughed. No one else did.

"How did you know that?" he asked.

"Silver bullets? Bitten? Cursed?" Raye rolled her eyes. "Have you completely missed every werewolf book, TV show, and movie ever made?"

"Apparently. Though I guess you haven't." He glanced at Franklin. "What's your excuse?"

"I deal with things like this all the time." He kept his gun trained on Raye's "mom," who had stilled at the sight of it. Raye stepped between them, then Bobby stepped between Franklin and her.

"Cass?" Franklin asked.

"I've got her."

Bobby glanced over his shoulder. The voodoo priestess had produced a shiny knife from Lord knew where. It sparkled silver as the moon lifted beyond the trees.

"Is everyone slightly nutso?"

"Seeing is believing, Doucet." Cassandra's fingers flexed on the hilt of the knife. "And believe me, I have seen."

"She's not a werewolf." Raye put out a hand and the knife flew from Cassandra's palm to hers. She scowled at the blade. "What does silver do?"

Cassandra contemplated her empty fingers for a instant before answering. "If you touch her with it and she doesn't burn, she's not your usual werewolf."

Raye laid the flat of the blade on her mother's nose. The wolf gave a disgusted huff, but she didn't burst into flames.

"See?" Raye handed the weapon back to the voodoo priestess.

"She might not be the usual werewolf, but that doesn't mean she isn't something else," Franklin said.

Bobby turned to the man. "Are you really with the FBI?"

Franklin appeared offended. "Of course!"

"No one would dress like that on purpose," Cassandra said. "He gets the specialty cases."

"There really is an X-files division in the basement?" Raye asked.

Franklin cast her an annoyed glare, and Cassandra snickered.

"You'd better get the wolf out of here before my backup arrives," he said.

Cassandra stopped laughing. "You didn't."

"Of course I did. What was I supposed to do after . . . " He used his gun to indicate the clearing.

"He's right." Cassandra rubbed her forehead. "The wolf needs to go."

"Why?" Raye asked.

"Our boss is coming, and he's the greatest werewolf hunter of all time."

"Don't start." Bobby had just gotten his mind around the witches and now they were talking werewolves. When did it end?

"My mother is not a werewolf," Raye insisted.

"Edward's more of a 'shoot now, figure it out later' kind of guy." Franklin peered into the trees. "And he'll probably be here any minute."

"Where was he?" Cassandra asked.

"He was on his way from Three Harbors."

"That's where my sister lives," Raye said, just as Pru snarled.

"Sister?" Franklin asked. Then things started to happen all at once.

The wolf loped off. A few seconds later, several shots were fired in the direction she'd gone.

Raye shouted, "Mom!" and Bobby had to grab her before she ran off too.

"You need to go to the hospital," he said.

"But—"

"She's over four hundred years old. She can handle herself."

"You don't know Edward," Franklin muttered, and Bobby cast him a stern "shut the hell up" glance. "I'll give him a call. Tell him not to kill the un-werewolf."

"You do that," Bobby said.

"I'd feel better if Henry were here," Raye murmured.

"He's not?"

She shook her head.

Bobby wanted to ask if Genevieve was near, but cops and EMTs spilled into the clearing, and the next hour was spent arresting people and trying to explain what had happened without using the words *spells, magic, voodoo,* or *werewolves*. It was surprisingly harder than he'd thought. He let Franklin do most of the talking. The fed had had practice.

Raye left in the ambulance with Cassandra. He'd seen enough of the priestess to know Raye would be safe until he got back to her side. Once he did, he didn't plan to ever leave again.

"Doucet!"

Chief Johnson had arrived. He didn't look happy.

"Just who are you guys?"

Cassandra waited until the EMT finished putting in my IV and went to sit a few feet away with his clipboard. Then she leaned in close.

"There's a group of hunters called the *Jäger-Suchers*." At my confused expression she translated. "Hunter-searchers. They've been around since the Second World War; so has my boss."

"He's gotta be ancient."

"He is. He began hunting werewolves, but as time went on, he branched out." She lifted her gaze to the EMT, who was giving my vitals to the hospital—probably still half an hour away, even at this speed—by cell phone, then returned it to mine. "He's gonna be pretty interested in this mess."

"He isn't a witch hunter too, is he? Because I have enough of those on my ass already."

Cassandra's lips curved. "He likes to employ the good witches."

"And the not so good ones?"

Her smiled faded. "He doesn't employ them."

"How did you meet him?"

"I tried to raise my daughter from the dead."

Hadn't seen that one coming.

"Did you?"

Cassandra shook her head.

"Can you?"

"Not anymore." I bit my lip, frowned, and she continued. "Raising Bobby's daughter is a bad idea."

Maybe so, but how did she know I'd had it? For that matter, how did she know about Bobby's daughter?

"Franklin is in the FBI," she said. "He can find out damn near anything. Edward can find out even more."

I was tempted to ask if she could read everyone's mind, or just mine, but she spoke.

"I would have done anything to have my child live again. I nearly did but . . . " Cassandra let out a breath.

"But?" I pressed when she didn't go on.

"I learned several things while I was trying to raise her. Everything happens for a reason. There are no accidents, and most importantly, there is a better place, and it isn't here. Bringing her back would have been for me and not her. It wasn't fair, and it definitely wasn't right."

"Okay," I said slowly, my gaze drawn to the corner of the ambulance where Genevieve had just materialized. "But what do you do when they don't go to the better place?"

Cassandra's eyes followed mine. "She's here?"

I nodded.

"Ask her."

I didn't need to. Genevieve had already told me what the problem was. Bobby believed it was his fault that his daughter was dead. I wasn't sure how I was going to make him stop believing that, but I'd have to try. And that would start with telling him all that his daughter had shared.

As soon as we arrived at the hospital, I was whisked off so that someone could stitch up the knife-shaped hole in my arm. The painkillers combined with the sudden absence of adrenaline until everything faded to black. When I woke, night had fled. The sun was shining. Bobby was there. So was his daughter.

There was something different about her. She was kind of fuzzy, and it wasn't because I was.

"Hey," I mumbled.

"Hey," Bobby returned, and took my hand. "Your dad just left."

For a minute I thought he meant Henry, but he couldn't see Henry. "My father?"

"Yeah. Sorry. Forgot you have two. John was pretty upset. Stayed here all night. I don't know if your—uh—other dad is—"

"He isn't." Which worried me. But I was in no condition to summon him now.

"Jenn's called at least ten times."

"She hasn't come?" How very un-Jenn of her.

"She's being questioned. She was the last one to see Brad before he snatched you. I'm sure she'll be here as soon as she's done." Bobby took a deep breath. "I love you."

"I— What?"

"Marry me?"

I glanced at Genevieve, who was fading fast. "Hold on."

"I will." He tightened his hand. "I won't ever let go."

"I meant Genevieve."

"Where?" he asked, then turned in her direction.

"You feel her, don't you?" He was more sensitive to ghosts than anyone I'd ever known. We'd discover why later. Apparently, we'd have time.

He shifted his shoulders. "I . . . " His breath rushed out. "Yeah. I do."

The little girl became more solid. "Tell him it wasn't his fault."

"It wasn't your fault," I repeated.

Pain flickered in Bobby's eyes. "Of course it was. I left her with her mom. Audrey was—" He took a breath, which shook in the middle. "Tell her—"

"You can tell her," I said. "Just because you can't hear or see her doesn't mean she can't hear and see you."

I patted the bed at my hip. "Come here, baby."

Genevieve sat where I indicated and lifted a ghostly hand to her father's face.

He turned his cheek into her palm. "I should have done more to get you away from your mother, sweetheart."

"She needed me, Daddy. I couldn't leave her."

I told him what she'd said.

Tears welled in his eyes. "I still should have taken you somewhere. Anywhere."

"The man in black wouldn't let you keep me."

I got a shiver. "Man in black?"

"That's what she called the judge."

"Did you try and get custody?"

"I did. But we were never married. Audrey didn't even put my name on the birth certificate."

Which explained the lack of info I'd found on Genevieve Doucet.

"I'm sorry," Bobby said. "I told you I didn't have children, but I—"

"I understand."

"I tried to save her, and I failed. She died."

"Mommy's waiting," Genevieve said. "My gramma too. I want to be with them."

"You need to let her go, Bobby. She doesn't belong here anymore."

"I'm not sure how."

Neither was I.

"Is he happy?" the child asked.

"I think he could be."

"That's all I want. I can't leave him when he's so sad."

Bobby's gaze remained on me. "What did she say?"

"She wants you to be happy."

"I will be. With you."

Genevieve leaned over and kissed him. He closed his eyes, and the tears fell.

"Good-bye," he whispered at the exact moment she did.

His hair stirred as she disappeared. He opened his eyes. I traced a tear from his cheek with my thumb. "You okay?"

"I think so. Ever since she died I felt . . . " He struggled to find a word.

"Haunted?"

"Yeah."

"And now you're not."

"No," he agreed.

"Except for that one guy." At least Geraldine had moved on.

He straightened. "What?"

"Cold case." I lifted my gaze to said guy. "We'll talk. Run along."

The guy went poof.

"Did he?"

"He did."

"About that marriage proposal . . . "

"Bobby, I . . . "

"You're going to say no?" He sounded almost more surprised about that than he'd been about the ghosts.

Of course I *did* love him. But—

"Just because your daughter's gone doesn't mean I won't still see the dead, and that bothers you."

"It did. But really, Raye, after all that's gone down, that's the least of our worries."

He was right. The *Venatores Mali* were still out there. They still wanted me dead. Probably more now than before.

"Mistress June?" I asked.

"No sign of her. Franklin and Cassandra are on it. And their boss . . . " He shook his head. "That was one weird old dude. But he said he'd find the woman. I wouldn't want to be Mistress June when he does."

"What about the others?"

"Clammed up tighter than clams."

I assumed that was tight. No idea. Never seen a clam.

"Brad?"

"You cracked his skull."

"Whoops."

"You don't sound sorry."

I wasn't.

His lips twitched. "Probably for the best that he's out of it, and in protective custody."

"Because?"

"Your little friend wants him dead. She scares me."

"She should."

His half smile faded. "If you don't want to marry me, fine." He didn't sound fine, or look it either. "But I'm not leaving."

"You have a job, a life in New Orleans." And I had both in New Bergin. I might have considered leaving with him, even for superbly haunted New Orleans, if it hadn't been for my sisters. I'd never met them, but I couldn't leave them behind.

"*You're* my life," Bobby said. "And I have a job here now."

"You what?"

"Brad's a little incarcerated, and Chief Johnson . . . well, he isn't up to dealing with all of this."

"Who is?" I asked.

"Me."

"You gonna tell him that?"

"Didn't have to. He retired."

"Just like that?"

"Can't say I blame him."

I didn't either, but—

"Are you sure?"

"I've never been more certain of anything in my life, Raye. But if you're not—"

"No." I stared into his eyes, and saw that in a world of complications, some things were so damn simple. Like this. "I'm sure too."

Of Bobby. Myself. Us. Everything. For the first time in a lifetime, I belonged.

To him.

Epilogue

Henry stood at the edge of another forest, in another town, watching another daughter.

The sky above split open, spilling lightning. The earth below shuddered with approaching thunder. Henry couldn't help it. He was both afraid and furious—two traits that often manifested in a storm.

The *Venatores Mali* hadn't raised Roland. Yet. But they weren't going to stop trying.

Pru appeared at his side. They gazed at their middle child, framed in the window of her apartment. She had no idea what was coming. They hadn't wanted her to, had hoped they would succeed in New Bergin and there would never be any reason to disrupt the life she had made here.

"Are you ready?" he asked.

Pru lifted her nose to the stormy night sky and howled.

Read on for an excerpt
from Lori Handeland's next book

Heat of the Moment

Available July 2015 from St. Martin's Paperbacks

Chapter 1

I glanced up from my examination of a basset hound named Horace to discover the Three Harbors police chief in the doorway. My assistant hovered in the hall behind her.

"Can you take Horace?" I asked, but Joaquin was already scooping the dog off the exam table and releasing him onto the floor. Before I could warn him to leash the beast—my next scheduled patient was Tigger, the cat—Horace had trotted into the waiting area and found out for himself.

Indoor squirrel!

Since childhood, I'd heard the thoughts of animals. Call it an overactive imagination. My parents had. That I was right a good portion of the time, I'd learned to keep to myself. Crazy is as crazy does, and a veterinarian who thinks she can talk to animals would not last long in a small northern Wisconsin tourist town. I doubted she'd last long in *any* town. But Three Harbors was my home.

Woof!

Hiss.

Crash!

"Horace!"

Tigger's owner emitted a stream of curses. Joaquin fled toward the ruckus.

"Kid gonna be okay out there?" Chief Deb jerked a thumb over her shoulder, then shut the door.

"If he wants to keep working here, he'd better be." The waiting room was a battleground, when it wasn't a three-ring circus.

I sprayed the table with disinfectant and set to wiping it off. "What can I do for you, Chief?"

"I've got a missing black cat."

My hand paused mid-circle. "I didn't know you had a cat."

She'd never brought the animal to me, and as I was the only vet within thirty miles, this was at the least worrisome, at the most insulting.

"Just because you picked up a stray," I continued, "doesn't mean the animal doesn't need care." Ear mites, fleas, ticks, old injuries that had festered—and don't get me started on the necessity for being spayed or neutered. "A stray probably needs more."

"Chill, Becca, the missing cat doesn't belong to me. Neither do the two other black cats, one black dog, and, oddly, a black rabbit that seem to be in the wind."

I opened my mouth, shut it again, swiped an already clean table, then shrugged. "I don't have them."

"If you did, you'd be my newest candidate for serial killer of the week."

"I . . . what?"

"After the first two cats went poof, I suspected Angela Cordero."

"She's eight years old."

"Exactly," Deb agreed. "But when the dog disappeared, I started to think maybe it was Wendell Griggs."

"Thirteen," I murmured.

"Missing small animals are one of the first hints of pathological behavior."

Apparently Chief Deb liked to read that healthy and growing genre, serial killer fiction.

"Missing small animals are usually an indication of a larger predator," I said. "Especially this close to the forest."

Three Harbors might be bordered on one side by Lake Superior, but it was backed by a lot of trees, and in those trees all sorts of creatures lived. Perhaps even a few serial killers.

My imagination tingled. If I weren't careful, I'd be writing one of those novels. Maybe I should. Writing might be good therapy for my overactive imagination. Ignoring it certainly wasn't helping.

"I know." She sounded disappointed. Apparently the chief would prefer a serial killer to a large animal predator. Worse, she was kind of hoping that the serial killer was someone we knew who'd yet to hit puberty.

This surprised and disturbed me, though I didn't know her well. We'd gone to school together, but Deb had occupied the top of the pyramid in high school—literally. Someone of her tiny stature and blond-a-tude had been a given for cheerleader of the year.

She'd worried me when she'd danced on top of those ten-people-high pyramids. Now I was worried that she'd fallen off, once or twice, and hit her head.

"Have you had any animals in here that have been bitten, scratched, mauled, or chewed on?" she asked.

"Not lately."

"Any farmers complain that they've seen coyotes or wolves closer to town than they should be?"

"Wouldn't they report that to you, not me?"

She tilted her head. "Good point."

Deb had cut her blond ponytail years ago and now wore her hair in a short cap that, when combined with her tree-bark brown police uniform, Batman-esque utility belt, and Frankenstein-like black shit-kicker boots, only made her appear like a child playing dress up.

Dress up.

I tapped the calendar. "Less than two weeks until Halloween."

"I *hate* Halloween." Deb kicked the door, which rattled and caused Horace to yip in the waiting room. Wasn't he gone yet? "Second only to New Year's Eve for the greatest number of morons on parade."

"You said all the missing animals were black."

"So?"

"A wolf or a coyote wouldn't know black from polka dot."

While dogs and cats, and by extension wolves and coyotes, weren't truly color blind, they didn't see colors the way we did. Most things were variations of black and gray and muted blue and yellow. Or so I'd heard.

"Might be kids playing around," I continued.

"Sacrificing black animals to Satan?"

"You think we have a devil-worshipping cult or maybe a witches' coven? In Three Harbors?"

She drew herself up, which wasn't very far, but she did try. "There *are* witches."

"From what I understand, they're peaceful. Harm none. Which would include black animals."

"*Something* weird is going on."

"Kids messing around," I repeated. "Though I doubt they're stealing black animals and keeping them safe in a cage somewhere just for the hell of it."

Which brought us right back to budding serial killer. Or two.

"Would you be able to give me a list of all the animals you treat that are black?" she asked.

"If the owners agree."

Wisconsin statutes allowed the release of veterinary records with permission from the owner.

"Why would anyone care about the release of the color of their pet's fur to the police?"

"Never can tell," I answered.

If there was one thing I'd learned in this job, it was that people were a lot stranger than animals.

At five-thirty, Joaquin flicked the lock on the front door and turned off the waiting room lights, then followed me through the exam room to the rear exit.

Trees ringed the parking lot that backed my clinic. Only my Bronco and a waste receptacle occupied the space. However, I'd had a night-light installed, and it blazed bright as the noonday sun.

"Sorry to leave you with the Horace and Tigger problem," I said.

"It was my fault for letting Horace run free."

It had been, and I bet he never did it again. Between patients I'd seen him sweeping up dirt from an overturned potted plant and wiping the floor beneath one of the chairs. It was anyone's guess if Horace had peed and Tigger had knocked over the plant or vice versa.

I'd never had a better assistant than Joaquin. His long-fingered, gentle hands calmed the wildest pet. He also had the best manners of any adolescent in town, not that there'd been much of a contest. From what I'd seen of the Three Harbors youth, being a smart-mouthed, uber-delinquent was the current fashion.

"You going home or did your mom work today?"

Joaquin lived in a trailer park outside of town. Not a long trip, but one that involved a sketchy stretch of two-lane highway, with only a bit of gravel on the side. I didn't want him walking it after dark, and at this time of year, dark had come a while ago.

"She's working."

"You're going straight to the cafe?"

His lips curved at my concern. "If you saw where we lived before we came here . . . This place is safe as houses my mom says. Although I don't really know what that means beyond really safe."

Three Harbors *was* safe, at least for people, which reminded me. "Have any of the kids been talking about . . ." I wasn't sure what word to use. Did they call Satanism something else these days? And if so, what? "Cults?" At his blank expression, I kept trying. "Sects? Devil worship?"

"That's why the chief wanted the list of black animals?" His voice was horrified. "Someone's killing them?"

"We don't know that."

"What do we know?"

I hesitated, but now that I'd opened the door, I couldn't

close it without freaking out Joaquin worse than he already was.

"There are several cats, a dog, and a rabbit missing. They're all black, which almost surely rules out a feral dog, coyote, or wolf."

He nodded. The kid nearly knew as much about animals as I did.

"I was thinking that since it's so close to Halloween maybe some kids were messing around. Hear anything?"

"No one talks to me at school." He twitched one shoulder in an awkward, uncomfortable, half shrug. "I'm Mexican."

Three Harbors didn't have a lot of Mexican-Americans. In fact, now that Joaquin and his mom were here, we had two.

"I don't fit in," he continued. "I'm dark and foreign and new."

Joaquin was a beautiful boy—ebony hair, ebony eyes, ridiculous lashes—also ebony—smooth cinnamon skin.

"Doesn't that make you exotic and exciting?"

"Not," he muttered.

"No one's talked to you?"

"Teachers. I heard one of the kids saying that I didn't speak English."

"And what did you say to that?"

"*Hablo Inglés mejor que usted habla Español, estúpido.*"

"You didn't."

"You understood me?"

"I'd have to be *estúpido* not to understand *estúpido.* Once I got that much, the rest wouldn't really matter. Have you been participating in class?"

"Have to."

"In English?"

He cast me a disgusted glance. "Have to."

"Then why would anyone think you couldn't speak the language?"

He rolled his eyes the same as every kid I'd ever met. "Hence my use of *estúpido*."

I pursed my lips so I wouldn't laugh. I liked this kid so much. Why didn't everyone?

Because kids were mean. I knew that first hand.

But were they mean enough to sacrifice helpless, harmless animals?

I hoped not.

I lived in an efficiency apartment above my clinic. When I'd taken over Ephraim Brady's practice after college, it was part of the deal.

My mother hadn't wanted me to move to town, but it wasn't practical to live on the farm when over half of my business was done in the office. Not to mention the small kennel where we housed post- and pre-op patients, boarders, and strays. In the winter, I might be prevented from making it into the office for a day or two, and then what? If I was already there . . . half the battle was won.

I exchanged my khaki trousers—which repelled animal hair better than most—for track pants, my white blouse—out of which anything could be bleached—for an old T-shirt. I covered that with an equally old sweatshirt, switched my comfy shoes for the expensive running variety, then grabbed a hat and gloves, put my cell phone in one pocket, my keys in the other, and trotted down the stairs and out the door. Time for my nightly wog—my twin brothers' word for the walk-jog I did to stay in shape.

Instead of wogging down Carstairs Avenue—the main street of town was named after my family. The Carstairs had lived in Three Harbors from the beginning, which, according to the welcome sign, had been in 1855—I took the path into the forest.

Three Harbors was a small town, but it was also a tourist town, and these days that meant bike paths and hiking trails. They were well lit and meticulously maintained. I still kept mace on my key ring. I couldn't very well jog with a nine millimeter. Even if I owned one.

The forest settled around me, cool and deep blue-green. The trail had lights every few feet, some at ground level, others high above. Still, I rarely ran into anyone after dark, and I loved it.

My feet beat a steady *wump-wump.* That combined with the familiar crunch of the stones beneath my shoes at first drowned out the other sound. But eventually, I heard the thud of more feet than two.

At the edge of twilight, loped a huge black wolf.